The brass door handle turned without a noise. His heart hammering, Dr. Fields pushed the door inward a couple of inches. Light spilled out into the falling night. He could not see much through the finger wide gap. There were shapes, moving shadows, swaying in flickering candlelight. Dr. Fields moved his face closer to the opening, hearing the surge of sound from inside.

"*Gul'ngh'fltqa,*" rose the chanting in soft, guttural unity.

"There is a way, and it can be opened," came a lone, loud voice, edged with a purring accent.

"*Itaq'ghl'n'hl!*" The sounds were like the grinding of broken ribs in a shattered chest. They made Dr. Fields shudder in the warm summer night air. He did not know what language they chanted, or if it was a language at all, but it ran through him as if those sounds contained something primordial, something that touched the deepest instincts within him. Though he had not bent his knee in a church for many years, he knew the power of faith, but he had also met his share of quacks and charlatans. He did not believe in the supernatural and superstition—they were just the remnants of lies that people had been telling themselves for thousands of years, lies to give solace or create fear. Reason and science defined the limits of the possible, everything else was delusion.

But, as he listened to the sounds, one word stuck in his mind: *unholy.*

An

ARKHAM HORROR™

Novel

The Lies of Solace
Book Two of the Lord of Nightmares Trilogy
by John French

Fantasy Flight Publishing, Inc.

For Liz — for walking with me through every step.

© 2012 by Fantasy Flight Publishing, Inc.
All rights reserved.
Paperback edition published in 2012.
Printed in the United States of America.

Cover illustration by Anders Finér.

ISBN: 978-1-61661-220-7

Fantasy Flight Publishing, Inc.
1975 West County Road B2
Roseville, MN 55113
USA

Find out more about Fantasy Flight Games
and our many exciting worlds at

www.FantasyFlightGames.com

The Lies of Solace

PROLOGUE

Cilicia, Asia Minor, 1190 AD

It did not take long for the peasants to die.

Most of the townsfolk had been in the fields, and it took a moment for them to see death coming for them. When they saw the knights, they began to run toward the town, spilling out of the green fields of ripening corn spread out along the riverbank, shouting warnings. The town, little more than a cluster of low mud-brick buildings inside an earthen palisade, looked down on the fields from a low hill in a bend of the river. A dirt road cut through the carpet of green to a gate in the town wall. Most of the running peasants were cut down before they could reach that wall. Some ran up the road, their eyes wild with fear as the iron-wrapped men rode them down. Others fled farther into the fields. Knights peeled off, driving their horses through the swaying corn stalks, shouting hunting calls as they ran their quarries down.

At the head of his men, Armand killed until he was in the shadow of the town's gate. It was small, its mud-brick arch low enough that he would have to duck to ride through. A cool gloom waited beyond. At first, his mind explained this away with a half-formed thought of an awning or shading trees within, but the more he looked at the gate and darkness beyond, the more it made him think of an open mouth leading to a hungering darkness.

"The way is open," said the Byzantine priest from so close that Armand almost brought up his sword to strike. The priest was staring at him, pale blue eyes cold and unblinking. Armand tried to swallow to ease his dry throat. The priest was corpse thin, as if his flesh had been sucked inward beneath the tallow-pale skin, drawing it tight over bones and sinking his eyes into pits. He wore layers of rich, sun-bleached cloth colored and patterned with dyes and embroidery. The priest had given no name when they first met, and when Armand had asked him what they should call him, the priest had smiled and asked if a dog needed to know the name of its master. After that, the knights had begun to refer to the priest as *Le Maitre*—"the master"—and the title seemed to please him.

The priest nodded at the gate, dismounted, and began walking toward it, his patterned robes blowing about him in the wind. "Come! Your reward is waiting, my friend."

Armand paused, then flicked a hand at those of his knights that were nearby. Some were still off hunting for survivors amongst the green stalks of the fields, but most were here. Armand and the rest of the knights dismounted. They would leave the horses outside the town walls; fighting in the confines of streets and houses was best done on foot. Armand hefted his sword and unslung a long shield from his back, its surface pitted and scratched from blows that had failed to take his life.

"There is no need to bring all of your men," said the priest, his eyes flicking over the rest of the knights. Armand looked at the town walls, then back at the bodies of the peasants in the dust.

"What about the Saracen garrison, the raiders?"

"There are no Saracens," said the priest.

Sudden anger overcame his fear of this priest. Armand wondered what had ever made him believe the Byzantine priest's stories of a shrine taken by Saracen raiders and their hoard of stolen silver. Take the shrine back for God, and they could keep the riches—at least, that had been the promise. Now, it seemed laughable that Armand had led these men here because of such a story.

"You lied," he snarled, taking a step forward. Behind him, a handful of his knights shifted their weapons and moved to his lead.

"I promised you rewards beyond your dreams," said the priest. "Those riches still await you." Armand looked at the man's robes and wondered if he was even a priest as he claimed. He could suddenly smell the lies coiling around this man like the sudden reek of an open grave.

"And for you, priest? What is there for you in this place?"

The priest hesitated and Armand could almost see the responses being weighed.

"The answer to a question," said the priest carefully, "a question that can only be answered here."

"You brought us here for that?" Armand snarled, bringing the tip of his sword up to point at the priest.

"It is not something I could have done myself," said the priest, gesturing toward the corpses of the townsfolk who had died trying to defend their homes. "They would not have let me pass. Now they have no choice." The priest walked over to a bloody heap that had been a man who had pleaded with Armand. Delicately, he raised the dead man's arm, turning it so that the palm was visible. Beneath the blood and dirt, there was a mark inked into the skin, its outline faded with age to dull grey. To Armand, the mark looked like a jagged outline of a man surrounded by symbols that made him turn his eyes away.

The priest let the hand drop. "The people of this town have bent their knees to older gods since before the land of your fathers was named. That service makes the land fertile and protects them from want in a land of thirst and hunger." He stood up and walked close to Armand, his voice dropping low. Armand could smell spice on the man's breath. "They keep an oracle here, an oracle who, when the stars are right, can grant the answer to any question. That time is now and the question will be mine." Armand found that he was looking into the priest's eyes.

"Come, even if I omitted facts before, have I not been honest with you now?"

Armand found himself nodding. He had always thought the priest had hidden something from him, and now he knew what it was. He believed him; after all why should he not? All he needed to do was look into the man's eyes to know that he spoke the truth.

"You have already done your service, is it not time for your reward?" said the priest, this time loud enough for his words to carry to the nearby knights. Armand nodded and turned to his men. They were watching him, poised like jackals for any sign of weakness or betrayal. Even with the soft, reassuring words of the priest in his head, he knew they would kill him if they thought he or the priest were trying to cheat them.

"Follow us," Armand said. He saw a flicker on the faces of some, read the distrust. "You heard the priest: our reward is within this godless town." Some looked ready to protest, but he turned and walked toward the waiting gate. With the clink of steel, his knights followed.

Beyond the gate, it was as if they had stepped from a summer day into winter twilight. The buildings were made of dull mud brick and piled on top of each other in an irregular jumble of walls and flat roofs. Above them, the sun was a dead white disk in a dark sky, casting a sickly pale glow. Shadows fell at impossible angles, their edges as ragged as ripped flesh. Dark flowing shapes crawled on the edge of sight, and the air tasted of frost.

Armand found that his hands were shaking on the grips of his shield and sword. He felt as he had when, as a boy, he had stepped into the forest at night and heard wolves howling in the distance: alone, but watched by things that he could not see. Behind him, he heard some knights mutter pleas to God. Armand motioned them forward and they followed him into the shadows, their eyes flicking in the unnatural dark, hands gripping blades and shields nervously. Only the priest moved without hesitation.

They followed twisting paths between the houses that led up to the brow of the hill. It was as silent as a tomb, and Armand wondered how anything could live in this place between the light of the world and the darkness of hell. He thought of the marks that the priest had shown them on the dead man's hand, and he found that he was whispering a prayer himself, the words misting the unnaturally cold air.

When they reached the brow of the hill, they found it was a clear space of bare, dead earth at least thirty paces across. At its center stood the stones of an ancient doorway, the last remnants of a structure that must once have covered the whole hill. The doorway was twice Armand's height and made of three massive blocks of finished stone: one capping the other two to form a blunt frame for the dark sky beyond. Someone had daubed twisting marks onto the stones, marks that were surrounded by handprints and smears that looked black in the half-light.

"Devil's mark," hissed a man close to Armand, and he heard whispers spread through the knights as they encircled the ancient stones.

The priest snorted at the words. Armand was about to ask what the marks were when the priest walked out from the circle of knights, his hand raised as if in crooked benediction.

"*Gwl' hq' lhl*, Oracle of Oblivion, Night's Exile!" shouted the priest, his voice raised as if in a high wind. "I call you by your name in the hour of your passing." The words hung in the air. Some of the knights called out as the priest spoke, threats and curses bubbling up out of their fear. None of them moved. They just stood staring at the old stone doorway as if tethered like cattle.

Armand said nothing; his eyes were fixed on the marks on the stone. He thought they looked like the outline of a man drawn by the tips of fingers. They looked like nothing—like a child's scribbling—but he could not look away.

Armand was still staring when a man staggered from the doorway. He seemed to step from nowhere, as if collapsing from the dark sky seen through the stone doorway. He was old, naked, and famine-thin, his sagging skin hanging loose off a bent frame of bones. His long fingers held a staff of twisted wood, its surface worn smooth. As the old man stumbled closer, Armand could see that his eyes were closed and his mouth was opening and closing soundlessly. The man stopped, swaying on the spot, just in front of the doorway. There was a moment of silence.

"I bring sacrifice and demand my due as a questioner." The priest turned, waving his hand across the throng of knights before the stone doorway. "They came of their own will, and have been given the choice to turn back." The priest smiled, and it was the smile of a wolf looking at a flock. "*Haq' lhl, drg, nagl,* they are yours in payment."

The words shook in Armand's head, the guttural syllables clawing at the warm docility he had felt in the presence of the priest. He saw the lies, the veil that had been pulled across his instincts, shredding as he looked at the smiling priest. He felt rage, and that rage tore through his fear in a red tide.

"Enough of this," he snarled, stepping forward and raising his sword to cut the grinning priest down.

Behind the priest, the old man's eyes snapped open.

The sword blow never fell.

Behind the lids, there was nothing but a black void. Armand froze as the old man shook where he stood, his thin limbs juddering faster and faster. A buzzing ring filled Armand's ears like a swarm of flies caught beneath a metal bowl. Beyond the stone doorway, the cold light of stars burned in a thousand scattered flecks of light.

The old man's mouth opened and darkness flowed out in a silent scream as his jaw stretched wider and wider. His skin split and flesh sloughed off his frame like wax melting in a flame. His form uncoiled in thick strands of muscle and sinew like wool being unwound from a spindle. Where a man had been, a shape stood. It looked like the outline of a human figure, a black silhouette, a flickering shadow cast by firelight. It had no dimension, features, or substance, but it stood in front of Armand and his knights like a statue carved out of midnight.

He looked at the shadow figure and felt his soul collapse; images passed in front of his eyes, impossible things, things that made him want to scream and laugh and murder and dream. Blood was running down his face from his mouth and nose as he fell to the floor, his limbs twitching. Above it all, he heard the priest's voice rise again, eager, triumphant.

Black tendrils flowed out from the figure, coiling through the air and across the ground, wrapping around the knights, squeezing, flowing into screaming mouths and wide eyes. Some thrashed like men caught in a fast flowing tide, others gave childlike whimpers as they were pulled down, the darkness closing over them like storm waters.

And then Armand realized he was alone with the priest on the suddenly silent hill.

"The payment is taken. I demand my due as a questioner," said the priest, his voice echoing as if they stood in a vast cave.

There was a pause, a gathering stillness. The priest was kneeling, his head bowed as if he was a pilgrim waiting for a blessing.

The shadow outline flickered, its shape changing as if it had no fixed dimension.

"What is it to be without death?" asked the priest, a slight tremble in his voice.

The shadow reached out with a dark hand and touched the priest on his head. He screamed and began to burn. Flesh boiled away in layers to reveal bones that charred from white to black, and organs withered within a blackened skeleton. The screaming ended and Armand felt something flow through his limbs, bathing him in agony, blinding him and filling his mind with white light and shrieking. He heard a high voice echoing inside his skull, pleading as it was smothered by a presence that whispered to it like a priest to a dying man. Armand could feel the sensations of his body receding. Then, he realized that the pleading voice was his own. He had one last instant of terror and pain and was no more.

The priest opened his eyes and raised his head from the dust. The noon sun beat down on him, and beyond the stone doorway he could see blue sky. He staggered to his feet; his limbs felt heavy. He looked down at himself and saw a blood-stained surcoat over a coat of chain mail covering a body made strong by war. By his foot, a pile of grey ash trailed smoke into the dry air on a thread of wind. All around him the town stood empty, the fields beyond suddenly withering under the sun.

The priest turned the face that had been Armand's to the blue sky and laughed.

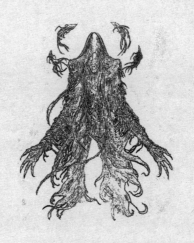

Part One

Fête of Shadows

Mr. Hugo Bradbury
and Mrs. Helena Bradbury
request the pleasure of your company

at
Stonegroves House,
Arkham, Massachusetts

for a grand Fête of Shadows

at
7 o'clock p.m.
Wednesday 14th July 1929

Please dress to the tune and style of the
wondrous and mysterious.

Each guest is required to show his or her
invitation upon arrival.

CHAPTER ONE

Dr. Fields

Easttown, Arkham

Y ou didn't need to come. I didn't want you to come, Father."
Dr. Fields looked at his daughter and didn't know what
to say. He had told young men that they would die before their
time, had watched his wife die inch by painful inch as the cancer
ate her from the inside, but faced with his only daughter standing
defiant and ragged in these cramped and filthy rooms, he did not
know what he should do.

He was a tall man, thin but healthy for his age, with blue eyes
in a face framed by grey white hair. In his best suit, he was the kind
of man to whom people gave respect and the time of day without
thought, the kind of man who they had been happy to bring their
aches, pains, and fears to for nearly thirty years. But standing in the
middle of the gloomy room, his hat clutched in both hands, his
feet neatly together, he looked more like a nervous child.

"I wanted to see you." He smiled, but could feel its weakness.
He flicked his eyes up to her face, so thin and hard it reminded
him of her mother in the last hollow weeks of her life. His daughter's matted blond hair sat in a tangle above a pinched sallow face

which spoke of meals left uneaten. Her eyes were hard and dark above a thin mouth set into an angry line. She wore a grey dress mottled with patterns that might have once been flowers and the oily smudges of old stains. She was not even thirty, but hard times and trouble had wrung youth from her and left her like a rag stained by bitterness and worn through by the harsh rub of life.

"I was worried about you," he said.

"Yeah?" she sneered, and turned away from him to search through a litter-piled sideboard for a cigarette.

He glanced around again. The apartment was on the ground floor and the bright light of summer came through the dusty windows in a gloomy haze. There was a metal-framed single bed on a sagging wooden floor, and a stove stained from heat and spills. Unwashed pots and dishes sat in a sink set into a narrow counter of wood across which mold had spread in damp brown patches. Piles of clothes covered furniture in tangled drifts that mingled with dust-covered pictures, bundles of books, and broken china. A heavy smell of damp, spoiled food, and dust hung in the air.

"You can't live like this, Amelia," he said, looking up at her as she found a pack of pre-rolled cigarettes and struck a match to light one. She exhaled a long plume of smoke.

"How I live is none of your business, Fath—" She bit off the last word, not looking at him.

"This place is not healthy," he said, casting his eyes over the squalor of the room. He saw a man's shoe half-hidden under a pile of dust-covered fabric. It was Henry's. Another part of a life that had fallen to ruin around his daughter, remnants of her past spread like the debris of a storm left at the tide's edge.

There was, he saw, one small area of order in the chaos and grime: a small table of cheap, stripped pine on which lay a neatly folded grey garment weighed down by what looked like a broach made of polished metal in the shape of two hands clasped together.

"Why did you come? My health?" She was glaring at him,

smoke curling from the cigarette as she held it to her mouth.

"Yes. Yes, in part," he said, trying to keep his voice level and soothing.

"That's not your concern," she snapped as she turned away from him again. She began shifting piles of clothes as if looking for something.

"I am your father: it has and always will be my concern," he said, a hard edge of authority and emotion coming into his tone—the father talking to the defiant little girl.

"You lost the right to say that a long time ago," she said, curling her lip.

"Look at this place, Amelia," he gestured around him, concern overriding the careful control in his voice. "Look at your life."

Suddenly she was facing him shaking with rage.

"Life, what life?" she bawled, her voice raw, her pale face flushed red. She kicked a pile of clothes and framed pictures. "This is it. This is all that I have." She looked at him, the hand holding the cigarette stabbing at the debris around the room, ash and sparks falling from its burning tip. "Scraps for the pawn broker so that I can get a few more cents to keep eating food and sleeping indoors." She had begun to cry as she shouted, and as she finished she slumped to the floor gripping her knees, her body shaking as tears streaked down her face.

He stood for a moment, uncertain what to do. He had always been unsure what to do with his daughter. The blood, pain, and suffering of others held no fear for him, but the girl on the floor crying filled him with hesitation and awkward uncertainty for everything that had been taken from her. He realized that he had not held her since she was a child. Even when her mother died, he had found a way through the pain on his own. He had held his face unmoving, his back straight, and let his daughter cry on the shoulders of others. He bent down, taking care to place his hat on the floor, and hugged her as she sobbed.

"Amelia," he said, his voice soft, but she kept on crying. He did not want to say anything else. For a moment, he glimpsed in his mind the father he might have been and wanted to hold onto the possibility that he could undo the past—his distance from his daughter and his poor choices. She continued to cry, but he found the resolve to say what he knew he must.

"Amelia," he began, pulling himself away from her so that he could look into her puffed and tear-streaked face. He thought that she looked like a child again—the same open wide eyes looking up at him that he remembered from a long time ago. "I came to see you because I had a letter from Dr. Zulock at Arkham Asylum. He says that you have not attended any treatments since you were discharged a month ago." She stopped crying.

"Dr. Zulock says you have taken up with a spiritual group rather than take his treatment." She pulled away from him, the tearful softness leaving her face. "It is important that you continue your treatment with Dr. Zulock. Your psychological state—"

"My state?" She was on her feet again, all her anger and defiance flowing back into her face. "My state? All you have ever been able to see is condition, disease, treatment, medicine. Treatment! There is no treatment, no medicine. You would have known that if you had been here when Thomas died, rather than at the end of a telegram." She was looking down at him, fists clenched at her sides, eyes wide with anger. He closed his eyes for a moment and let out a breath.

"I have never been sorrier than when you lost your child." He looked at his daughter, wishing her to believe him, knowing that she would not.

Her son, his grandchild, had contracted influenza in the waning months of the great epidemic. As the fever ran higher, he'd begun to cough up bright yellow goblets of phlegm. He had coughed for days. Then the coughing had stopped and his fever had run higher and higher. It had not stopped until the night the hospital doctors came to find Amelia Knowles and her husband Henry to tell them that their only son had died. Henry Knowles had found comfort in a bottle soon after, and a month later had taken a train to Innsmouth and had walked to the end of the peer at dusk, a whiskey bottle in his hand. His body was never found.

"Thomas. My son was named Thomas."

"I know. I was not here but—"

"No you weren't, and when Henry went, you still weren't," she said, her voice hard.

"I...," he began, but he did not know what to say. The truth was that when he'd heard the devastating news he had been afraid, afraid of facing the cold wave of grief that he had felt when he had held his wife's hand as she died years before her time. Worn to shreds by the long war against the Spanish flu epidemic, a war he had been fighting patient by patient, he had had nothing left. For him, there had been nowhere to go for comfort, and at that time he had had nothing to give his daughter. So, he'd locked the door to his office in Boston and wept for his grandchild alone, leaving his daughter to the comfort of others. A week after the death of his son-in-law, Dr. Fields had received a private note from his old friend Dr. Giles Zulock of Arkham Asylum. The note had said that his daughter had suffered a psychological break and been committed to the asylum's care for her own safety.

"What good could you have done anyway?" she asked.

"Amelia, listen, you need treatment."

"I have all the help I need, and I need none of yours."

"This group you have taken up with—I don't know what they are, but I do not like what I hear." He had gone to see his old friend when he arrived in Arkham, and Dr. Zulock had warned him that his daughter had not only refused treatment after being discharged, but had taken up with some sort of religious sect. They were called "the Hand of Solace," he'd said. The group claimed to offer help to those who had suffered great loss, though what they did exactly, Dr. Zulock had not known.

"More doctors whispering. What are the whispers saying, Daddy?" She was speaking in a mocking, baby-like whine, a sneer on her lips as she watched him.

"That this group is like a church without God, and that they prey on the bereaved and broken. I do not know what they want from you but—"

"They don't want anything."

"Amelia, I wish I could believe that, but I don't," he said, a pleading note in his voice.

"You don't?" she asked, her voice mocking.

"No. I think it would be better if you did not associate with them anymore."

Her face was a mask of incredulous anger.

"You want me to leave them? To leave them, and go back to Dr. Zulock with his hypnosis, talking about my nightmares until I feel better?"

"Amelia…," he pleaded.

"Yes, yes, of course. Of course you want me to do that, Daddy. Leave the people who can do something and go back to something nice and safe. Somewhere a doctor signs a form and you can talk to him about how treatment is progressing." She turned away from him, walking to the small table with the folded grey garment and metal brooch. Her voice had become formal, cold, like a bank manger dealing with a regrettably unacceptable request. "Well, thank you for your concern, Dr. Fields, but I will find all the help I need in the hands of others." She picked up the polished metal brooch, turning its silvered surface in the light.

"What happened to you?" He could think of nothing else to say; he felt beaten, defeated, lost.

"What happened to *me*, Father?" she asked, her voice now calm and hard. "*Hell* happened to me, while you were looking the other way." She put the brooch down, walked to the door, and opened it. "I want you to leave now."

"Please listen, Amelia—"

"I have listened, Father," she said. "I have listened to you and your words are as worthless as your medicine."

He picked up his hat from the floor. She held the door open. The hallway outside was bright with the light of summer.

"Amelia. Please."

"Goodbye, Father." She did not look at him as he stepped outside.

"Amelia. Take care." The last word was lost as she closed the door.

Twenty minutes after he'd left, Amelia left her apartment. As she stepped down from the entrance hall of the rotting, gabled building, she was smiling. Sunshine spilled over the high peaked roofs into the narrow Easttown street, glinting off her matted hair. Tucked under her arm was a neatly folded grey garment and gripped in her hand was a brooch in the shape of two clasped hands.

The street was quiet and the air smelled of the drains warming under the cobbled sidewalks. She began to walk, looking as if she enjoyed every step and breath; she looked like a different girl from the one who had sobbed on the floor and shouted at her father. She looked like someone on a journey with hope and joy at its end.

From the shadows of the gap between two houses, Dr. Fields watched his daughter and felt his thoughts fill with worries and fears. For a second he wondered if he should just leave. Then he thought of the grey garment folded neatly on the small table away from the detritus of his daughter's life. He thought of the brooch of clasped hands and the worries that Dr. Zulock had shared with him about the Hand of Solace. A chill spread up his back. *No*, he thought. He would not fail his daughter again; he would not let her face the demons of life alone.

Dr. Fields slid from the shadows and began to follow his daughter through the sun-soaked streets of Arkham.

CHAPTER TWO

Raker

Boston

The coffee arrived half cold in a chipped mug. Raker dumped sugar into the tepid brew and stirred it in, watching the granules dissolve. The diner was quiet, the smell of grease and cigarette smoke stale, the worn seats in the few booths empty. A fat man three empty stools along the counter was blinking at the sports page. Grease stains spotted the front of his post office uniform and he was resting his elbows either side of a half-eaten plate of food. Out beyond the glass front of the diner, the street was folded in the warm dark of a summer's night. On the other side of the street, Raker could see the train station, the stone pillars set into its curved front framing high windows that spilled light onto the street. At the peak of the station's curved front, the hands of a half-visible clock lay in the small hours.

"Anything else?" asked the girl on the other side of the counter. She looked tired, thought Raker, like him. He noted the creases on her face that came from worry rather than age, the wary look of someone waiting to see what dream would wither next. He knew that look: it was the one he had been dodging all his life—sometimes, he even managed it for awhile.

"No, thank you," said Raker. He smiled. "Keep the change." She looked at the money in her hand and back at him. He read the question on her face: *sure you don't need it yourself?* He had to admit that he did not look his best. The brown suit he was wearing did not quite fit, he needed a clean shirt, and his corn blond hair needed a cut and comb. He had not had a chance to get himself cleaned up in the last couple of days, and the suit was one he had borrowed in the hope that it might make him more difficult to recognize. But, he thought, he could be in a worse state—a lot worse.

He flicked another glance at the clock and at the time on his train ticket; time seemed to be limping past. He wanted to be gone from Boston, gone now. Gone before the people he owed found him. He wanted to be moving before they figured out that he was not going back to his apartment. They would come after him, he knew. You did not just run away from the amount of money he owed. He was doing the smart thing, going where no one knew him, vanishing. He snorted to himself. *First smart thing you've done in awhile*, he thought.

He looked at the well-thumbed photograph he had been turning over in his hands: a pretty face, hair cut short enough to cause outrage, lips drawn back to laugh, a flash of mischief in the eyes. He grinned to himself and flicked the picture over to look at the words written on the back:

> To my Charlie,
> So you don't forget
> —V

Her name was Vivian, but she liked to be called "V." They had met at a party two years ago, the kind of party where the shadowy world of people who lived on the edge of the law and the very rich met over glasses of expensively illegal liquor. He smiled at the memory, still bright in his mind. She had been in Boston staying with friends for a few months—a cluster of bright young people who thought that it was great fun to touch the underbelly of the world, confident in the knowledge that they could retreat back to their safe, moneyed lives. Vivian had been different, though. She'd had a thoughtful distance from her dilettante friends that no one else seemed to see—at least no one apart from Raker. They had talked and laughed. She was so clever and she did not judge him; she made him better somehow. They had had six months—a glittering, unreal six months—then she had said that her mother and brother had bought a house in an old town only two hours away by train and they wanted her home. Raker had wondered if they were trying to stop her less-than-respectable lifestyle. She had smiled grimly at that and said she would write.

Raker ran a hand across his chin, felt the two days of stubble on his jaw, and put the photo in his pocket. He had dreamed of buying enough respectability that Vivian's high society family might accept him, so he'd tried to make his own money. For a man like him, the only way to do that was on the wrong side of the law. Prohibition had created endless possibilities for fast and tainted money. He knew it had not been honest. *Find someone making pure, honest money and you will be looking at a poor man,* he'd thought. Then, a few months ago, Vivian had stopped writing, and he had started taking more risks, bad risks, as if the danger would make his doubts and fears about Vivian fade.

What did her not writing mean? Had she forgotten him? Or was it that damn family of hers? The ice-eyed mother and the slab-bodied pig of a brother—had they found out that she still wrote to him? The thought would not shake, though, and had clung to his thoughts as soon as he'd known he would have to run. He looked at the train ticket again. He would find out why she had not written soon enough. After all, he had no one else he could run to.

"Deep thoughts, Raker?" asked a soft voice next to his ear. He had time to raise his head and catch a glimpse of a bulky shape behind him before a hand grabbed his head and slammed it into the counter. He tumbled off the stool, the diner spinning around him. The girl behind the counter was screaming. His nose and mouth were thick with blood. The fat postman farther down the counter was scrabbling for the door. Raker could see a figure standing over him, a long, dark coat over wide shoulders, flat face half shadowed by the brim of a hat. Another figure stood two paces behind the first. Raker saw the glint of a length of iron bar held loose at the second man's side.

"They want their money, Raker," said the first man, his voice low, unhurried, reasonable. *Schmidt*, thought Raker. The man's name was Schmidt. Raker had seen him once or twice, heard about him: a hard man, a breaker not a killer. Not that that was any comfort. Raker opened his mouth to reply. Schmidt's patent leather shoe lashed into his ribs. "No, not yet, Raker. You don't get to talk yet." Schmidt looked up and jerked his head at the girl behind the counter. "Go home. You ring the police, someone will come for you." Raker watched the girl scamper for the door and run once she was through it. The second man locked the door and carefully pulled the blinds down over the windows. Through the pain in Raker's head and his sucking, cracking breaths, he tried to think. Things were about to get a lot worse; he knew how this kind of routine worked.

Schmidt had taken two steps away from Raker and taken his coat off, folding it over a stool. Raker could see the relaxed bulk of the man's muscle moving under his shirt. He looked down at Raker with small, dark eyes.

"You know how this goes," said Schmidt, unfastening his cuffs and carefully rolling up his sleeves. "Thought you would have made it out of town by now, given us a chase." Schmidt looked at the other man. "Get him up." Raker watched as the man placed the iron bar on the countertop before he stepped closer. Raker noticed the man was licking his lips.

"Get up," the man growled. Raker made a feeble move to stand. "I said get up!" The man's kick was heavy, but not fast, and Raker was ready. He caught it before it reached the full force of its swing and yanked hard. The man fell, crashing onto the floor with a yell of surprise. Raker was on his feet, turning to where Schmidt stood. A punch hammered into the side of Raker's head. He reeled against the counter, feeling his head fill with a fluid dullness. Blood flowed around his left eye as he saw a blurred shape moving close and fast. He jerked to his left and felt the punch graze his forehead.

On the floor, the second man began to pull himself to his feet. Raker reached across the counter, feeling with his fingertips, his blood-blurred eyes locked on the two men. One more blow and there would be nothing but pain and splintering bones and his sobbing pleas. His fingers touched iron.

Schmidt punched again. For a big man he was fast, bulk and muscle flowing with hammer force. Raker brought the iron bar around and felt it shake as it thudded into Schmidt's chest. He went down with a swallowed cry, scattering chairs as he fell. The second man was on his feet, moving forward, fists balled. Raker took a fast step forward, lashed his foot into the man's groin and brought the iron bar down on the side of his knee with a splintering noise. There was a long, boiling scream as the man crumpled into a ball holding his leg, sobbing. Raker looked around, suddenly feeling the blood hammering through his limbs, making his hands shake. Schmidt was still down, gasping, his face white, flecks of blood and spit on his lips and chin. Neither man would be coming after him. He dropped the iron bar and stepped back to the counter.

His train ticket still sat next to his half-empty coffee, a spatter of his own blood over the destination. Scooping it up, along with his hat, he made for the door, pulling it shut after him as he walked across the road to the station. Every part of his body screamed to run, but he knew that people would look at a running man and ignore a walking one. He pulled his hat low trying to hide his bloody face. Glancing at the clock, he saw that he only had a few minutes before the train left.

The station was nearly empty—a few lonely travelers sitting in the cavernous station hall, a half-asleep man behind the ticket counter. His footsteps echoed on the polished marble floor as he walked quickly past the glass-fronted shops and wooden benches toward the platforms. He occasionally glanced behind him, wondering how long it would be before Schmidt or the other man were found or called for help. He hoped neither had seen the destination on his ticket before they'd slammed his head into the counter. He thought about what Vivian would say when she saw him.

At the entrance to the platforms, an inspector frowned at the blood spots obscuring the destination on Raker's ticket.

"Where are you headed?" asked the inspector, eyes moving over the blood on Raker's face.

"Arkham."

CHAPTER THREE

Jacqueline Fine
Long Island Sound

There was pain, bright pain, and a stream of sensations and images flowing through her: a house glittering under the cold stars, blood running across white stone, grey figures, and a man with an old face and cold eyes, so very cold...

Blackness and a voice as dry as dust: "Welcome to Arkham, Miss Bell..."

She was falling through bright light...

A bell attached to a glass-fronted door rang. There were letters on the door, neat black letters in paint; she was stepping through the door and there was...

Dead flesh, mounded and sliced, slack grasping hands...

The smell of must and old paper...

"Help me," said a man on a shadow-covered floor. He raised his hands and she could see the blood...

A cold-eyed man was smiling at her from so close she could kiss him. Except it was her face twisting in surprise as she looked at herself...

There was a shadow on the road in front of her. It stood before her, *a hole cut out of daylight into darkness. Then, it had a face, a face of paper skin and ink black lines. "There is no way out, no solace," said the voice. The old man smiled at her and his face changed, sliding from age into beautiful cruelty. It was a different face, but the smile was the same; it was a smile of savagery and pleasure.*

There was no sky and…

…she could see again.

"Jacqueline?" asked the man's voice. "Jacqueline, are you all right?"

Jacqueline…that is not my name, she thought. She could see a concerned face looking at her from underneath the brim of a cream boating hat. It was a kind face, grey blue eyes fixed on her with genuine concern, a curl of blond hair straying across a tanned forehead. He wore white slacks, an open-collared shirt, and deck shoes. "Jacqueline, darling?" asked the man looking straight at her.

But that is not my name, she thought as panic flooded through her. She did not know who or where she was. She was sitting in the shadow of a parasol, the blue sky clear above, the grass green beneath her chair. A few yards away, the reflection-flecked water lapped against the edge of a wooden dock. Far out on the gleaming water, sails scudded past in the warm wind. On her other side, a smooth lawn rose to a large house that sat beneath the sun, its walls sharp white. She had a glass of iced tea in her hand, its surface trembling in her grip. The broad-brimmed hat sitting tight on her short, black hair seemed like an iron clamp on her skull, and the black and white print dress brushed like something dead over her skin. It felt as if she had woken from a dream to find herself halfway through someone else's life.

"Darling…," began the man, reaching out to take her hand. She pulled it away as if his touch was red hot. She was alone in a strange world, and all she knew was the message of the living nightmare she had just experienced: something terrible was drawing close, walking from the future to become the present. It would happen; she knew it. *It must not happen.*

The man sat with a worried expression on the other side of a table spread with china plates and a tray of brightly iced cakes.

"Jacqueline?" he asked.

But that is not my name, she thought again as memories dropped into her mind. *I am Elizabeth Bell*. It took a heartbeat more for her to remember why. "Jacqueline Fine" was her assumed name, the name she had begun a new life with, away from music halls and the booze stink of clubs. It was the first lie she had told to leave her old life. Remembering it brought the rest of her memories back in a steady trickle.

Walter Fane—the man's name slipped back into her mind like a fragment bobbing to the surface of the sea after a storm. He was her fiancé, and he believed she was someone she was not. He thought her the orphaned daughter of a Canadian intellectual, well-bred but without money. That was a lie, of course—he would never have asked her to marry him if he knew the truth. Her father had been a stage magician and a drunk who had dragged her across the continent from town to town and stage to stage, assisting with his show. When she became older, she'd had an act of her own as a child fortune teller and medium. She'd been good at it; she could convince people she was the real thing. It was when she was drawing a bigger crowd than him that her father had started hitting her when he drank. Around that same time, she'd started to dream of the future. It was small things at first, moments that she'd dreamt and then happened. Then she'd begun to see more and more. Three days before her father died, she'd dreamt of him falling down the stairs. She'd done nothing to stop her dream from happening, and had cried as the rain came down and the gravediggers shoveled earth over her father's coffin.

Alone, and with nothing and no one, she had remade her life. She was clever, charming, and good at lying. Her first two decades of life had given her those skills, and she had used them to make herself into Jacqueline Fine. She had covered her old life with lies and ignored the tug of dreams that might be of the future. The lies had given her happiness, until now, until this dream of terror and blood.

She looked at Walter's simple, happy face and felt a stab of guilt. She loved him, and he loved a lie.

"Yes, yes, I am quite all right," lied Jacqueline. "Thank you." She smiled at Walter, careful to let nothing of what had just happened show through to the surface of her expression. For a second, she had gone tumbling through visions and sounds and returned back to where she had been with barely a heartbeat pause. She had had moments like this before—glimpses of living nightmares— but not for a long time and never this strong. And in the past it had never happened in daylight, or when she was awake.

"If you are sure, darling," said Walter, with only the slightest twitch of an eyebrow. "You looked most peculiar for a second. I hope it is not the heat."

Jacqueline shook her head, thinking. Something had been said just before the waking dream, something that had an echo in what she had seen, a link. She could not remember what it was.

"No, just the light reflecting off the water; for a moment it quite dazzled me." Jacqueline smiled, again thinking of what had just happened. Ever since her father had died, she had ignored the rare moments of strange visions and dreams, and had forced herself to ignore the echo of those visions in things that happened around her. If she admitted they were a part of her then the part of her that she hid—the part with a different name and a childhood spent in misery—would be real. But this vision was not like anything she had ever dreamt. She had felt the malice, the warm stink sensation of blood.

"Did you hear what I said before?" asked Walter, leaning forward, worry replaced with excitement.

He is a good man, thought Jacqueline. Not too bright, kind, unquestioning: just right for her. But he would leave her if he knew who she really was.

They had been engaged for five months, and it seemed that both he and his family had not seen through her carefully constructed story of good breeding and an unfortunately dwindling family fortune. She had the accent, carefully practiced and edged with culture to prove it, after all. Nothing was left of the girl who had followed her father from theatre to theatre doing card tricks and mind readings. That person was gone. At least, that was what she had convinced herself.

"No, sorry, darling. What's the news?"

He gave a grin and picked up a thick, oblong card from the table.

"We have been invited to a party." He turned the card over to show Jacqueline the looping print and the embossed emblem of a domino mask at the bottom. She tried to read the words but he turned the card back over, his eyes playing over it excitedly. "It's a Masque of Shadows."

Jacqueline felt a sudden cold sensation across her skin. She could remember part of what Walter had said before the dream vision had flooded her. There had been a word, a name that had sent her tumbling into the nightmare.

"Who's hosting, darling?" she asked.

"Oh, an old friend from college. His mother just bought a new house." She could see the excitement running through him. "It's going to be incredible. Everybody is talking about it, and we are invited."

"Where is it?" She held her smile in place over a surge of fear. As soon as she asked the question, some part of her knew what he was going to say and did not want to hear the answer.

"It's in Massachusetts, just outside Arkham."

CHAPTER FOUR

Dr. Fields
Merchant District, Arkham

The House of Solace was one dying building lost amongst others. Two stories high with a flat roof, damp crawled up the walls, mottling the crumbling red of the bricks, and dust misted its windows. The green paint of its doors and frames was flaking to show the wood beneath, like bones beneath charred skin. It had been a warehouse, built decades before in a time when wealth had floated into Arkham with the river tide. That time had long passed, and if it were not for the neatly painted sign, a glance would have said that the building was deserted and empty. The sign hung above the high loading doors that faced the street. It was a simple sign painted in uncomplicated letters on a white board. "House of Solace" was written above a stylized symbol of two hands clasped together. The buildings that pressed close to it on all sides were equally run down and dilapidated, remnants of a forgotten type of commerce left like carcasses on the shoreline of a crueler age.

From across the narrow street, Dr. Fields looked at the rain-stained windows of the House of Solace and worried. He had followed his daughter through the streets of Arkham, passing from the mildew squalor of Easttown, across the river, past the shop fronts of Rivertown, and into the narrow roads and close-pressed decay of the old Merchant District. He had followed her, doing his best to stay unseen, hanging back out of sight, ready to duck into alleys or doorways if she looked around. But she did not look around; she just strode with purpose and without worry, her worn shoes clicking on the sidewalk. Doubt followed Dr. Fields with every step. Was he doing the right thing? Should he respect her wishes and leave her alone? Was he right to doubt the intentions of the Hand of Solace? The questions looped endlessly through his mind, repeating then resolving into clarity before dissolving into uncertainty again.

Now, faced by the dilapidated facade of this House of Solace, those worries and more crowded his mind with conflicting voices. He had seen his daughter go inside through a small door to the left of the loading doors, unlocking the side door with a large key. Other people had followed. Some looked respectable, their clothes neat and clean, but most looked ragged, tatters and stains mottling their clothes, dirt marking their faces. Each entered through the small door his daughter had unlocked.

Dr. Fields looked at his pocket watch. The light was fading fast in the shadowed street and he had to squint to read the time. No one had entered the building for over ten minutes. He glanced back at the high, dust-smeared windows of the House of Solace. Light the flickering color of lamps or candles played across the grimy glass. He glanced around. The street was silent, the shadows from the buildings spreading softly down its edges. As quietly as he could, Dr. Fields crossed the road to the front of the House of Solace and began to edge toward the small side door.

When Dr. Zulock had written to say that he was concerned that Amelia had stopped attending treatment and become involved in some sort of spiritual group, Dr. Fields's main concern had been with Amelia refusing proper psychiatric care. After he had talked to Dr. Zulock earlier that day, his worries had taken a different focus, one that had pushed him to follow his daughter to this building that named itself a House of Solace.

The handle of the door was polished smooth and bright from use. Dr. Fields felt the cold brass under his fingers as he closed his hand around it. This close to the loading doors, he could hear muffled noises from inside. It sounded like singing or chanting, rising and falling without clear rhythm, like the pulse of a failing heart. He felt a surge of fear at what he was doing.

From what Zulock had said, the Hand of Solace was a type of spiritual group. What their beliefs were, Dr. Zulock had not known, but he had gathered that whatever they were, they were definitely not Christian. Their concern was with suffering and its victims, whom they purported to offer hope. They had begun recruiting from amongst the former patients of Arkham Asylum, and once a handful of his patients were amongst their number, Zulock had begun to become concerned. He found that they also sought out those who had lost loved ones or seen their lives ruined; they hovered around the edges of suffering like vultures offering soft words and printed leaflets on the possibility of hope. What concerned Zulock most was that none of those who became involved with the group would ever talk about what it did or how it helped them. All they would say was that it gave them hope.

The brass door handle turned without a noise. His heart hammering, Dr. Fields pushed the door inward a couple of inches. Light spilled out into the falling night. He could not see much through the finger wide gap. There were shapes, moving shadows, swaying in flickering candlelight. Dr. Fields moved his face closer to the opening, hearing the surge of sound from inside.

"*Gul'ngh'fltqa,*" rose the chanting in soft, guttural unity.

"There is a way, and it can be opened," came a lone, loud voice, edged with a purring accent.

"*Itaq'ghl'n'hl!*" The sounds were like the grinding of broken ribs in a shattered chest. They made Dr. Fields shudder in the warm summer night air. He did not know what language they chanted, or if it was a language at all, but it ran through him as if those sounds contained something primordial, something that touched the deepest instincts within him. Though he had not bent his knee in a church for many years, he knew the power of faith, but he had also met his share of quacks and charlatans. He did not believe in the supernatural and superstition—they were just the remnants of lies that people had been telling themselves for thousands of years, lies to give solace or create fear. Reason and science defined the limits of the possible, everything else was delusion.

But, as he listened to the sounds, one word stuck in his mind: *unholy*. His mind felt numb with what was happening on the other side of the door, the possibilities filling his imagination, calling to him.

"The Obsidian Key will unlock peace," came the lone voice.

"*Vd'ul'na!*" The reply was louder and Dr. Fields saw with panic that the door he stood by was opening wider. He looked down to see his hand still on the door handle. Someone was opening the door; they must know he was there. Any moment they would look out and see him crouching in the darkening street. The crack of light was now a broad strip through which he could see a high-ceilinged room blurred with incense smoke and lit by shifting light. The door swung wider, the sound of its hinges lost under the guttural sound of chanting. He saw the backs of figures clad in grey robes, their bodies smothered under the thick fabric, formless, swaying. The sound wrapped around him. He felt something half revolting half soothing, like a wet-mouthed whisper at the back of his head.

"A way must be opened," called the lone voice. Dr. Fields felt something in that clear, purring voice that pulled on him. He realized that the door was swinging wider and wider. The room beyond was filled with grey, hooded figures all looking toward a figure in a white robe. A cowl hid the figure's face as he stood with his hands in the air, wide sleeves falling from thin, pale arms. The dozens of burning candles made the white of his robes glow, and for a moment, Dr. Fields thought that the figure looked like an angel, like a fire white angel in a grey world.

"And it shall be opened!" came the drone reply. Dr. Fields felt his lips moving to form the reply even though he did not know the words. It was as if he was on the edge of something warm and comforting, something that wanted to help and only wanted you to listen in return.

With cold shock, he realized he was about to step into the room. He looked at his hand on the door and realized it had been *him* pushing it open. He gasped, feeling the world snap back into shape around him. A figure at the back of the grey-robed throng turned its head. Dr. Fields caught sight of an eye and mouth under the shadowy fold of cloth. The eye went wide with surprise and the mouth began to open.

Dr. Fields turned and ran before the cry came, his aging muscles burning as he rushed down the silent streets, his heart hammering. After a few minutes, he stopped in the shadow of an empty house, its blank windows filled with teeth of shattered glass. Gasping for air, he looked to see if anyone was behind him, but the street was empty. A sharp pain was hammering between his eyes, and as he brought his hand to his face, he felt warmth on his hand and tasted the sharp tang of blood running from his nose.

He had been right, he thought, right to come here when he heard about the Hand of Solace, right to follow his daughter. He thought of the soft, warm feeling that had drawn him to open the door, and the strange sounds of the chanted replies. Beyond this, there was something more, something he had glimpsed in that candle lit room, something that made the words "they give us hope" feel like the words written on a tomb.

"What have you done, my daughter," he whispered to himself. There had been something about what was happening inside the House of Solace that shook him more than he wanted to admit. *Unholy*, the word whispered in his mind again. He told himself to remember that the hypnotic effects and the suggestive power of ritualized gatherings were well-documented; to call something "unholy" was to give credence to irrationality and lies.

Still, the experience had made him more afraid for his daughter. It was as if he was watching her fall down an abyss into oblivion. He had to do something; he had no doubt of that now. The police would not help him; no matter how much they might find a religious sect distasteful, such organizations were hardly unknown. They might talk to his daughter if he insisted, but she showed no outward sign of being disturbed. They would do nothing. No, he needed to break the hold that this Hand of Solace had on her. He needed to understand the lie that had given her hope. It was a matter beyond the bounds of medicine and science; it existed in the charlatan world of the irrational. He had nothing but distaste for such things and little knowledge of them; he would need help.

He thought of a man he disliked but who had some association with one of the old, supposedly esoteric societies that existed in New England. *Mortimore*—that was the man's name, a fellow medical doctor. Mortimore once had asked Dr. Fields to join the society when he was younger and it seemed his medical career could amount to greatness. The reply he had given had been polite, but he had not managed to keep his distaste from his tone. Mortimore was in Arkham now, successful and wealthy from what Dr. Fields had heard. No doubt the connections offered by his membership in the society had helped.

No matter, thought Dr. Fields. He would have to swallow his distaste and ask Dr. Mortimore if he and his associates knew anything of this Hand of Solace. He would swallow his pride and ask the favor of the society that he had snubbed. Whatever it took would be a small price if it helped save his daughter.

He had heard that the society had its main branch here, catering to the busy professional lives of its membership. He was not certain where it was exactly, but he was sure that once in the French Hill district he would find the place he needed. Wrapped in faux mysticism it might be, but the Silver Twilight Lodge did not hide itself completely from view.

CHAPTER FIVE

Raker
Easttown, Arkham

It had taken a fold of bills to get into the back room at Hibb's Roadhouse. There was a front room set with tables served by the same watery-eyed old man who had looked at the stains on Raker's jacket and the ragged bills for a long time before grudgingly showing him the other room. It was in the cellar, hidden down a set of worn stairs behind a plain door that looked as if it led to a closet. At the bottom of the stairs, a thick, weighted curtain muffled the sound of the room beyond. The space was small, a few tables scattered around, the floor covered by tattered rugs. The smell of sweat and spilled beer was strong enough to cut through the cigarette smoke.

There were a few people, some on their own nursing small glasses of amber liquid, others clustered together in muttering groups. There was a quiet, surly mood to the place. A few customers eyed Raker when he walked in; others seemed to notice nothing but their own thoughts. There was no bar, just a bored-looking woman too old for the cut of her dress and a low-grade heavy dealing cards to himself at a table. Just to the side of the heavy was another door that Raker guessed led to where they kept the booze. He picked a table and asked for a beer.

Raker did not want to drink. Booze was expensive and he avoided it where he could, but people talked more when there was liquor in them. He wanted information about the Bradburys before he went up to their door—the kind of information that fell out in loose talk—so he had found a place where tongues wagged.

He'd walked around Arkham after getting off the train in the dawn light. He did not like the town, its buildings old and creaking with age, their high gables pointing toward the lightening sky. He felt like they were looming over him, silent, watching. He had been to New York, had walked the streets next to the cliff-like skyscrapers and felt dwarfed, but there was something about Arkham that made him feel small and vulnerable. He'd once heard someone say that just before dawn you saw everything as it really was. If that was true, the Arkham he saw looked like a sunken, hollow face that you could only tell was alive by the gleam in its eyes.

The woman brought Raker his drink and he paid her without a word. He was already gauging the other patrons. There were two hard drinkers and a cluster of men with a muscled look who spoke together in low, accented English. Dock workers, he guessed. Beside these characters there was a pair of uneasy-looking men talking in hushed tones, and a man in a worn but good quality suit sitting on his own in a corner. The glass in front of the man was empty and he was looking around the room, casting a wide smile around like a searchlight. The smile was slightly fixed and there was a glassy sheen to the eyes that looked out from behind round glasses. He looked like a banker or a clerk, unused to his surroundings, but with a reason to drink. That meant he would be unguarded.

That's my man, thought Raker, and walked over to the guy's table.

"Mind if I join you?" asked Raker. The man looked up and beamed at Raker, his eyes not quite focusing.

"Sure." Raker noted the controlled slur in the man's voice. That was good; it meant that the man was not a seasoned drinker, and was already on his way to being drunk.

"You want a drink?" Raker indicated the man's glass with his own and turned to call the waitress over without waiting for the reply. "Another for me and my friend here." The woman nodded and Raker turned back to the man.

"Thank you..." The man looked like he was about to ask a question.

Raker cut him off, this was all about momentum, about leaving the other person with no time to think about why they had a new best friend. "Just got into town; never been here before."

He let the conversation run on for awhile. Apparently, the man was a banking clerk and lived alone. His name was Franklin. Raker carefully avoided giving his name in return. There was something that was worrying Franklin, something he had seen while walking in the woods a few days ago. He seemed spooked. Raker didn't really care why the man was jittery enough to go to a drinking hole, but from what Franklin said, he knew a lot about the town. Raker smiled to himself. He had found what he needed: an informed local.

He let Franklin mutter more about how he could not stop thinking about the swirling patterns on trees, then dropped in the Bradburys' name as casually as he could, mentioning that he had come out here to work for them. Franklin nodded and took a sip of the third drink Raker had bought for him.

"The Bradburys, up at Stonegroves—that them?"

Raker frowned as if surprised that the man knew them. The address Vivian had given him had been Stonegroves House.

"Yeah, that's them." He paused and hoped Franklin would fill the gap.

"Yeah, they have a lot of money." The man gave a hollow laugh. "Mrs. Bradbury inherited a fortune from her father and another from her husband. At least, that's what I heard."

"Seems so, to buy a place like that." Raker grinned, keeping his tone casual as if only mildly interested. Franklin took a slug from his glass and leaned closer.

"Spent a fortune on it. Been empty for a decade you know— man that built it hung himself a month after it was finished." The man's voice had become an excited whisper. "Body found swinging in the big hall. Never found out why… Been empty until the Bradburys bought it." Raker feigned interest. He wanted to know what the Bradburys were like, not about local tales. Franklin shrugged. "Strange that they stayed after the thing with the girl."

"What?" Raker felt as if cold water was suddenly running through his veins. The relaxed, friendly expression was gone from his face. Could he mean Vivian? Franklin carried on, oblivious to Raker's change in demeanor.

"Only been here a couple years and they are already like the lord and lady of the town. She's most particular when she comes into the bank. And her son? Wouldn't want to say it to his face, but he's a nasty piece of work. Just shows you breeding isn't everything." Raker was not really hearing what Franklin said. He could only think of the offhand way Franklin had said "the thing with the girl."

"What did you say before about a girl?" Raker could not keep the urgency from his voice. The question must have broken through the alcohol dulling Franklin's wits. He gave Raker a sharp look, suddenly wary, the atmosphere of genial gossip gone.

"Sorry, I shouldn't, shouldn't have mouthed off." Franklin's voice was cold and careful. "You work for them and I am sure they are fine people." He slung back the last of his drink and stood, picking his hat up off the table.

"No, it's okay, but what about the girl?" asked Raker, the note of desperation clear in his voice. Franklin shook his head and looked away, avoiding Raker's eyes.

"Can't say, don't really know. Thank you for the drink." Franklin put his hat on and began to walk away.

"Wait…," called Raker, aware that people were watching the exchange. Franklin turned back and looked at Raker with bloodshot, drunk eyes.

"Good luck, whatever it is you are here to do." He touched the brim of his hat, the gesture slightly unsteady. "Be careful, friend. Arkham…it can get under your skin."

CHAPTER SIX

Jacqueline Fine
French Hill, Arkham

A bell rang as she pushed the door open.

"Hello?" she called, one hand still on the glass-paneled door as she peered into the gloom. It was the same shop, she was sure: the neat but worn letters painted on the glass of the door, the ring of the bell, the gloom filled with the shapes of bookcases and cabinets. It smelled of dust and mold, like the inside of a house left to rot under spider webs.

She had recognized the door as she walked through the sun bright streets of Arkham. She had said to Walter that she wanted to look around the town. He had been happy to stay playing croquet with his friend Harry and his wife, whom they were staying with. So she had walked through the streets of Arkham, looking for something that would match the dream, for some thread of the future to grasp.

It had taken two hot hours and her attention had been wandering when she'd seen the shop front. Her glance had caught the wide windows filled with dusty statuary, dark furniture, and empty candlesticks. She'd stopped and stared at the shop front, the glass-paneled door set between two windows, both showing a collection of dust-dulled objects arranged on sun faded red velvet. A sign hung above the door mirroring the words painted on the glass pane beneath: *Curiositie Shoppe*. In her vision, she had not seen what was written on the door, but every other detail fit. It was what she had been looking for: a fixed link with her vision, a place to start.

"Hello?" she called again, and stepped through the door. It hinged shut behind her and the bell above the doorframe rang again. To Jacqueline, it felt like the door of a cell clattering shut behind her. She remembered that she had decided to do this, to follow her vision and try to change fate. Still, she felt as if every step she took into the future bound her more tightly to the nightmare vision she had seen.

Can I change the future, or do I make it certain by trying? It was a question that had robbed her of sleep, but she knew that she had to try. Her *sight*, long dormant, had never lied in the past. It had only ever shown the truth of what was to come. Now, it showed a future of death and shadows, a future she knew was waiting to be born. She was the only person who knew, so she was the only person who could do anything. *I have to do this*, she thought. *I can't let that future happen.* But she did not know what would cause the future as she had seen it, nor how she could divert it. That was why she had come looking for somewhere to pick up a thread of the future, to begin to unravel it.

Inside the Curiositie Shoppe, it took a moment for her eyes to adjust from the brightness of the street. There seemed to be no other light than the sunlight from the windows which faded to a soft charcoal gloom the farther from the door she looked. The shop had a low ceiling but seemed to go a long way back, the space crowded with dark wooden bookcases and glass-fronted cabinets. Statues carved from bone and ebony stared at her from around the sides of tall vases enameled in patterns like green fish scales. Pictures hung on every clear space of wall, drab oils of men and women with sour, elongated faces. On a display easel hung a riot of patterns, thick paint smeared across the canvas to dry in clots of glossy color. She was not sure what the picture was of, but she did not want to look closer to find out.

As her eyes adjusted, some of the objects in the cabinets resolved into necklaces of tarnished silver, grinning painted masks, and jars of fluid in which floated soft, pale objects. There was no order to how the objects were arranged: a polished bone cup sat alone, while the shelf below was crammed with moldering books. Crates of cobweb-covered objects lurked behind shelves and under tabletops. Over it all, the smell of dust and mold hung like a shroud.

"See something you like, madam?" The voice came from so close behind Jacqueline that she had to stifle a scream. She turned around to see a round-shouldered man in a faded brown suit. The man was short, his back curved by age, and his arms hung loose by his sides, the fingers open. White hair ringed his bare, liver-spotted head. In the gloom, Jacqueline could not tell what color his eyes were.

"No," she stammered. "That is, I was just waiting for something to catch my eye." The man smiled, showing a wide crescent of yellow teeth. Jacqueline thought it looked like the smile of a skull.

"Of course, of course," said the man. His voice had a soft sing-song quality, each word pronounced precisely. "We have a wide collection of rare objects and books, from many places and many ages. My name is Mr. Thomas. I have the privilege of being the owner of this establishment. It will be a pleasure to help you. Do you have anything in particular in mind?"

Jacqueline looked around while her mind raced. She had only come into the shop because her dream had led her there. Now she was here, she had hoped that the thread of the future would lead her further. She had no idea what she was here for or why—she had presumed that it would become clear. She looked around, eyes flicking over the objects, books, and pictures, looking for something to pay an interest in. She was about to reply, when she saw the book.

It sat open in a glass-topped cabinet only a foot away. The pages were wide and yellow with age, their ragged edges showing the marks of the knife that had first cut the leaves. Of the two pages, one was covered in treble column print, while the other showed a reproduction of a woodcut illustration. A card with writing on it in neat letters sat by it: *Reserved for collection.*

Jacqueline felt cold, as if she had just opened a door into a landscape of ice.

"Madam?" came Mr. Thomas's voice, and Jacqueline realized that she had been staring, mouth open as if about to say something. "Is there something that you would—"

"Yes," said Jacqueline, not taking her eyes from the book and the picture on its pages. "That book there, the one in the cabinet."

"Oh, I am afraid that I already have a customer for that piece." Mr. Thomas walked to the cabinet, his movements precise, as if he was running on clockwork. "Though, I am not surprised that it caught your eye." He unlocked the cabinet with a small key and pulled on a pair of black felt gloves. "Sixteenth century, written by an Englishman, though this edition was printed and bound in Holland. It is an exquisite example of the craft of the time." He picked up the book and turned it to show the opened pages to Jacqueline. "Written in English, which is strange given the subject matter. One would normally expect Latin, or perhaps Greek."

Her eyes flicked over the closely printed letters. Although the words were written in the Old English spelling, she realized she could understand what the phrases meant as though they had been written for her to comprehend, though they gave her no pleasure as she picked them out: *hunted unto the end…angel of shadow…great slaughter across Valencia…*

"What is it?" she asked in a dry voice. Her eyes returned to the woodcut on the opposite page. It showed a man in robes, a beard curling from his mouth, his hands raised in a strange gesture. Behind him, towers fell and fire filled the sky; at his feet, severed limbs and heads covered the ground. Above the broken towers, strange, squid-like demons flew through the sky. Time had clearly been lavished on the details, and the expression on the old man's cruel, handsome face was clear and easily read. It was a satisfied smile.

"*Culworth's Heretics*. It is a set of accounts of the greater heretics of the preceding century. One of the few examples I have come across, certainly the only one of this quality. It was banned in its own time, of course, a fact which only increases its rarity." He ran his gloved hand over the page as if stroking a cat, his voice edged with a reverent purr. "While its title might indicate that it deals with those condemned by a branch of Christianity, Culworth chose to focus on accounts of sorcery and witchcraft. Some of the accounts are highly detailed. Some have even speculated that Culworth himself was present at some of the events he described." Mr. Thomas turned a relishing smile on Jacqueline. "He was eventually burned as a necromancer."

Jacqueline's mind was spinning. She did not understand how the book could be connected to her dreams, but the proof was on the page in front of her. The face staring up from the woodcut was the man that had smiled at her in her dreams: the old man with the cruel smile. The woodcut was imperfect but it was undoubtedly him; this man in a four-hundred-year-old book of sorcerers had smiled at her from a nightmare future. She needed the book. No matter how much it cost, she needed the knowledge that it contained. She needed to know how it connected to the future she was trying to prevent from happening.

"How much is it, Mr. Thomas?" she asked with her best attempt at a calm, interested smile.

He shook his head and gave an apologetic sigh. "As I said, I am afraid that it has already been reserved for a buyer." He turned and placed the book back into the cabinet.

"May I ask who?"

"Another young lady, in fact. She came in several months ago. Most engaging. She had been doing some research in the university library. She'd heard that I might be able to obtain a number of more obscure titles."

Jacqueline was not really listening, her eyes following his hands as he lowered the glass lid of the cabinet and locked it with the small key. She had money, Walter had seen to that. Would money persuade this man to sell the book to her?

"Strange," he said, looking down at the open book in the cabinet. "It was the very same pages that caught her eye when she looked through it." He turned back to her. "But then, it is a singular illustration."

"Mr. Thomas, has this other customer paid you an advance for the book?"

He frowned at the question.

"No, given her family there was no need." He gave her a sharp look. "It has been some time since we came to an agreement, but I am sure she will be in to collect it."

Jacqueline swallowed and made her play.

"I am most interested in purchasing that book, Mr. Thomas." She reached into her purse and withdrew a fold of crisp, green bank notes. "I will pay an advance in cash and write you a check for the full amount here and now." He looked at her, his eyes narrowed but lingering on the banknotes. "And I will pay twice the amount you were previously offered." His eyes went wide and she knew she had him.

"Well, it has been some time, and there was no exchange of monies." He ran his tongue over his yellowed teeth. "You will pay twice as much, madam? Even not knowing how much that is?"

Jacqueline nodded. "Yes."

"I think that will be an acceptable arrangement," he said with a slow nod, and took the book back out of the cabinet. He then took it to the counter and began wrapping it in brown paper. Jacqueline watched him, thinking that she would have to come up with a story to account for the purchase to Walter. Unfortunately, he had no interest in books, much less rare sixteenth century manuscripts on necromancers; otherwise, she would have said it was a present for him. She would think of something.

Mr. Thomas finished wrapping the book and looked up, a polite smile on his face. She had her checkbook and pen ready. She was just about to begin writing when a thought struck her.

"Mr. Thomas, the person who had reserved this book. The girl who was struck by those same pages as me..."

Mr. Thomas looked puzzled, his eyes fixed on her pen poised above the surface of the check.

"Yes," he said. "What about her?"

"What was her name?"

"Oh," he smiled, his face relaxing. "Bradbury. Her name was Vivian Bradbury."

CHAPTER SEVEN

Dr. Fields
French Hill, Arkham

He had been waiting for an hour. They had shown him into a reception room off the foyer and closed the door, leaving him to the comfortable quiet and the ticking of the clock above the unlit fireplace.

The Silver Twilight Lodge in Arkham sat in discrete elegance on a treelined street of the French Hill district. It was an old building of brick with the sharp gables common in the older neighborhoods of Arkham. Looking up at it from the street, the only thing that struck Dr. Fields as odd was the absence of windows on the second and third floors. Smooth brick filled the spaces where windows should have been, giving the building a blank look, like a human face without nose or eyes. A short path led through a low wrought-iron gate to stone steps and a wide blue door. The words "The Hermetic Order of the Silver Twilight Lodge" were worked on a silver plate fixed to the polished door.

He had knocked on the door and been answered by an immaculately dressed footman with a stiff face and cold eyes. The man had taken his request to see Dr. Mortimore with a curt nod and left him waiting in the marble-floored foyer. He had waited, feeling alone and unwelcome, listening to the sharp noises that even the smallest shift of his feet made on the white marble. A brass five-pointed star was set into the floor, its effect subtly dominating the space. The walls were cream; plaster busts of grim men looked down at him from stucco-edged niches.

After a few uncomfortable minutes, the cold-eyed footman had returned and said that Dr. Mortimore was here and would join him shortly. The reception room he'd been shown to was little better than the foyer. It was empty and he sat alone next to a small table topped with polished green stone. A slight smell of pipe tobacco hung in the air. The wooden floor and dark wall panels seemed to press in on him. Sitting in one of the leather upholstered chairs that dotted the room, he felt like he was waiting outside a court for a jury to reach its verdict.

The door clicked open after an hour. The man that stepped through had aged since Dr. Fields had last seen him, but only in that his hair had receded into a dull grey and the skin over his sharp face looked taught and pale. His grey suit was precisely tailored to match his lean figure. He looked at Dr. Fields with green eyes, the same way he always had, like a snake at a mouse.

"Lyman, how pleasant to see you," he said, extending his hand. Dr. Fields stood, forcing a smile onto his face.

"Daniel," said Dr. Fields, shaking Mortimore's hand. "Thank you for meeting with me."

"Oh, not at all. Please." He motioned to the chairs. "It's a pleasure to see old colleagues." He settled into a chair. "Would you like something? Coffee? I am sure we can even run to something a little stronger."

"No, thank you."

"Quite right, bad for one's health and respectability." Mortimore took a silver cigarette case out of his breast pocket and lit one with a match. "How is your wife? You have a daughter, don't you?"

"My wife passed away, several years ago."

"Oh, I am so sorry." The ring of sincerity to the words was hollow, but Dr. Fields nodded in thanks. Mortimore let out a long exhalation of smoke. "But today, what can I do for you, old friend?"

"I wanted to ask you about the Hand of Solace."

Mortimore went very still, his green eyes fixed on Dr. Fields, the hand holding the burning cigarette frozen halfway to his lips.

"I am sorry, but I am not sure what you mean."

"They are a spiritual organization here in Arkham. They seem to recruit from the desperate and destitute." He kept his eyes steady under Mortimore's green gaze. *There's no point in holding anything back from this gamble.* "My daughter has become mixed up with them. I am very worried about her and this…" He paused, considering his next word carefully. "…cult."

"Very unfortunate, but I don't see how I can help."

"There is something about the Hand of Solace, something… *esoteric.*" He let the word hang. "If I could understand something about them, it might help me get my daughter away from them." Mortimore said nothing, his face set, unreadable. "I thought that with your long-term connections with a well-known esoteric society you might have some insight." Mortimore stayed silent, smoke coiling from his burning cigarette. "Well, can you help?"

After a long pause, Mortimore stood.

"Please, wait here." He walked to the door and left Dr. Fields again with the stillness and the ticking clock. He had a feeling that he might have just done something terribly ill-advised. Mortimore had reacted as if he had put a gun on the table.

There is nothing else I could have done, he thought. A lifetime of treating everything beyond the bounds of science with contempt had left him unequipped to begin to understand what the Hand of Solace might have made his daughter believe. He needed to understand what he faced, even if he did not believe it. He suddenly remembered the strange words that he had heard through the crack of open door, and the feeling of being pulled.

The door clicked open and Mortimore stepped back in. Dr. Fields came to his feet. The expression on Mortimore's face was stony.

"Well? Can you help me?"

Mortimore did not seem to have heard him. He put his hands on the back of one of the chairs and began to talk in a clipped voice. "You are, and always have been, a fool."

Dr. Fields rocked as if slapped. "What—"

"Your arrogance and self-righteousness is equaled only by your ignorance." Mortimore was looking at Dr. Fields with something between fear and contempt.

"I came to a friend…," he began carefully.

"We have never been friends," snapped Mortimore, "and you have nothing but contempt for me. You loathe the organization in which you stand, while asking for help, the nature and implications of which you cannot comprehend."

Dr. Fields nodded slowly; he could not deny the truth of Mortimore's words. He had always disliked and distrusted organizations that had an element of exclusivity not based on merit, and he distrusted secrets. The self-proclaimed mystical aspect of the Silver Twilight Lodge had just added to the reasons to treat the offer to join it with a derisive laugh. Now he wondered if that laugh, uttered all those years ago, had not also been ill-advised.

"You will not help," he said in a flat voice, his shoulders slumped.

"He did not say that, Dr. Lyman Matthew Fields, son of Bartholomew." The voice was strong, resonant with authority, and came from behind him. Dr. Fields turned, his face showing his shock at the sound of his full name and the name of his father. He had seen no one else enter, but a man now sat in one of the leather chairs a few yards from his back. The man wore a suit and waistcoat of charcoal black. He looked at least a decade younger than Dr. Fields and Dr. Mortimore, but there was something about the grey eyes that made Dr. Fields feel like a child looking at an old man. Silver buttons gleamed down the man's front, and rings circled every finger of the hands that rested on the arms of the chair. A not unpleasant smile twitched across his slightly pudgy face.

"My name is Carl Sanford. Please sit." The voice was lower than before, but measured and weighted with authority. He pointed to one of the chairs, his movements fluid and precise. Dr. Fields lowered himself into the chair, his eyes on the man called Sanford. Mortimore moved to sit just to his left, on the edge of Dr. Fields's sight. "You are a man of science and reason, Dr. Fields," began Sanford. "You see the world filtered by received wisdom and tested truth. So why are you here?"

"My daughter—"

"Has become entangled in something that she does not understand." Sanford paused, nodding slowly. "I know this. I asked why *you* are here."

Dr. Fields felt a flare of anger, but fought it down. He had come here for their help, for what they might be able to tell him. For that, he would swallow his indignation.

"The Hand of Solace—I came here in the hope that you knew something of them, of their nature, something I could use to persuade my daughter away from them."

Sanford looked at his fingers, spreading them and letting the light play over the stones set into the rings. "We know of them, and something of what they are about, but there are things and people even I dare not cross." He looked up at Dr. Fields, his eyes unreadable, as if they were glass set in a skull. "Again: why are you here?"

Dr. Fields shifted; he was suddenly certain he should not have come, that no matter how the House of Solace had disturbed him, this was not the place to come for help.

"I thought you might help me understand…," he began, but Sanford flicked his hand dismissively.

"No, that is not it." Sanford leaned forward. "You were brushed by something you could not fit into your neatly ordered universe, and so you came running here, to the only other place you could think of that also does not fit." Sanford nodded slowly, his glass blank eyes still on Dr. Fields.

He is right, thought Dr. Fields, the thought rushing into his mind before he could consider it more deeply. *My god, he is right, and I have no choice. This is the only place that might be able to help.*

"Will you help?"

Sanford frowned and leaned back in his chair. "Help who? You?"

"Yes, and my daughter." To his left Mortimore snorted. Sanford looked amused.

"Let me be frank, we care nothing for you or your daughter. You are straying into a domain we avoid."

Dr. Fields wondered what Sanford was talking about. *"A domain we avoid"?* It was as if the round-faced man thought himself a predator and the Hand of Solace the hunting ground of another.

"I do not know what you mean—"

"No, of course not," said Sanford with a slight shake of his head. "Which is why, Dr. Fields, I cannot explain anything to you, even if I was inclined to, which I am not."

"Then, thank you for this conversation. Good day." Dr. Fields got to his feet and took a step toward the door.

"Please, Dr. Fields, I am being honest with you." Dr. Fields paused and looked at Sanford. The humor had left the man's face. "Honesty is something that you will come to value more than you know. I also did not say that there was nothing I would do."

Sanford reached into an inside pocket of his jacket and pulled out a thin bundle wrapped in black velvet. He unrolled it across the low, marble-topped table, the objects inside chinking against each other as the velvet unfolded.

"What are these?" asked Dr. Fields, looking down at the shining objects. There was a dagger, no longer that six inches, its blade slightly curved, its handle of yellow bone. There were signs cut into the blade, sinuous signs that might have been letters or words but were from no language Dr. Fields had ever seen. Beside it was an amulet of green stone fastened to a silver chain, its polished surface running with fluid reflections as if it were oil.

"They are as they seem," said Sanford, watching Dr. Fields pick up the dagger, his eyes running across the signs on its blade.

"I have no use for violence, or trinkets," said Dr. Fields, placing the dagger back on the sheet of velvet, but his hand lingered next to them on the tabletop.

"Perhaps, and perhaps not," said Sanford. There was a note in his voice that Dr. Fields could not place.

"What are they?"

Sanford began to fold the velvet over them, his pudgy hands not touching either object. "Protection and possibility." He finished folding the cloth and left the neat roll of black on the tabletop. "Which and how is up to you."

"Riddles." It was Dr. Fields's turn to sneer.

"Truth," said Sanford. Dr. Fields gave a tired shake of his head. The fear and doubt of before had faded and been replaced with a heavy feeling of fatigue and disappointment. What had he expected? Some babbled chanting had spooked him and he had come running to a group of people who believed in magic. He thought of the dagger and the amulet now folded away, wrapped in darkness. What else could he have expected? His eyes stayed fixed on the black velvet parcel on the green marble table.

"Is this the full extent of your help?" He looked at Sanford, who nodded. Dr. Fields began to walk to the door. It was almost an absentminded movement that picked up the bundle off the table and put it in his pocket. Even as he did it, he did not know why. His hat was on his head and he was reaching for the door handle when Sanford spoke from behind him.

"The answer is that you lie to yourself, Dr. Fields." He turned back, his eyes locking on Sanford's. "That is why you came here. Because inside you, beyond reason, you know that there is something else, something that you know not."

Dr. Fields paused, then pulled open the door and walked out without a word. In the hall, he hesitated as he pushed open the front door, the footman nowhere to be seen. He looked back at the half-open door to the room he had just left. Sanford and Mortimore knew more than they were saying, but if they thought he was gone...

He let the front door click shut and moved around the edge of the hall, keeping out of sight of the half-open door until he was pressed against the wall just beside it. Slowly, he moved his head until he could see past the doorframe. Mortimore was standing just behind Sanford's chair, frowning as if worried.

"Is it worth the gambit?" asked Mortimore. "We have never challenged *him* openly, and that fool is marked for nothing but oblivion." Carl Sanford turned to look at the man who looked older than him. Mortimore flinched from the look. "You have cautioned us never to cross the path of the master of the Hand, yet you guide a fool to his door with a cloak of ignorance." Mortimore pointed toward the open door that Dr. Fields had walked out through. "He will be devoured, and the master of the Hand will know that he came to us." Sanford looked away, steepling his fingers.

"Perhaps, but there are other possibilities. Is another person waiting to be born in that man?"

Mortimore sat down next to him and took a fresh cigarette from his silver case. "And while he stumbles into the tiger's den, with our tools in his hands, what do we do?" The silence hung for a moment as Mortimore struck a match and fresh smoke filled the air.

"We wait, my brother. We wait."

CHAPTER EIGHT

Raker

French Hill, Arkham

Raker strode through the gates of the Stonegroves estate and up the white gravel drive under the shadows of red maples and oaks. Around him, the landscape unfolded into an expanse of trimmed green grass shimmering under the sun. The air was soup warm, filled with a haze of tree pollen and flitting insects. Above, the deep blue of the sky cupped the baking land.

The driveway was long and sweat was making his shirt cling to his back by the time he was halfway to the house. He knew that he did not look great but he had done the best he could. He wore a clean suit and shirt without grime, or worse, the dull smudge of blood stains. The shoes on his feet were freshly buffed and his face freshly shaven. But it was too hot and he had had to walk from town. He had taken his jacket off and it trailed down his back from where his fingers hooked through its collar. The suit and shirt were new; he had bought them that morning from a store in town. It was the best he could buy, but it had been cheap because it was a heavy winter suit in an unfashionable cut of light grey. It also did not fit very well.

Above him, growing closer with every uncomfortable step, was Stonegroves. It sat on the crest of a hill amidst smooth trimmed grass and terraced beds that flavored the warm breeze with a patchwork of flower scent. The house rose in three floors of white stone capped with a red tiled roof whose sharp gables stabbed into the cloudless sky. The sun was shining full on the front of the house making its walls seem to glow, and throwing deep shadows across the pillared balconies on the higher floors. Arched windows, ringed with carved gargoyles, opened to darkness inside. Looking up at the house, Raker thought that they looked like empty sockets in a dry skull. Despite the heat, he felt himself shiver at the thought. He had only looked at it from the outside but he did not like the house. It was as if there was something subtly wrong with it, as if it was somehow tricking the eye.

The man he had bought his suit from in town had said the house was haunted. The land was bad, he'd said, and the house had used old stones in its foundations. Stones that had been there since before the ships came from Europe. He remembered that the man who had built it had hung himself in its great hall a month after it was finished. He thought of the drunken banker in Hibb's Roadhouse and his remark about how it was strange that the Bradburys stayed. His pace along the gravel drive quickened.

He hoped that Vivian was here, that she would see him, that the reason she had not replied to his telegrams was that she had been away, or that they had not arrived. If he could see her, he was confident that he could overcome any doubts that had entered her mind.

As he passed a wide lawn of smooth grass a gardener looked up from clipping a topiary bush and gave Raker a suspicious look. Raker nodded and smiled and the gardener raised his hand in unsure acknowledgement. When he came close to the house he had to pick his way past a press of vans, their sides lettered with the names of a dozen classes of merchant: provisioners, decorators, florists, and other tradesmen that Raker did not recognize. Men were moving between them and the house, hauling crates and parcels, forearms bared to the heat, sweat staining their shirts. It seemed as if Stonegroves was being stocked for some grand extravagance. He had always know that Vivian's mother was rich, but looking at the quantity of deliveries and the size of the house he realized he had underestimated just how rich. He was suddenly acutely conscious of his ill-fitting suit and the sweat that had soaked into his shirt.

In the shade of the columned portico, he spent a few seconds adjusting his suit, possibilities and excitement running through him as he fussed, delaying the knock on the wide black door. Unsatisfied with how he looked but realizing that he looked as good as he possibly could, he stepped forward, his hand rising to grip the curled brass of the knocker. The door opened before he could knock and Raker looked into the stiff and age-creased face of a butler in full dress.

"Good afternoon," said the butler, his voice the essence of formality, his grey eyes level and expressionless. "The trade entrance is around the back. See the housekeeper and she will tell you where to put your delivery." The relevant information clearly delivered, the man began to close the door. Raker put his hand against it. The man stared at it, shock at this breach in etiquette radiating across his face. Raker smiled.

"I am here to see Vivian Bradbury. Can I come in?" The butler began to splutter something but Raker had already pushed the door open and stepped inside. The foyer was the biggest room in any house Raker had ever seen. It was one wide, long hallway, its walls hung with mirrors that reflected the light of lit chandeliers. The illusion that the corridor extended into infinity was only broken by doors to unseen rooms leading off to either side.

"This is unacceptable." The butler's voice was ragged with surprise and anger. He had taken hold of Raker's sleeve and was tugging on

it. "You must leave, you must leave now." The man was smaller than
Raker and older, but he kept on tugging, the veneer of formality shattered by Raker's lack of respect. Raker did not move.

"I would just like to see Vivian Bradbury." Raker held his voice
light and friendly. "I am a…friend, from Boston. She does live
here, doesn't she?" The old butler stopped tugging and looked at
him. Raker thought he could see a pleading in the man's eyes, or
was it something else? The man seemed to crumple in on himself,
and let go of Raker's arm.

"She is not here, and she will not see you." There was a tone to
his voice that Raker could not place; it sounded almost like sorrow. The butler looked down, not meeting Raker's eyes.

"Is she out? Is she coming back soon?"

The butler shook his head. "Please, sir, go. Just go." Raker
noted that the man had called him "sir" for the first time.

"I must see her," said Raker, voice low, eyes fixed above a smile.

"Let him in, Lenthorpe," said a woman's voice. The old butler stiffened, his air of crisp formality snapping back into place,
his face set and his back straight. Raker turned to see a woman
standing a few paces away by an open door that led into another
part of the house. She had a hard, angular face, her iron grey
hair neatly curled around her head. Her back and posture were
straight and commanding despite the fact that she was a head
shorter than Raker. She was dressed as if she had just come from
sitting in a garden: she wore a pale-colored dress and held a wide-
brimmed hat in her hand. His first thought was that she looked
like Vivian but older and hardened by years to blade sharpness.
Then he realized that she must be Vivian's mother, Helena Bradbury. She looked at him steadily with green eyes.

Raker realized that he still had his hat on and began to take it off.

Her clear, sharp voice cut across him. "That won't be necessary;
you're not staying."

"Hello, Mrs. Bradbury," said Raker, a wide smile appearing on his face as if by reflex. "My name is Charles Raker. I am here to see Vivian." Helena Bradbury raised an eyebrow, her face saying that Raker's brand of easy charm did not impress her.

"You don't need to give me the crocodile smile, Mr. Raker. She is not here, it's that simple. You can't see her because she is not here," she said, her voice clipped and iron-edged.

She has not asked me why I want to see Vivian, thought Raker, *and she knows who I am.* He kept smiling, but inside his heart sank.

"I just came here to talk to Vivian, Mrs. Bradbury," said Raker, his voice carefully respectful. "I…I am a friend from when she was in Boston. I have not heard anything from her for awhile." He met Helena's look and saw something beneath its glass hard surface, something that made him suddenly worried. "I really would like to speak to her."

"I know who you are, Mr. Raker. I know about your unfortunate association with my daughter while she was in Boston, and I said she is not here—"

"When will she be back?"

Helena shook her head, briefly closing her eyes.

"Mr. Raker, you cannot see my daughter. That is all there is to it."

She must be here, thought Raker. *They know who I am. They know about Vivian and me…that is why she has not written: because they found out.* He shook off the other thought that had opened in the back of his mind when he had looked into Helena Bradbury's eyes.

"She's here, though, isn't she? Please let me talk to her. Just five minutes," said Raker, stepping toward Helena Bradbury.

"No. Mr. Raker, you have your answer and I will give you no other," she said.

"If she is not here now, can I leave a message?"

"You just don't listen, do you?"

"I just want to see her."

"This is my house and I am telling you she is not here. Whatever happened between my daughter and you is now over." Raker was about to reply when a shout came from the hall behind him.

"Is this him?" Raker turned to see a big man striding down the hall toward him, face flushed with anger, shoulders bunched under a white cotton shirt. Helena Bradbury moved past Raker quickly, intercepting the big man with a hand on his arm.

"It's all right, Hugo. Mr. Raker is just leaving," she said. Hugo shrugged his mother's hand off and took another pace forward. Raker took a step back, his shoulders shrugged loose, legs tensed ready to fight or run. Hugo Bradbury was taller than Raker, and looked to be all muscle under his clean cotton shirt and grey summer slacks. He had a wide, flat face with a hard jaw, and small dark eyes. Rage radiated from him like the threat of an oncoming storm.

"I cannot believe that you would show your face here," said Hugo, his voice low and heavy with menace.

He wants to kill me, thought Raker. The shock of it almost made him stagger. He knew violence and knew that the anger in Hugo was a barely restrained murder rage. But why? They clearly knew who he was, but was his romance with Vivian reason enough to cause such hatred in her brother? Something more was driving this rage, something hidden from him.

"Look, I don't want any trouble, and I am sorry that I barged in here." He looked at Helena. "I just want to see her—"

"I should break you in two," growled Hugo, his eyes wide in his flat face. Something in Raker snapped. He had had enough; there was something he did not understand, something under the surface of what had been said. It frightened him, but it also made him angry. He should have tried to calm Hugo down, tried to talk them both around, but life had taught Raker that when someone meant you harm you didn't roll over and play nice. Keeping his hands loose by his sides he stepped closer to Hugo, meeting his glare.

"Go ahead," he said softly, watching instincts war in Hugo's black pupils. He could tell that the bigger man was teetering on the brink of trying to smear his face into a bloody pulp. Hugo did not move.

"Hugo, it's all right," said Helena Bradbury, her voice soothing. "Mr. Raker came to see Vivian. He does not know that she is not here and won't take my word for it." A look passed between mother and son.

"He thinks she is here?" asked Hugo, looking carefully at his mother. She nodded. Raker felt his own anger come surging up.

"I will find out where she is. I will see her and there is nothing you can do about it." Both Helena and Hugo turned to look at him and after a heartbeat pause Hugo laughed. It was a humorless laugh, the kind of laugh that broken men make.

"There is nothing we can do? There is nothing we can do," laughed Hugo, shaking his head and then stepping away.

"Mr. Raker," said Helena, then paused and began again. "Please, there is nothing for you here anymore. For your own good, and for Vivian's sake, please go." The hardness in her voice was still there but the edge of anger had gone. Raker did not look, but kept his eyes on Hugo's retreating back, wondering at the anger and despair in Hugo's words. Why was Hugo ready to assault him? Why was Vivian not here? What was the dead look in both Hugo's and his mother's eyes? Nothing seemed to fit. He felt as if he had stepped into a world that looked like the one he knew, but run into hidden rules that he did not understand. What he'd glimpsed in their eyes was the look of people trying not to weep or rage at the side of an open grave. He felt as if a snake of iced steel was circling his guts.

"Is Vivian all right?" he asked before he could stop himself.

"Please go, Mr. Raker," said Helena Bradbury again, and he knew that he would get no answer to his question. He turned and walked toward the front door. Lenthorpe the butler had it open and the sun was streaming in.

"And Mr. Raker," said Helena Bradbury as he was about to step through. He turned to look back at her. "There will be no need for you to come back here." He gave a half nod and walked out into the light of a world that seemed different.

He had taken several steps when a voice called to him from the portico that shadowed the front door.

"Sir," the voice was low, and he turned to see Lenthorpe standing in the shadows, a worried look on the old butler's face. The old man beckoned to him, and after a second, Raker stepped back under the portico where a thick stone pillar hid them from anyone looking out of a window.

"Yes?" asked Raker.

"You were asking about Miss Vivian," said Lenthorpe, his voice quiet, eyes darting around as if afraid of being seen.

"Yes, is she here, Lenthorpe? Can you get a message to her?" Raker felt a surge of hope but as he spoke the old man's face slumped and he looked down, not meeting Raker's eyes.

"No."

"I can pay well, Lenthorpe," said Raker, reaching into his jacket pocket for his bill fold.

"I do not want your money, sir." The old man looked back up into Raker's face, his expression causing Raker to drop his hand to his waist.

"Then what?"

"I know who you are, sir. She was very fond of you," said the old man. "They may blame you, but I don't. I used to take the letters she wrote to you to the post; she made me promise not to tell the mistress." Raker could see tears forming in the wrinkled edges of the man's eyes. "I don't think it had anything to do with her time with you. They do, but not me. It's not right that you don't know, sir." Raker felt the steel ice grip his insides again.

"Know what?"

"I…" The old man was not meeting Raker's eyes.

"Come on," said Raker.

"Dr. Lemaitre," said the old man. "Talk to Dr. Lemaitre."

"Where can I find this Dr. Lemaitre?"

The old butler had begun to walk back to the front door, and when he replied he was looking away from Raker.

"At the asylum, at Arkham Asylum."

CHAPTER NINE

Jacqueline Fine

Miskatonic University, Arkham

"That would require access to the restricted collection," said
the library assistant with a cold expression. Jacqueline suppressed a sigh of frustration. The assistant was a woman of middle
years with a tight bun of hair drawn up above a thin face. Jacqueline had felt her disapproving gaze ever since she had entered
the library. Whether it was her fashionable dress or the fact that
she obviously did not fit in with the quiet solitude of the library,
she could not tell.

Jacqueline had decided to come to the library almost as soon
as she had left the Curiositie Shoppe. She needed solitude to pick
through the contents of *Culworth's Heretics*, and she knew that
she might need other references to find out about the man in the
woodcut. A library was the obvious place to go and the university
the most logical place to find one.

Walking through the campus in the summer sun, she had
had time to gather her thoughts. The face in *Culworth's Heretics*
matched the face of the old man in her dreams, of that she was
certain. Understanding who that man was would help clarify his

significance to the future. The blood and shadows of her vision lurked at the corners of her mind, worrying her. Her vision of the Curiositie Shoppe had fit her visit perfectly and that worried her: was she unraveling a vision of the future so that she could stop it happening, or making it happen by her actions? She still did not know, but she felt like she had no choice but to follow the threads she had grasped. She felt trapped, unable to choose any path but the one she followed.

The sight of the library had done nothing to soothe her worries. Three floors of weathered grey granite, it looked more like a reliquary than a library. Gargoyles snarled down at her from above arched windows and Latin script wound around the double doors at the top of a wide set of stone steps. Looking at it, Jacqueline felt as if the building was looking out at the rest of the sunny world, brooding on its secrets.

Inside the doors, it was cool and smelled of cold stone, leather, and paper. The light was dim; the bright sunlight passing through the windows seemed to become weaker, diluted by dust. Looking around she could see rows of dark wooden shelves. Each was twice her height and rails ran along the shelves for sets of steps. Rectangular reading tables filled the spaces between the shelves. Smiling at the hard look from the spinster-like woman behind the front desk, Jacqueline had found a very quiet desk and begun to read.

It had taken her an hour to read the section on the man in the woodcut. What she'd read had shaken her, but she now had a name for the man from the woodcut, the man from her dreams. She needed to find out more about him, and she knew that she'd need help finding what she needed in the library. Her education had been haphazard and she had taught herself most of what she knew. She read a lot and took pride in that, but she had never looked for cross references in an academic library. So she had folded the book back in its wrappings and gone to the front desk to ask the spinster-like assistant for help.

"Is that going to be a problem?" asked Jacqueline with her best and most friendly smile.

"Are you a student here?" The woman seemed unimpressed by the smile, and was looking at Jacqueline over the top of her glasses like a disappointed school teacher. Jacqueline thought about trying to bluff that she was a student, but the look in the library assistant's eyes said that it would not go well.

"No, I'm sorry but I am not."

The woman raised an eyebrow.

"University rules are particular on access to the library. Technically, miss, you should not be here. Those same rules are even more particular concerning access to the valuable and rare books that we hold within the restricted collection." The woman began sorting through books piled behind the desk, her hands moving with almost tender care as they touched the covers. "If you are a visiting researcher, may I ask if you have a letter of introduction?"

"No, but—"

"Then I am afraid that it is quite out of the question." Jacqueline heard the ring of finality in the woman's voice, but she could not walk away now.

"Very well, thank you for your time." She made a show of fumbling with the parcel that contained the book, as if it was slipping out from under her arm. With a tut of exasperation she put it down on the desktop and stripped off the brown paper wrapping as if she was going to re-wrap it.

"Where did you obtain that?" asked the woman in a hushed, almost reverent tone, her eyes fastening on the cracked leather binding and the title worked in worn gold leaf on the spine. Inside, Jacqueline smiled to herself with satisfaction. It had been a gamble, but Jacqueline had always been gifted at reading people, and she had seen how the woman touched the books behind her desk.

"Oh, it is part of my research; I am writing a book on one of the incidents described in it." The woman was still looking at the book like a mother at a loved child.

"It is yours?" Jacqueline nodded. "May I look inside?"

"Yes, of course." She smiled as she said it and the woman opened the book with reverent care, her eyes playing across the pages.

I have her now, thought Jacqueline.

"I'd heard that Miskatonic University's library was the finest for such things. I did not think to bring a letter because—"

"What was the reference again?" The woman looked up, a frown on her face, but the stiff disapproval had gone.

"It was the name of one of the heretics who committed a series of blasphemous atrocities." Jacqueline reached out and turned the pages of the book until the woodcut of the face from her dream was looking up at the library assistant. "The name his followers gave him was 'Lemaitre.'" The woman nodded and reached for a sheet of paper and began to make notes. She looked at Jacqueline and gave a smile.

"I am sorry. I did not realize you were a serious researcher." She gave another admiring glance at the open book. "As I said, books relating to this area are often held in the restricted collection, and you would normally require written permission, but in this case and with my help, I am sure that is not necessary." She came around the other side of the desk, picked up *Culworth's Heretics*, and gave an apologetic smile. "My name is Carol, by the way."

"Jacqueline," she said with a broad smile, and followed Carol through the silent library.

The restricted collection was on the third floor, tucked into a corner of the building that seemed even quieter than the rest. Its shelves were made from the same heavy, dark wood as those in the rest of the library, but each shelf was covered in a tarnished brass grille locked closed by a padlock. Jacqueline could see the thick spines of leather-bound tomes through the grilles.

Worn names in gold leaf on cracked leather looked back at her. There was an atmosphere about the shelves that went beyond the musk of old paper and aging leather. Her teeth were tingling and her skin prickled. Her mind filled with images of deep oceans and vast plains, empty apart from the ice blowing on the wind. She knew that there were forces beyond science and reason, had known it since she had begun to dream the future, and here she felt as if her nightmares were going to coalesce from the dusty air. That secret truth nearly made her turn and walk out of the library. She could feel that what was locked onto these shelves was greater and more terrible than anyone could guess.

Carol seemed unaware of the potent atmosphere around the locked shelves. She took a bunch of keys from a pocket.

"Let's begin."

It took them hours for the first links to appear—a reference here, a date there—but bit by bit the books piled on the library table grew. Some of the intuitive jumps the older woman made amazed Jacqueline. The notes on Carol's notebook spread from page to page and the library became quieter and quieter. Carol seemed to be in her element, but Jacqueline felt a sense of dread grip her with every additional detail they discovered.

"Lemaitre" was the name of the man in the woodcut, or that was the name that history had given him. The old man whose face she had found in the Curiositie Shoppe and seen in her dreams now looked out at her from dozens of fragments of time. A sorcerer, diabolist, warlord, and mass murderer, his bloody and grisly trail wound its way across centuries. In the twelfth century, he had been a priest in the Byzantine court and led a band of crusaders on an unholy quest from which none returned. In the fifteenth century, the Ottomans took a fortified tower on the borders of Walachia and found magical equipment and a charnel pit filled with hundreds of corpses. The surviving slaves named their master as Lemaitre. The Ottomans burned the tower.

Through every account in every language the details changed
and the description of the man altered, but it was the same monster. Apart from anything else the name "Lemaitre" followed him
in one form or another like a curse of growing potency. There was
also the mark of black magic, sorcery, and diabolism which all
the fragments said were concerned with one terrible and ultimate
goal: true immortality. Sacrifices to faceless gods in shunned
corners of the world, skies turned red at the correct turning of
the stars, bargains made with alchemists and mystics for lore or
artifacts that were said to hold the key to the gates of life and
death; the path across history was like bloody footprints on a
dusty floor. It made Jacqueline feel sick and afraid. The man who
waited in her dreams of the future had been real. Was he dead?
She and Carol had spent most of the day searching down every
scrap that the university library had to offer and she had found
no answer to that question. The implication was clear: Lemaitre
pursued immortality and had lived many times the life of a normal man without succeeding. Her dreams told her that he was
going to try again, and soon.

"I need some air," said Jacqueline, pushing a heavy book away
from her and standing up. She swayed for a moment. All the
lines of words and symbols in so many books, it was almost as if
they had crept inside her head to float through her eyes in sickly
glowing afterimages.

"Are you all right?" asked Carol, who had looked up from a bound
ledger that was open in front of her. She was also pale-faced and her
eyes looked watery and bloodshot behind her glasses. Jacqueline took
a breath and steadied herself.

"Yes, it's just…" She thought about telling Carol of her dreams.
At least then someone else would know. "It's just a bit stuffy in
here," she said, and forced a smile onto her face. Carol gave a tired
smile back.

"Yes, it is." She shuffled a pile of paper and handed it to Jacqueline.

Carol's neat handwriting covered every sheet. "I have made notes for you, all of what we found."

"Thank you, Carol," said Jacqueline, feeling a sudden rush of affection for the older library assistant.

"That's all right. You will have to remember to take your own if you mean to make a good job of being a writer." Jacqueline was about to say something, but Carol had already turned back to the ledger on the table in front of her.

"This is strange," she said, pursing her lips and running her finger down a wide column filled with signatures. Carol had said nothing about the trail of implication that said an ancient sorcerer had existed across Europe and Asia for centuries. She had taken it in her stride as someone used to helping people sort through information that included all manner of unexplained peculiarities. Jacqueline wondered if she was about to say something about it now, but the older woman straightened and pushed the ledger across the table. The page was divided into columns, each filled with names and dates written in different hands. In the first column were the names of books and in the columns to its side were numbers and dates.

"It took me some time to notice, and it was only when I was logging our use of the restricted collection that I realized…" Jacqueline frowned at the ledger, trying to see what Carol was talking about. "All of the volumes we have examined were accessed several months ago."

"Is that unusual?" asked Jacqueline.

"I mean each of the *exact same* books that we have gone through today were looked at by *one* person. By someone following the exact same links." Jacqueline looked up at Carol. "Do you have a rival in your subject?" Jacqueline thought of the *Reserved* card by the book in the Curiositie Shoppe, of the lady who had promised to come back and pick it up.

"What was the person's name?"

"Very odd. Again, not a student but an independent, like you," said Carol, turning the page of the ledger to show the signature running along the bottom of the entries in smooth flowing script. "It is signed 'Vivian Bradbury.'" Jacqueline felt suddenly very cold.

Carol closed the ledger. Underneath it was a slim folio notebook that Jacqueline had not noticed before.

"There was a notebook jammed behind one of the volumes. It's the same handwriting as the signature. I have not had a chance to read all of it. Some of it seems quite personal." She opened the notebook and took out a folded square of yellowing newsprint. "And there was this."

"May I see it?" asked Jacqueline, a slight tremor creeping into her voice.

Carol passed her the square of newsprint and slid the notebook to her. "Keep it—if she is who I think she is, she won't need it."

It was a photograph cut from a newspaper: a row of solemn faces, some sitting stiffly on chairs, others standing behind them. A large, elaborate doorway could be seen behind them. They were all men, some younger, most in their middle years, all with an air of earnest seriousness. There was a caption at the bottom: *Dr. Zulock and his staff, proud receivers of the governor's visit, 1924, March*, and then the names of those photographed.

Someone had circled one of the men's faces at the back in blue pencil. The man was young, his graceful good looks clear even seen in a grainy image. Jacqueline did not recognize the face but she recognized the name in the caption: "Lemaitre." It was the name of a monster seeking immortality, a monster who looked up at her from grainy print with a new face, a monster who was alive and here in Arkham.

CHAPTER TEN

Dr. Fields
Southside, Arkham

Dr. Fields stared at the door and hoped that he had been wrong. The room was small, one of the smallest in the boarding house. In the dark, it felt like the walls were pressing in to touch him. He sat on the bed with his shoes on and his jacket hanging from the post of the narrow iron frame. Behind him, the single sash window was shut and fastened—he had checked it several times—but the curtains were open, spilling silver moonlight into the room.

Someone had followed him. He had not realized it until he was almost back at the boarding house. After he had left the Silver Twilight Lodge, he had walked for some time, not paying any particular attention to where he was going. The buildings had changed around him, people had passed by, and the sun had faded lower in the blue summer sky. He had been angry, angry at the arrogance of Mortimore and Sanford, angry at his own stupidity in going to a bunch of people who seemed to believe in hokum. As for Sanford's *gift*, he had nearly thrown it in the river. He had let his anger boil as he walked the streets of Arkham.

Better that than let the despair that was circling his thoughts into his mind.

His anger had almost burned out when he realized that some-one was following him. The sky was darkening to the blue of watered ink and he had begun to feel the fact that it had been some time since he had eaten and longer since he had slept. He had taken a room at Ma's Boarding House when he'd arrived in Arkham; it wasn't the usual type of place he'd stay, but it'd been the first one recommended to him by a passerby. It was a worn and dingy place, but good enough. He had not slept the first night; it had felt like something too mundane, too normal for the circumstances he was facing.

He was just realizing that he would have to go back to the boarding house to rest when he caught a movement out of the corner of his eye. He'd turned sharply, but there was nothing there but the quiet Arkham street, spreading with shadows under a darkening sky. The impression was still with him, though: the glimpse of something furtive moving along the side of the street. He could not have told how big it was or its shape, but he had a fading memory of grey and a rippling as if of heavy fabric. After several seconds of staring into the edges of the street, he had turned and walked on, but the feeling of being watched and of something moving just out of sight had not left him.

At the boarding house, he had climbed the stairs to his room quickly, sweeping past the lady of the house without a nod or greeting. Once he was in his room, he had locked the door, checked the window catches, and seated himself on the bed in the dark. Nothing had happened, and after half an hour he had begun to drift into a half dream of shadowy figures and silent plateaus of red dust.

He had come alert with a start, his eyes wide in the moon bright-ened darkness. Now he stared at the door. There was something out-side his room; he could see its shadow smudging the light of the crack under the door. It was not moving. He let his breath out quietly. There was no noise; the boarding house was silent around him.

Maybe it's just another guest, he thought, *or the owner come to see if I want something to eat?* He stayed still, though, feeling as if a winter chill had seeped into the summer air. The door handle turned slowly and he heard the lock creak as silent pressure pushed at the door. He realized that he was not breathing.

Frost began to form on the door handle, the crystals glittering in the moonlight from the window. He let out a gasp and his breath plumed like smoke in the cold air. Frost was crusting the door and floor. The light under the door had vanished; in its place was a shadow, spreading like tar under the door. The half-remembered guttural, drum beat chants of the House of Solace were in his head. He could hear the jagged sounds, the pleading voices shouting next to his ears. The frost glittered in the dark air as the shadow spread toward him.

A memory of light glittering on silver lying on velvet flicked into his mind. There was no space for doubt, for careful reason or rational reflection. Dr. Fields pulled the velvet bundle from his jacket pocket and pulled the amulet and dagger from their soft wrapping. He thrust them out toward the spreading shadow. He had not known what to expect, had not known why he had done it. Something beneath the part of him that had laughed at stories of devilry and warlocks hoped that the smiling Sanford was not a liar.

There was a sudden absence of noise, as if he was underwater. He tasted blood in his mouth and his eyes stung. The shadow flowed back on itself, draining out of the room. In its wake, the frost melted to a damp sheen.

Still holding the silver dagger and the green stone amulet, he stepped toward the door. The light coming under it was bright and clear and he suddenly realized that he could hear the grumble of a gramophone somewhere downstairs, and the distant snarl of a fox from outside. For a second, he wondered if he had had a waking nightmare brought on by stress and exhaustion. He reached out and touched the door handle. It was cool but clean of frost. Slowly, he unlocked the door and pulled it wide. The light of the lamp on the landing outside shone on his face. There was nothing.

He was about to turn back into his room when he looked down at the floorboards outside his door. Any thoughts of dreams or delusion died in him. There on the bare boards were marks like the footprints of something that did not walk like a man scorched into the wood.

He stepped back into his room and locked the door. He did not want to think about what had just happened, but in the moonlit dark he decided what he would do the next day. He would go to the House of Solace and find the truth of what they were. Amelia had to listen to him if he could show her that truth.

Curled in the dark, a silver dagger in his hand and green stone amulet around his neck, Dr. Fields stayed awake until sleep and dreams swallowed him.

CHAPTER ELEVEN

Raker

Easttown, Arkham

He'd needed a drink. More money got him into the back room of Hibb's and a series of thick measures in a cracked glass. The liquor burned as it went down. He did not normally drink to get drunk, but walking back into town, it was all he could think of doing. He had hoped that it would numb him, dull down and cut out the thoughts that boiled through his head. It had not worked. All he could think about as the rough alcohol burned his throat was the look in the Bradburys' eyes and the sorrow in the voice of the old butler. Arkham Asylum: his thoughts came back to it again and again like liquid swirling at the bottom of a tumbler.

If he had been brave or angry or anything other than empty he would have gone straight to the asylum, but all he could do was think of the tears in the corners of the old butler's eyes.

An asylum, the thought screamed at him again, its implied questions rushing after it: Was Vivian at the asylum? If she was, why? What could have happened to her to drive her to…to…

He did not want to know, did not want to go and find the

answers. It was as if everything he had ever believed in was a joke, as if he had been existing by a set of rules that were a lie. There was nothing to cling to, no normality to anchor him. Going to the asylum would make things certain, would lock him into a reality that he was not sure he wanted to be a part of. He took another gulp of the sour booze and coughed as it slid down.

But she might be there. There might be something he could do. She might be all right.

"What can I get you?" The bored waitress's voice was just close and loud enough to make him look around. Raker had chosen a small table tucked in the corner where the shadows from the dim electric bulbs did not quite reach. The back room speakeasy was busier than it had been the first time he had been here. More men and the odd woman sat around tables in serious huddles. None of them looked to be having a good time. It seemed a place for quiet misery or grim bitterness.

"Whiskey, straight," said a voice from the next table. It was a flat, sober voice, and something about it cut through the fog of worry and liquor. Raker glanced at the man who had spoken. He was lighting a cigarette with apparent nonchalance. A heavy face was topped with a neat smear of dark hair. His suit was good but on the flashy side, his tie a bright flare of red silk, and the hands that cupped the cigarette had thick, ringed fingers. The man looked out of place, like someone from Raker's old life picked up and dropped into his present.

Raker looked away. Despite the cold, hollow feeling in his stomach, he recognized the electrical tingle that suddenly itched the back of his skull—the instincts of living a life among the wrong people telling him that danger was close. They had found him. He had left two men bleeding on a diner floor in Boston. It would not have taken much for the people who he owed to figure out that he had been waiting for a train. Perhaps they had found the waitress from the diner, or the inspector who could have remembered a blood-stained man running for the Arkham train. He had not been clever or careful enough.

As casually as he could, he stood up and began to walk toward the curtain that hid the stairs. It was possible that the man had not known he was in the speakeasy room, that he was just here for a drink, or that it was nothing to do with him at all. He was halfway to the curtained exit and nothing had happened. He glanced out of the side of his eye at the man in the red silk tie. The man was looking straight at him, coal black points in cold grey eyes. Raker ran for the curtain. Behind him, the man was out of his seat, the table in front of him shoved to the side. Something glittered in the man's fist. He did not need to see the knife to know it was there. These were professionals, the sharp edge of the Boston underworld that Raker had chosen to cross and flee. A knife inside and a gun waiting outside, that was how it worked, that was the way it was done.

Raker was at the curtain, pulling aside the weighted cloth and running up the stairs, his head hammering with adrenaline. He was out in the front room of the roadhouse, barging past people, deaf to the shouts, hearing only the running footsteps behind him. He was at the door, the handle in his hand. There was a shout from behind him; it might have been his name. He yanked the door open and was running out into the cool night air. There was a dry crack and something whizzed close to his head. The gunman waiting in the darkness outside the roadhouse had taken his shot. There were running steps behind him. He kept running, twisting down the next road junction he found.

He ran until he was gasping for air and the sound of running feet behind him had vanished into the low noise of a city at night. Breathing hard, he tucked himself into a dark doorway and watched the way he had come, his heart hammering, the liquor he had drunk an oily ache around his eyes. A few people passed but no man in a red tie or hurrying pursuers. He waited all the same.

He should leave Arkham: that would be the smart thing to do. They would have a man watching the train station, but there were other ways of getting out. That was what he should do… but in the shadow of the doorway he knew that he was not going to do it. He would go to the asylum when it was light and see this Dr. Lemaitre. If Vivian was there he would help her, or at least see her and let her know that he was there. If something had happened to her and there was someone to blame he would find them. And then God help them.

CHAPTER TWELVE

Jacqueline Fine

Uptown, Arkham

Jacqueline arrived at their friend's house as the sun set. Set back from the sidewalk, it was four floors of expensively modest style that belied its size. It belonged to Harry, a friend of Walter's. Harry and his wife were coming with them to the Bradburys' party, and had kindly put them up for the duration.

Walking up the steps under the bright light of the doorway lamp, she paused for a moment before knocking. She had walked slowly back from Miskatonic University, turning the discoveries of the day over in her mind. She had left *Culworth's Heretics* in Carol's delighted keeping. It would have only caused more questions than she wanted. She had Vivian Bradbury's notebook, and Carol's notes if she needed them, but she thought she would not. The details of what she had learned were too fresh and raw for her to forget.

She had already decided what she was going to do next, but it would involve Walter, and that weighed on her conscience. She was following Vivian Bradbury's footsteps into a future which she had glimpsed and which held pain and madness. Every step she was taking seemed to carry her into that future; she had not found a way of turning aside from it. Now she was going to walk deeper into it, hoping that she would find a way of stopping it, and she was taking someone she loved with her. That worried her more than anything else.

She knocked and smiled at the footman who opened the door to her. The entrance hall was as wide as the house, tiled in blue and white, with a wide wooden staircase sweeping up to a railed landing. Jacqueline could hear the sounds of laughter from somewhere upstairs. She was taking off her hat and gloves when Walter came down the stairs. With one look she could tell what he was going to say.

"You have been out for hours. I was worried." There was a small frown above his grey eyes. She liked it when he looked worried for her, liked the way it folded his brow. *I am sorry*, she wanted to say, *sorry, but we are about to walk into something that might be terrible.* But she could not say that, too many lies—including her ability to see the future—told for too long would unravel, so she smiled instead. It took effort.

"I have been looking around Arkham." She walked over to Walter who stood uncertainly on the bottom step of the curving wooden stairs. He was half dressed for dinner, wing collared shirt open at the top button and without his dinner jacket. "Remarkable place, so many nooks and crannies and old buildings."

"But it's nearly dark, and we were wondering what to tell the housekeeper about serving dinner." He was still frowning.

"I lost track of time." She put a hand on his arm and kissed him on the cheek. "I went to look around the university and this lovely lady gave me a tour of their library." He looked less worried at that but raised an eyebrow.

"Are you coming over all bookish? Will I have to install a reading room once we are married?" He smiled, his worry vanishing. It was one of the things she liked about him most: worry and moods seemed to pass over him as quickly as a summer shower.

"No." She laughed. "No, it was just interesting. It's a shame you were not there." He chuckled, taking her arm, and they began to walk upstairs.

"Not really my thing, but I am glad you found something to entertain you. It's been rather dry here—endless talk of who is going tomorrow night and worries about costumes."

"Oh yes." She paused. "The party…"

He glanced at her. "You're not getting cold feet are you?"

"Oh no, far from it," she said, and smiled. In fact, the party was half of what had been occupying her thoughts as she had walked back from the university library. The name of the people who were hosting it was Bradbury, and the name of the young and moneyed woman whose steps she seemed to be walking in was Vivian Bradbury. Vivian Bradbury had known about Lemaitre, had unpicked his history of massacres and sorcery, and she knew that he was here in Arkham. Lemaitre still smiled from Jacqueline's dreams with an old face, and from a grainy photograph with a different face, a young and beautiful face. These were not coincidences—they were ropes tying them together.

"What is it to celebrate?" she asked, keeping her voice casual. Walter shrugged.

"Not really sure… I think it might just be the Bradburys showing off."

"Showing off?" They were at the top of the stairs, where it broadened out into a wide, carpeted landing. He pulled a lacquered cigarette case from his pocket, tapping a cigarette on the top before putting it between his lips.

"Oh yes, showing off how many people they know, how many people want to be at their gatherings." He lit the cigarette and exhaled, his eyes suddenly bright with excitement. "Almost crass, but it will be the greatest fun—you'll see. Costumes, the best champagne, entertainers, music, and all dressed up like something from a show of horrors." He gave a grin. "You can bet that no cops will raid it either, wouldn't dare, not with their connections." She stayed quiet for a moment as they walked past the doors to the sitting and dining rooms.

"How well do you know them? The Bradburys, that is."

He shrugged again. "Not very well: I went to college with Hugo, and met his father once before he died. Never really got on with Hugo. Strange that he invited us, but then our parents knew each other, so I guess that explains it. Hey, I'm not complaining—the only people that are sore are the people who didn't get an invitation."

Jacqueline paused, trying to make sure the next question was as casual as possible. "There is a sister too? Vivian or something."

Walter glanced at her, a small frown back in place. "How did you know that?"

Inside she cursed. "You told me." She laughed mockingly. "Remember?"

He made a show of grimacing.

"You know my memory's bad; don't tease."

She laughed and he grinned.

"But there is a sister?"

"Yeah, never met her. Smart, though, real smart, that's what Hugo used to say. Why all of the interest?"

She had the answer ready and gave a small shrug. "Just thought that if I was going to meet her at the party, I better find out if she is terrifyingly pretty or really dull. Is she going to be there?"

Walter shook his head. "Don't think so, and it might be best not to mention her when you meet Helena Bradbury or Hugo."

"Oh, why is that?"

"Talking to Harry today, he says she got into some kind of trouble. You know, got involved with someone on the wrong side of the tracks. Came back here, but had some kind of mental breakdown. The Bradburys don't like to talk about it much." Jacqueline thought of the reserved but unclaimed book in the

Curiositie Shoppe and the notebook hidden for months in the university library. What had happened to Vivian Bradbury? What else had she found out?

"Anyway, enough." They were at the stairs that led up to the next floor. Turning to her, Walter squeezed her shoulders reassuringly. "I know you, I can see through all these questions." For a second, she was terrified that he was about to say that he had found out about her past, about all of the lies that made her acceptable to him and his family. He smiled. "This is just nerves at meeting all these people. Don't think about it. You'll be fine, and anyway, the New England set can be fun—you'll see." Jacqueline nodded, inside thinking about the party and the Bradburys. They might know something, or perhaps there were other fragments of Vivian's trail in the house. That was the next step on the path. She just wished that the path was not so clear and defined. The more she thought about it, the more the future felt like a tunnel vanishing into blackness, atrocity visible to her in the distance like the inevitable light of an oncoming train.

"Yes, yes, I am looking forward to it very much. It's all I can think about, actually."

He smiled at her and started up the next set of stairs. "Come on, dinner's coming up soon and we have to get dressed."

She followed Walter, still thinking about the sides of a tunnel closing tight around her as she walked through the dark.

Chapter Thirteen

Dr. Fields
Merchant District, Arkham

He had watched the House of Solace as the sun rose through the clear sky. The morning hours had passed, the day growing hotter and making him glad of the cool shadows of the alley he watched from. Dr. Fields had waited until it was light to leave the boarding house, the cold fear of the night before making him watch his back as he walked through the streets to the Merchant District. He had seen no one follow him, and had found the House of Solace silent under the sun. No one had gone in or out while he watched and no movement or light had flickered behind the grime-smeared windows.

The decision he had come to in the night had not faded. There would be some hidden truth in the House of Solace, something unknown that would shake the faith of those lured into its lies. He was sure of it, but he still hesitated. When he had watched his daughter enter the House of Solace, she had used a key, and when he had arrived he had carefully tried the handle of the little green door and found it firmly shut. If he wanted to see what was inside, what this Hand of Solace was about, then he would have to find another way in; most likely he would have to break in.

Dr. Fields had never broken the law in his life. If he did this, there would be no going back; he would have sacrificed one part of what he believed was right and good for something else. He would be entering a grey realm of morality where his only guide was his sense that what he was doing was right. He thought of Amelia, of the false fanatic hope in her eyes. He had nothing beyond instinct and the feeling that he was watching his daughter fall down an abyss into oblivion. But that feeling was enough.

He walked across the street, past the locked door, and down an alley that ran along the side of the building. It was very narrow, so narrow that his shoulders scraped the mold-covered walls to either side. The light was dim, coming from the slit gap between the buildings three stories above his head. He edged forward, eyes scanning the wall and the litter-covered floor for an entrance. When he had almost reached the blank wall at the end of the alley, he found it: a tiny set of steps, almost choked with litter, which led down to a door.

With care, he moved down the steps, keeping his movements as quiet as he could, and tried the door. It was locked, or jammed shut, but he felt a sponge-like give in the wood. He smiled grimly to himself. He would literally have to break in. Wedging his shoulder against the door and his foot on the brick steps, he shoved his weight forward. He was past his prime, but the rotten wood of the door was weak. There was a soft splintering and the door buckled inward. A second lunge and it was fully open—a small, oblong opening into darkness.

He pushed himself through into the musty gloom. It was dark and Dr. Fields stood for a moment to let his eyes adjust. He could see nothing beyond the tenuous arc of light that extended from the broken door behind him. He took a step forward and thought he heard something scurrying in the dark at the corner of his sight. He took another step, raising his hands so that he would feel anything he could not see. Another step and he felt rough brick and crumbling mortar beneath his touch. He began to move to his left, keeping contact with the wall. After half a dozen steps, his hand vanished into black space. He moved back a step and felt the solid presence of the wall again.

"A maze of darkness," he murmured to himself, and then wished he had not. He was wondering if he was going to have to feel his way through the basement of the House of Solace, when he remembered his matches. He patted his pockets until he found them. He struck one, the sulfurous flame flaring at the tip of his fingers. The gloom pulled back from the sudden light and he blinked; he was in some sort of passage or corridor. The wall in front of him ended in a corner around which the passage continued.

Coaxing the flame of the match to stay alight, he followed the passage around the corner. He saw five doors on either side of the corridor. A wooden door closed each opening. His match burned out and he had to strike another. He was about to try the first door when a thought came to him and his hand stopped on the cold metal of the door handle. All the doors were shut; not left ajar, none rotting or half-broken, but *shut* with definite purpose.

He shook himself. Of course people used these rooms, and the building was occupied, after all. His light nearly burned out, he turned the handle of the first door and stepped into the room beyond. The thick smell of musty damp filled his nose. It was cold down here, away from the sun, and the damp of the river was slowly seeping into the roots of the building. Something glinted bright in the last light of the burning match. He struck another; the sudden flare of light showed him a cellar room. The floorboards above formed the room's roof, and its walls were unrendered brick with a damp sheen that reflected the light. But it was what was in the center of the room that made Dr. Fields stare unmoving until the match burned down to his fingers.

Steel hooks, knives, and cleavers hung from the ceiling, all shining steel and waiting edges. They were not individual instruments, but bundles of identical butcher tools all new and unrusted under a skim of grease. Beside them hung leather aprons, dozens of leather aprons, clean and fresh. Stacked neatly beneath them were elbow-length gloves, also of thick leather. There was enough to clad and equip half the slaughtermen in the county.

The match went out and Dr. Fields yelped as the last flame touched his fingers. He suddenly wanted to be away from the implications of the instruments that hung silent in the dark room. He fumbled back out into the dark passage and stood for a moment, thinking of the other doors waiting for him a few feet away. He reached for his matches and hesitated. For a second, he felt like a child hiding his eyes from the nightmare: *what you don't see does not exist*. If he did not strike the match, did not look, whatever was behind the doors would not exist for him. He could walk away, never know, never have to consider what the things he would see meant.

"Amelia, what hope did they promise you?" he whispered, and struck another match.

The next room was a mirror of the first except that no knives hung from the ceiling. Instead, two dull grey boxes stood on the dusty tiled floor. Each was a cube, a foot on each side. When Dr. Fields moved close enough to touch them he noticed a high, single noted hum, like the unbroken beating of an insect's wings. The sound was coming from each of the cubes. He could see that a thin crack ran around the sides of both cubes perhaps two inches below the upper surface, as if they were boxes with hingeless lids. If they were boxes, he could open them. He began to grip the top of one to start levering it off. His fingers touched the dull grey substance of the cube and went still with surprise. The cube was warm to the touch and there was something else—a sensation that ran through his flesh like the painless cuts of razors. Slowly, he took his hand away and backed out of the room, never taking his eyes off the two humming grey cubes until he shut the door on them.

He looked in the other rooms. Two were empty, but the last was stacked with crates, their sides neatly stenciled with letters and numbers. The air in that room smelled of metal and oil, and when he pulled up the top to one of the crates he saw gunmetal gleaming under his match light.

He closed the door on this room and considered what he should do next. No. What he *needed* to do next. Room by room his fears for his daughter had reformed and multiplied into a pattern that he did not fully comprehend but which he could not ignore. Something terrible was going to happen, something *inhuman*.

Fumbling around another corner at the end of the corridor he found a flight of stairs. He could see light at the top, seeping around the edges of a door. One quiet step at a time he climbed the stairs until he stood in the semi-darkness at its top. He listened, his hand on the door handle, his ear pressed against the wood of the door. He was reasonably sure that the building was empty, but someone could have entered while he was searching the basement. His pulse thumped in his ears, but otherwise there was silence. He turned the handle and pushed the door softly open. Weak light washed over him, making him blink.

He could see a passageway lit by daylight coming from large, open arches that ran along the right-hand side. The walls were painted in flaking blue paint and the floorboards were bare. Slowly, he moved forward, tensed for the noise of a foot on a floorboard or the sound of a voice. Through the arches were rooms that seemed to be stores for ceremonial paraphernalia. He saw candles stacked in neat bundles, and grey robes—like the one he had seen in Amelia's room—hanging from nails in the walls.

After a few yards, the wall to his left opened into a wide space that must have been the loading area when the building was a warehouse. He could see the bare supports of the roof high above him; the light came filtering through the dusty windows he had seen from outside and from broken skylights above. On the bare concrete floor he could see the remains of marks in charcoal, their shape and pattern scuffed. Banners of grey and black hung from the walls, covering the old, peeling paint. Embroidered on all of them was the symbol of clasped hands above a stitched slogan: "Solace and Hope," "Truth and Hope," "Solace in Our Hands," and many others. If he had not known better, he would have thought them the banners of a religious self-help group. They looked so mundane, so harmless. He thought of the knives in the cellar and suppressed a shiver.

Beside the closed loading doors he could see the small door he had listened at when he had followed his daughter here the day before. This wide, high space had been filled with people in grey, hooded robes, the air filled with guttural chanting. Apart from the marks on the floor, it seemed now like nothing but a converted meeting hall in a rotting building.

Standing in the center of the open space, he turned, looking up to the back of the building. There was another floor, a walled-in mezzanine, under the beams of the roof. Perhaps it had been another storeroom when the building had been a warehouse. He could see the beginnings of a flight of stairs beyond a doorway close to where he had emerged from the cellar. The stairs led up to the mezzanine that ran the width of the building.

Above the archway, someone had painted the symbol of an open palm in black paint. At the center of the palm, there was a mark like a dead starfish. It made him want to vomit to look at it. He felt his hand close around the green stone amulet in his pocket. The symbol above the door reminded him of accounts he had read of warning signs painted on posts and doors in older, less civilized times. Whoever had painted this symbol above the door had done so because of what lay up the stairs, in the room above.

He walked toward the stairs; in his pocket, the green stone amulet felt hot, as if it was warming from within. He kept his eyes away from the mark above the arch, but as he took the first step, he could have sworn that something passed over his skin, as if unseen talons had brushed him. The green stone was blood hot in his palm. Not looking back, he climbed the stairs into the gloom.

CHAPTER FOURTEEN

Raker

Downtown, Arkham

"It's past time for visitors," said the gatekeeper. "You need to ring ahead, get on the list." The gatekeeper waved a clipboard at Raker from inside the window of the small gatehouse. Next to the gatehouse, a twelve foot high wall enclosed the asylum grounds. A wrought-iron gate of bars and spikes closed with a locked loop of chain was the only opening in its weathered surface. Beyond the gates, Raker could see the dark edifice of Arkham Asylum, brooding, waiting.

Raker suppressed a surge of anger at the officious old man. He had come to Arkham to find his fiancé and so far all he had found were threats, avoidance, veiled hints, and a look in people's eyes that made him not want to consider what it implied. The butler had said to come to Arkham Asylum, and to ask a man called Dr. Lemaitre about Vivian. That could only mean that she was a patient here. He could not think how the bright, carefree, clever girl he loved had come to this place, but it was the only answer that made any sense. Raker was going to find out for certain. He was not going to be turned away by any gatekeeper to the realm of the insane. He did not look his best after a sleepless night walking Arkham's streets, but there were ways to overcome appearances. Raker smiled at the gatekeeper and reached inside his jacket.

"Look, is there nothing that can be done…?" Raker asked, slipping a fold of bills out of his pocket and casually tapping on the window ledge of the gatehouse. "I have come a long way and I just want to see someone." The gatekeeper's eyes were fixed on the hand holding the folded bills, his eyes flicking in time with the tapping. The man was old and looked like he had been doing this job for a long time and seen little joy, from the badly shaved jowls under a weak chin to the bile yellow eyes in a flattened face of wrinkles, topped with a stained peaked cap. To Raker, he looked like a man to whom life had given few chances.

"I suppose I could call up and find out if someone would see you," said the gatekeeper, running his tongue over tobacco-stained teeth. "No harm in that."

"No harm at all," replied Raker with a smile. "Tell them that I am here to see Dr. Lemaitre about Vivian Bradbury."

The old man picked up a worn Bakelite earpiece off a stand and wound a handle on a black-fronted box with a speaker horn set into one side of the wall on the inside of the window. Raker heard him talk into the receiver and hoped against hope that he could get in without having to wait until the next day. The hoods who had nearly nabbed him the night before would be out looking for him, and he doubted he could avoid them for another day.

The gatekeeper put the earpiece back on its stand and smiled a greedy smile at Raker.

"You're in luck. The doctors will see you." The man looked at the bills still in Raker's hand. "I just need to let you in." Raker peeled off a note and slid it into the gatekeeper's hand. The man looked at it, and raised an eyebrow. It took three more notes before the man finally pocketed them with a sour smile and shuffled out of the gatehouse with a ring of keys in his hand. At the gate, he unlocked the saucer-sized padlock that secured the length of chain looped through the thick vertical bars. He shoved one half of the gate open, the heavy iron squealing as it moved. Raker stepped through.

The asylum loomed in front of him, its three peaked gables sharp and dark against the summer blue sky. It was a large building of red brick, weathered and mottled by lichen and vines so that the gargoyles that leered from its cornices and roof snarled with blurred features. Five floors of narrow windows looked down on Raker with a dead gaze. Its ground floor was blank stone broken only by a peak-roofed porch over dark oak doors that were shut to the world. Between the asylum and the twelve foot wall that enclosed its grounds, there was a smoothly clipped lawn—featureless, sterile, and dull.

Looking at the building, he felt as if he was crossing a line beyond which his world would change and him along with it. Every line and feature of Arkham Asylum made him think not of a place of confinement, but of a place designed to ward people away: to keep them safe from what was inside.

"Don't wander," called the gatekeeper from behind Raker. "They might not let you out." The man cackled and Raker heard the chain rattle as it was locked around the gate again. Raker did not look around, but strode toward the asylum's gothic porch, his feet crunching on the gravel drive. In the minutes it took to walk to the door he thought of the questions he should ask. All he could think was, *Where is she?* and, *Is she all right?*

A male orderly was waiting for him outside the door when Raker reached the porch.

"You're here to see Dr. Lemaitre?" asked the man in a flat drawl. He was at least five inches taller than Raker, with a flat and clean-shaven face. His bare forearms were fleshy, but in a way that Raker could tell there were hard muscles underneath the soft skin. The short-sleeved white uniform seemed to contain rather than cover his bulk. Raker thought that the man looked more like a wrestler than a nurse.

"I am here to see Dr. Lemaitre about Vivian Bradbury," said Raker, making a halfhearted attempt at a smile, which the orderly just stared at as if his face was made of lead.

"I will take you through the asylum," said the orderly as if he had not heard Raker. "There are over a hundred and fifty patients here. Some of them do not see the same world as you or me. Some have tried to kill other people. Some have succeeded." The orderly raised a bunch of heavy keys on a metal ring and waved them at Raker. "This is their place; it exists for them, not for you. Understand?" Raker nodded and the orderly carried on. "You will not deviate from the route we take. Do not talk to any patients we may encounter. Do not give them anything. Do not take anything they try to give to you." He paused and looked at Raker with pale grey eyes. "Do you understand these rules?"

"Yes," said Raker.

"Then follow me," and the man opened the door into the asylum.

Beyond the heavy door was a tall, walled atrium tiled in a herringbone pattern of black and white. A female nurse nodded at the orderly from behind a reception desk and seemed to ignore Raker as he signed the visitor's register. They then passed through a locked metal gate, beyond which the hall continued. They took a turn through a set of double doors and walked down a corridor until it met a wide stairwell. A broad wooden staircase curled up from the floor to a landing that hung ten feet above the white and black tiled floor. Looking up, Raker saw that the ceiling was painted with animals moving through a landscape of jungle leaves and trees—gazelles, zebras, monkeys, and garish birds, all rendered in burning bright pigments. A tiger peering down at him from the distant corner of the ceiling caught his eye: its eyes glimmered red, its ivory white teeth grinning from behind blackish green foliage. He took two steps forward and watched as the painted eyes seemed to follow him.

"Because that's not creepy," he muttered to himself.

"Ceiling was painted by a patient," said the orderly as he moved past Raker. "It's called *The Jungle of the Mind*. Was part of his treatment, so they say."

"Did it work?" asked Raker, following the orderly up the first steps of the dark wooden stairs.

"Maybe," said the orderly without looking at Raker. "He vanished after he finished it." Raker looked into the tiger's eyes that tracked him as he climbed the stairs.

"Dr. Lemaitre's office is at the end of one of the secure wards," said the orderly, stopping at the top of the stairs for Raker to catch him up. "Remember the rules: a lot of the long-term patients are held in this ward, and they benefit from not being aggravated."

He did not even wait for Raker to nod, but led him through a wide, arched door into a long corridor that stretched into the distance, electric lights reflecting from the green tiles lining the walls, the highly polished wooden floor clicking beneath their feet. Pale, uniformed orderlies moved slowly along the corridor past them, some wheeling figures in bath chairs, others leading people by the arm. Raker could hear a jumble of mumbled words as they passed—snatches of lost monologues spoken to unhearing ears. The rasping scent of ammonia was thick in the air. They passed doors, some closed by heavy ratchet locks, others open to show white-walled cell-like rooms beyond.

Glancing into one room, Raker saw a man sitting on an iron-framed bed. He had an earnest and serious face weathered as if by sun and sea salt. A straitjacket bound his arms and he was staring at the wall, his eyes wide. Then, as Raker looked at him, his eyes flicked up; they were bloodshot, the pupils dilated.

"Must not sleep, must not sleep," the man mumbled. "To sleep is to dream, and the dreamer wakes." Raker had paused, caught by the man's intensity. "For he sleeps and dreams, and dreams." He nodded knowingly at Raker, who felt the orderly's hand on his arm.

"Don't forget the rules: no talking to the patients." He led Raker on.

"What was that about?" asked Raker.

"This is an asylum," said the orderly with a grunt that might have been a laugh. "He came off a boat that had been drifting in the ocean. He was the only one on board. Hasn't slept in all the time he has been here. Just raves about dreams."

"He must be a rare case," said Raker.

"Not in Arkham."

Raker spared a last glance for the man who was still staring at the white wall, and followed the orderly. They came to the end of a narrower corridor and stopped in front of a door. Raker noticed that the door was made of lighter wood than those of the patients' rooms they had passed, and there was a brass plaque screwed to its center that read: *Dr. Joseph Lemaitre*. The orderly was about to knock when the door opened. A grey-haired man in a white coat over a brown suit backed out while talking to someone still in the room.

"It is unacceptable, Lemaitre. You must understand, quite *unacceptable*. I will have to consider a letter to the board of trustees." The man was flushed, color smudging his cheeks beneath circular glasses. It was the flush of anger. "I have already written to her father. She should not have been discharged and now is refusing treatment and has taken up with this…this…*occult* group." He jabbed a finger at someone out of sight beyond the door, but Raker had the sense that the man was afraid, and only anger was giving him the courage to say his piece. "If harm comes to her it will be on *your* head."

"Thank you, Zulock," said a silken voice from beyond the door. Raker thought he could hear an edge of French in the voice's rhythmic tone. "As ever, I will give your opinion the greatest consideration." The second man to step out of the office was perfect: a white medical coat hung off his slim frame and his gold-blond hair curled above a face that reminded Raker of marble statues of saints. He exuded aesthetic perfection, radiating it like a candle. "But now if you would excuse me, Zulock, I have another matter that I must attend to."

With a smile, he looked away from Zulock, who turned and stormed off, anger visible in his every step. The blond man's dark eyes fixed on Raker.

"You are the man who has come about Vivian Bradbury," he said.

"Yes," said Raker. There was something about this man that he did not like, something just below the perfect surface. "Is she here? Can I see her?"

A quick look that Raker could not quite read passed between Lemaitre and the muscled orderly.

"You had better come in, Mr. Raker," said Lemaitre, motioning into the room beyond the door. Raker thought about arguing, about pressing his question, but at least this man seemed willing to see him. A nagging feeling that something was wrong followed him as he stepped through the door.

The room beyond the wooden door was large and had a high ceiling. Heavy bookcases rose from the edges of a red carpet so thick that Raker felt as if he was walking on a light covering of snow. Portraits of serious-faced men flanked a narrow stone-framed window opposite the door, in front of which was a wide desk topped in dark leather. The room smelled of aging books and pipe smoke. A wide couch in cherry-colored leather sat to one side next to two high-backed chairs.

Lemaitre motioned Raker toward one of the high-backed chairs and took the other, settling himself and smiling again at Raker.

"There are certain restrictions of confidence my profession places on me," said Lemaitre, nodding as if to emphasize truth, "but under the circumstances… How much do you already know about Miss Bradbury's condition, Mr. Raker? I take it that is what you are here to find out?"

"Almost nothing; I saw the Bradburys, but they did not even tell me she was here."

"Ah. So you know nothing of the reasons for her committal to this establishment for treatment a few months ago?"

Raker felt that sense of something being wrong become stronger, but he shook off the feeling and focused on the next question.

"No. Look, is she all right?"

"She was suffering from episodes of hallucinatory experiences combined with delusions. Severe and from—"

"Delusions?" Raker cut through the doctor's words. "I don't think so; that's not possible." Vivian had been like a bright light, carefree and sometimes compulsive, with a temper that could flare like a bush fire, but she had always been rooted, aware of the limits of her frivolous lifestyle. She was difficult to charm and almost impossible to fool; it was one of the reasons he loved her.

"I am afraid it is the truth, Mr. Raker." Lemaitre's voice was solemn. "She was suffering from severe delusions, hallucinations, and acute paranoia. I had known the family on a personal basis for some time and can personally attest to the rapid deterioration of her psyche." He glanced away and Raker caught an expression that looked like sorrow on the man's sculptural features. "She claimed that there were forces circling around her family's house, that an immortal sorcerer was planning some great atrocity." Lemaitre gave a humorless laugh. "A colorful and highly developed fantasy."

"That can't be right," said Raker. It was not just what Lemaitre was saying; something was wrong, had been wrong ever since he had come into this office, but he could not grasp what. Raker felt as if soft gauze had been pulled over his senses, muffling his instincts.

"No, of course it is not, Mr. Raker." Lemaitre shook his head as if in sympathy. "It was a delusion, but the madness that gave rise to that delusion was real. Her family found her condition difficult to credit or understand, her brother in particular." Raker was not listening. He felt as if he was at the center of a room that was dissolving, hope draining from him. This man was saying that Vivian had gone mad, the butler had said to come here, and the man in the speakeasy had talked about "that business with the girl." It all fit, it must be true, and the Bradburys blamed him because their daughter came back to them from Boston and then went mad. As much sense as it made, some part of him still would not believe it.

"I must see her, Doctor," said Raker.

"I am afraid that you cannot," said Lemaitre, softly, sorrow and sympathy heavy in his smooth voice. "Miss Bradbury did not respond well to treatment; in fact, her condition seemed to worsen. She—"

"No," said Raker; he could almost feel what Lemaitre was about to say.

"Vivian Bradbury hung herself in her room two months ago." There was a heartbeat pause in which Raker felt the world around him snap into a new pattern, one that explained everything: the end to Vivian's letters, the remarks made by the drunk banker in the roadhouse, the look in Helena Bradbury's eyes, Hugo's anger, and the fear that had been coiling inside him since he had reached Arkham.

"She is dead?" Lemaitre nodded, but Raker was shaking his head. "No, she would never have…"

"But she did."

It has to be true, thought Raker. On some level, he had known it from the moment he had gone to the mansion, but it was as if his mind had turned away from the possibility and blinded itself to the implications. It was true, and it suddenly changed the world around him. It was a world that not only made sense, but was real, and a world in which Raker felt utterly alone.

"Why would she…," he began, but Lemaitre answered smoothly before he could finish.

"Her delusions became unbearable." Lemaitre leaned forward earnestly.

Raker felt the warm, muffling dullness around his thoughts become thicker, and found he was nodding. This doctor was telling the truth, of course he was. Why would he lie?

"Her mind was broken." Lemaitre nodded gravely.

Raker shivered, and the warm, muffled feeling was gone. His senses and instincts snapped back into place, sharp and clear. What Dr. Lemaitre was saying made no sense; it did not fit with the girl he had loved. He knew it was impossible, as sure as he knew that Lemaitre was lying. He shook his head.

"I want to see the other doctor," growled Raker, "the one who was here before. I want to hear what he says."

"You will not accept the truth that I tell you." Lemaitre leaned back in his chair, the earnest manner gone. "That is unfortunate, Mr. Raker." It was at that moment that Raker realized what had been wrong since he had started talking to Lemaitre.

"I never told you my name," said Raker, his voice tight. He suddenly felt trapped and afraid. "And you never asked me who I was or why I was asking about Vivian." Lemaitre smiled. Raker was on his feet, edging toward the door, eyes on Lemaitre as if the perfectly formed man were about to pounce. "You already knew who I was. You wanted to know what I knew. Vivian did not go mad. Something else happened to her, and you talked to me because you wanted to know what I knew and how far I would go."

Raker took another step backward from Lemaitre. Something moved behind him. He began to turn. A heavily muscled arm looped around him, pinning his arms, and a thick hand clamped over his mouth. He could smell the antiseptic stink of the big orderly. The man must have been just outside, waiting. Raker tried to get a grip on something, to break the man's hold.

"Yes, Mr. Raker. Yes, I know who you are. The Bradburys are close friends of mine. We have a mutual undertaking that I cannot allow you to disrupt." Lemaitre smiled, relaxed while Raker struggled against the orderly's grip. "She is dead, that is true.

I had hoped that you would be satisfied that Vivian Bradbury had taken her own life. That you would believe me and go on your way. But you would not believe me. That is rare. You are a dangerous man, Mr. Raker, dangerous to me."

The orderly's hand was tightening against Raker's mouth and nose; his arms and legs had no strength, and the room was fading before his eyes.

"You could have not become involved, Mr. Raker. You could have not needed answers. Now, like Vivian before you, I cannot permit you to leave alive."

The last things Raker saw before the room faded were Lemaitre's dead eyes.

CHAPTER FIFTEEN

Jacqueline Fine

Uptown, Arkham

It poured into her mind in a hot cloud of sensations tinged with the sticky touch of fever. It was not an image but a whisper, like the caress of a warm breeze blowing across the surface of her drifting mind.

"Take my hand, wanderer," it said, the words echoing like the chiming of a bell. Then a face appeared, beautiful, framed by black hair, feminine lips opening a crack in an alabaster pale face, green eyes glittering beneath a grey hood. "Take my hand, wanderer," it repeated, lips moving out of time with the words. She looked into the face and the lips moved. They were saying something else…she was sure she could understand if she got closer. "Take my hand, wanderer," said the voice. The face grew closer and closer until it loomed before her like a cliff of pale flesh, the eyes glowing and sparkling with the light of turning galaxies. The mouth moved again, but this time she heard the words it spoke.

"There is no solace," it said, and she saw that the eyes were wide with fear and the lips red with blood, and that the face was her own.

She opened her mouth to scream and the mouth in the monstrous face split wide. Silence poured out, drowning her in darkness, and in the darkness was an outline of a shore, a man walking on the margin of an unmoving sea beneath still clouds. She was running after the man, stumbling in wet sand, seeing the mark of his feet like a path in front of her. She needed to reach the man, to ask him a question. She looked up and the figure was in the distance, running toward her yet getting no closer, and suddenly she wanted to be no closer and turned to run, and the man was there in front of her, and he had no face.

She saw a shattered mountain covered with stone faces that gazed at the red light of dying stars in a fading sky. Amongst the faces, there was a figure in a grey robe, arms wet red, a golden-haired man at its feet. The red-handed one laughed, and she felt the savage joy of every note like a rush of breath through her own lungs. It was her; she was laughing at the sky, laughing as the blood dripped from her hands, and she tumbled after it through a cascade of images that tasted of burnt iron and raw flesh: blood on a stone floor, flowing like molasses, sizzling hot, a black pool whose edges turned to darkness in which things skittered and crawled, a man in white with the face of an angel who stepped through a door that was a mirror.

With a snap, the door closed and she could see herself, and she had no face.

She was awake, her mouth still open, the scream dying in her throat. She was lying on a bed, the covers soft beneath the weight of her body. Light was streaming in from an open window to her right, its curtains stirring in a warm breeze that smelled of green leaves and dry grass. A face was looking down at her, worry in its grey blue eyes.

"Walter," said Jacqueline. "What is the matter? Was I screaming?" She sat up, still feeling the nightmare like a painful bruise on the inside of her head.

"Yes. I heard you from down the corridor. Are you okay, Jacqueline?" He had that puzzled look of concern on his face that was at once endearing and frustrating.

"Just a nightmare, darling." She reached out and patted his

arm. "I am sorry I scared you. What time is it?" she asked, glancing at the bright day beyond the window.

No matter what she said to Walter, the dream lingered in sickly half memories in her mind. It had been worse than before, more real, closer. She had the lingering feeling that something had touched her in the vision, something from beyond. It was as if something vast, uncaring, and incomprehensible had slid past her, leaving her tumbling in its wake: a small soul sinking in an ethereal sea.

"It's midday," he said. "I asked the servants to let you sleep. You seemed so tired last night." He gestured to the black turban and elaborate silk dress that was laid out at the foot of the bed. "The others are getting ready soon." He smiled. "Apparently, it takes a great deal of time to array oneself for such a party."

"I pushed myself too hard yesterday, but I will be ready, Walter darling. No need to worry." She smiled, but the worried frown stayed on his face.

"You were screaming—"

"Just a nightmare, like I said."

"You were screaming something about having no face..."

"You are so sweet, my dear," said Jacqueline. She climbed out of bed, pulling a blue silk robe over her nightdress. "But it was just a dream." He still looked worried. *Not as worried as he should be*, she thought. "I have to get dressed, darling. Really, don't worry. It was just a dream." He nodded and smiled uncertainly before making for the door.

"You would tell me, wouldn't you?" he asked, his hand on the door handle. "If it was something else, I mean."

"Yes, yes, of course I would," she lied. He nodded, still uncertain, and pulled the door shut behind him.

Jacqueline let out a long breath. Her headache was getting worse. She hated lying to Walter, but she had no choice. One truth would lead to another and then her life with him, their future, would unravel. And how could he believe that truth? That she saw the possible future, and in those future possibilities, something outside understanding waited, bloody and hungering? Then she would have to tell him that she was not the well brought up girl he thought, that she had lied to him ever since they had met. She did not know which prospect frightened her more: him thinking her mad, or him knowing that she had deceived him.

She moved over to the open window and looked out across Arkham, breathing in the warm air. The room was on the third floor of the tall townhouse. Outside, she could see the pitched roofs and sharp gables of the city laid out under the sun. The Miskatonic River was visible as a glittering band winding through the low buildings. It was beautiful, but there was something about it that she did not like, something brooding that persisted even under the summer sun.

Turning back, she looked at the costume laid out for her to wear that evening. It was a costume inspired by pictures of oriental fortune tellers, all layers of rich fabric and a black turban to wind around her dark hair. Walter had thought it wonderful and perfectly fitting for the occult theme to the Bradburys' costume party. The irony of the costume was not lost on her, but then she had worn costumes and masks of one type or another all her life.

She moved across the room to the mirror-backed dressing table. Perfume bottles and makeup pots littered its polished wooden surface. She looked at her hand on the table; the tremor was there in the tips of her fingers, a slight, uncontrollable vibration.

I am more afraid than I have ever been, she thought, *and I can tell no one.* She looked up at the mirror, her eyes unfocused. *Who would believe me?* As her eyes slid back into focus, Jacqueline saw herself blinking out of the mirror. For a moment, it was almost as if it was another person looking out at her from a silver window. She shook herself, perceiving the reflection again for what it was, a reflection caught in glass. She looked at her face and remembered the face in her dream, her face, whispering words that had felt like a warning.

CHAPTER SIXTEEN

Dr. Fields
Merchant District, Arkham

The gloom closed over Dr. Fields as he climbed the stairs. Step by step he climbed, his blood hammering in his ears, certain that at any moment someone would walk out behind or in front of him. As his eyes adjusted to the gloom, he saw a dim light ahead. It was a muddy yellow, like sunlight shining through grime-thick glass, or the light of an old lamp. He could make out a square opening just above the last step of the stairs. He realized that the stairs must emerge in the middle of the room's floor. The green stone in his pocket was still warm against his fingers but its heat was bleeding away. For some reason he found it comforting. Compulsively, he checked that the silver dagger was in his jacket pocket. It was still there, wrapped in soft velvet. Crouching on the top step, he glanced over the lip of the opening into the room above.

The room was large, and must have run the entire width of the warehouse. Grimy windows along one wall indicated that it must be at the back of the building. No other doors led off it. Around the edges of the room, on old tables and overturned crates, candles of all shapes and sizes burned with a greasy light, casting shadows up the walls. He turned, his eyes searching for movement or human shapes. There were none; the room was empty. He took a breath and stepped up onto the wooden floor.

The room was like a chapel without a god. On the walls, a thousand faces of tragedy stared down at him as he moved around the room. Some were photographs, indistinct faces of men, women, families, children looking out of the past through the grainy images. Others were cuttings from newspapers, curling newsprint telling of the sinking of great ocean liners, the coming of war, armistice, Spanish flu, crop failures, revolution, and starvation. Amongst these, the dead and undone looked out, their misery captured in a shutter's click and the flash of a bulb. He could also see oddments hanging from nails amongst the wallpaper of suffering: a medal, a watch, a scrap of fabric, a scarf, and many others.

A floorboard creaked under his foot and he jumped at the noise. He looked down so that he could step around the loose board. Marks covered the floorboards. They looked like they had been burned into the wood. It took him a moment to realize that the marks were dates and names, hundreds of them. He looked across the room. The burnt words and numbers crawled across every inch of the floor. He had been wrong: this was no chapel, it was a shrine to grief.

He looked back to the wall, his eyes taking in hundreds of mementos. Each one was a loss to someone, a wound in their lives that could never be closed. Something caught his eye amongst the tattered memorials. He stepped closer and picked up one of the lit candles. There was a scrap of blue blanket tacked to the wall over a photograph of a man holding a baby. The frayed edge of the cloth scrap hid the man's face, but the edge of his jaw and one eye were visible. Dr. Fields reached out slowly, the tips of his wrinkled fingers trembling. He lifted the cloth away from the photograph. Henry Knowles looked out from the glossy sepia-tinted surface, his smile bright and clear. Dr. Fields looked at the small bundle in Henry's arms, at his grandson. It must have been taken shortly after Thomas was born. There was a date written across the corner in Amelia's spidery hand. It was the date Thomas had died. Dr. Fields had no doubt that if he searched, he would find that date burned into the wood of the floor.

"I am sorry," he said in a quiet, cracked voice. The sound surprised him; the words had come to his lips without him realizing. He looked away from the photograph. He had known that the Hand of Solace preyed on those consumed by grief, but standing in the candlelight, under the eyes of a thousand scraps of memory, he realized that he had not understood its power. The grief in this place was like a physical force pressing against his thoughts.

"Hope," he muttered to himself. "They offer hope." That was what they held out to those whose grief papered the walls. So far, though, he had seen no clear sign of what that hope might be. That was what he needed to find: the heart of the lie that had snared his daughter. He looked around the room, eyes searching for something other than sad memories. At the far end, there was a section of bare wall. A pair of clasped hands had been drawn onto the flaking plaster in charcoal. Beneath the symbol stood a wooden lectern, its surface worn and scratched. Two iron-stemmed candleholders bracketed the lectern. The candles in them were tall and burning bright, as if they had been lit recently. A book lay closed on the lectern, its cover gleaming like polished ebony.

He crossed the room, moving with quiet care until he was looking down at the book. It was the size of a household Bible, perhaps a little larger. Its cover was not leather but polished stone that felt cold to the touch as he opened it. The pages inside where thick and had a soft texture like fine leather. The words on each page looked handwritten, and strange illustrations wound amongst the letters: spiraling snakes, geometric designs, the silhouette of a human figure. They were all drawn in black ink so that they seemed part of the words in places. The language seemed to be a form of archaic English, unfamiliar but understandable. With a deep breath, Dr. Fields began to read.

The book's message unfolded slowly across pages of convoluted language and through half-expressed hints. All Dr. Fields could think as he read more was that it was the work of a madman. It told of principles that existed beyond human understanding. The world that mankind understood was only a narrow slice of reality, a keyhole view into a universe that was far larger and stranger than could be perceived. Seen from the point of view of this wider reality, science, faith, and even time held no special precedence. The reality of human existence was not fixed but mutable. Those who possessed knowledge and will could bend it as they wished.

The book spoke of god-like beings, of avatars and heralds, and civilizations ruling the earth long before the rise of man. It wound through myth and allegory, telling of a being named only as "the Exile." A being that could answer any question and break any lore of time and space. It was a hungering god, a being of dark humor and thirst that could not be comprehended by man. To stand before it was to risk annihilation. Riddles and stories told of men who had sought the Exile and been granted an answer to their desire. Most of these tales seemed to end in death and terror. Dr. Fields could not tell if these tales were fact tangled in archaic terms, or allegorical ramblings filtered through a crazed imagination. He had a feeling they might well be both.

Buried amongst the allusions to sunless cities and dream-like kingdoms, there was a reoccurring reference to an "Obsidian Key"—"a god snare," the book called it. He almost smiled as he read the phrase "lost at the end of time, under the gaze of dying suns and dead gods." It was like a fairy tale, he thought. Like the drug dreams of Coleridge, or the mythscapes of *Arabian Nights*. Then he remembered that what he was reading was in some way bound to the lie that the Hand of Solace believed. The difference between the quaint and the terrifying was belief. The memory of the guttural chants heard through the crack in the door rose in his mind. He shuddered.

A phrase caught his eye as he scanned a page: *and even to the undoing of time shall be within the grant of the Exile.*

He re-read the line, realization spreading through him like ice. He looked down. Under his feet, the dates of loss and tragedy spread across the floor.

No, he thought. *They can't believe this. They can't think that these tales of gods and magic would grant them that; they can't.*

He looked back at the book, turning pages in a daze. Phrases flicked past his eyes: *god snare, summoning, beyond time, blood price, between worlds, beyond eternity.* The words blurred into a cascade of meaning, and over and over again the Exile and the Obsidian Key wound through the madness written across the pages like the tracks of a snake in the sand. It was an answer, an answer to what the Hand of Solace had offered his daughter. They had promised the impossible: they had promised that the past could be unmade. They had made her believe something that could not be. In her grief, Amelia had chosen madness over the misery of reality.

His hands were shaking as he closed the book.

"Father?" He spun around. Amelia was standing a step away from the opening in the floor. She wore a wide-sleeved grey robe. The hood was pushed back from her head, her tangled blond hair catching the light of the candles. Her eyes were wide with surprise. He could see that she had an unlit candle in her hand. "What are you doing here?" Anger began to curl her mouth. "You should not be here."

He moved toward her, trying to look calm. He had to get her out of here. They could talk then; he could explain what he had found in the basement. Now that he knew the insane lie at the heart of the Hand of Solace, he could persuade her. He *had* to persuade her.

"Amelia, come with me quickly," he said, extending a hand for her to take. She did not take it but looked at him with cold eyes.

"Not now, Amelia, you have to come with me. Now." He extended his hand farther and looked into her eyes, imploring. "These people are not what they seem," he said softly. He thought of the oiled gunmetal glimmering under the guttering light of his match in the lightless basement. "I have found things, Amelia; no matter what they have told you, this Hand of Solace is hiding something from you." There was a flicker in her eyes.

"What have you seen, Father?" she asked in a flat voice.

"Things that make me frightened. I don't think you realize what you have gotten involved with."

She nodded once, stiffly. He took another step and gently took her left hand. She looked up at him, and for a moment she was a little girl looking up from under a curled fringe of blond hair.

"I can't go, Father. Not now," she said, shaking her head.

"You must." He gripped her hand and tugged her. "Come on!" He felt her resist for a moment and then yield. She came close to him as he began to make for the steps down out of the room. "We will have to go out the way I came in through the cellar. If…" His voice trailed off and he went very still.

The knifepoint was pressed into his back just below the ribs. He could feel the tension held in check behind the point. Behind him, his daughter removed her other hand from his and placed it on his shoulder. Her voice when she spoke was as cold as the steel at his back.

"I am sorry, Father, but I am not leaving, and neither are you."

CHAPTER SEVENTEEN

Raker
Downtown, Arkham

Raker's first thought was that he wanted to vomit. His head felt light, as if it was full of swirling mist that coiled against his closed eyelids. Sensations returned like residue left on the inside of his skin by a draining liquid. He felt something hard under his arms and back, as if he was sitting on a chair. There was a taste of bile in his mouth. Where was he? He tried to open his eyes but they only flickered heavily and then stayed shut. He tried to move his arms, to feel around him, but they would not move. He could feel muscles tensing but no corresponding movement.

Half memories oozed back into his awareness. He had been going to the asylum. The butler had said to go there. But why would he need to go to an asylum? He was looking for Vivian in Arkham. He did not need to go to an asylum, did he? Images flicked through his mind's eye like riffled cards: a patterned black and white floor, an iron gate, a tiger watching him from behind painted leaves, a slim, handsome man with blond hair and a cold smile.

His eyes snapped open. He was in a small room. White tiles covered the walls. Mold wound over them and there were dark stains on the floor. Above him, a bare light bulb hung from a twist of wire. He was bound to a wooden chair by tight leather cuffs at his wrists and ankles. He faced a metal door, its edges and frame scabbed with rust. A dark eye was watching him from a hole in the door.

Raker felt a sudden surge of rage. Vivian was dead. She had found out something, something about the blond doctor, the one called Lemaitre. What she had discovered had killed her. At least, that was the implication of what Lemaitre had said. He yanked at the leather cuffs, straining to pull them free of the chair. The leather bit into his arms but held. He let out an angry grunt and collapsed back.

A laugh came from the other side of the door as it hinged inward. A ring of keys banged against metal as they swung from the key in the lock. The corridor beyond was dimly lit, but he could see worn green tiles on the floor and walls. Dr. Lemaitre stood in the corridor, the heavily built orderly just behind him. Lemaitre still wore the white medical coat, his left hand in the pocket of a finely tailored suit, the other resting on top of a black-shafted cane. The corner of Lemaitre's mouth twitched as if at a joke.

"Welcome back." Raker strained at the restraints again. Lemaitre tutted softly. "No, no. Mr. Raker, please be calm or you will do yourself a premature injury." Raker pulled harder but the leather held. "Wasted effort, you see," said Lemaitre, and stepped forward until he was just in front of Raker. He bent down until he was looking Raker directly in the face. "Now, Mr. Raker, I have a pressing prior engagement elsewhere, but I am still a little concerned that—despite your blundering naïveté—you might know more than you should, and if you do, that means others might as well. I cannot afford such a possibility." He smiled, showing a thin line of teeth. "So, I will leave you with Camberwell here."

He nodded toward the orderly by the door. "He will find out if you know more than you think." The orderly called Camberwell moved up behind Lemaitre, who straightened up. Camberwell had a worn canvas roll of tools in his hand. Raker could see the glint of surgical steel inside the folded fabric. "Oh, and there is no point calling for help. Even if anyone does hear, people scream in this place all the time."

Lemaitre gave a final reptilian smile and walked out of sight. Raker looked to the orderly who had spread the leather roll of tools on a low, metal table to the side of the cell. He could see the light gleaming on surgical steel handles and glass vials. Camberwell glanced at him with a look of bored indifference as he screwed a three-inch needle onto a glass-barreled syringe. Raker knew that whatever was about to happen, he would not be allowed to survive. There was something going on that had cost Vivian her life; now, it would claim his also. He flexed his leg and arm muscles, not to try to break free, but to sense any weakness or give in his bindings.

The orderly turned around, the fluid-loaded syringe held in his right hand. His eyes twitched over Raker's arms and legs and he shook his head. He stepped closer and clamped a hand over Raker's forearm and yanked the sleeve of his shirt and jacket up to the elbow. Raker gripped the arm of the chair, keeping the soft skin of his forearm pressed against the wood. The orderly gave a bored sigh and gripped hold of two of Raker's fingers, then pulled and twisted. There was a grating crack as the finger joints popped. Raker screamed as the pain whipped up his arm. He did not even feel as Camberwell turned his arm over and stabbed the syringe into a vein.

For a moment, the pain became stronger, as if it was acid spreading through his blood. Then, his vision rippled as if he was looking through spilled oil. The pain was still there, but it was distant, like a memory that he could put to one side. He could feel his pulse thrumming through his ears, echoing like the crash of waves. A dull, warm heaviness suffused his body. The room around him slid in and out of focus. It was like he was very, very drunk but without drifting into unconsciousness. He tried to speak; his tongue felt thick in his mouth and the voice that came out sounded like it was coming from a long way away. Someone was asking questions. Words were echoing like rolling thunder all around him. The sound was deafening. He heard himself shout for it to stop, but it was like someone else was speaking for him. The thunder-like voice cut out suddenly.

His head must have lolled against the back of the chair, because he could feel something hard pressing into the base of his neck. Above him, the glowing filament of the light bulb spun through kaleidoscopic patterns. Another needle pricked his arm and everything became soft and light. He could hear a voice again, but this time it was soft and slow like a shout heard through water. Another voice was answering. Was it him? It might have been, but he was not sure. The voices talked, one asking questions, the other answering in slurred sentences. They were talking about Vivian, about the Bradburys, about why he had come to Arkham.

That must be me, a part of him thought. *That must be me answering questions. I shouldn't do that; they are going to kill me once they have finished their questions.* But he could not stop the distant voice, which he now knew was his, from answering.

Time stretched, flowing like molasses. The sensations of his body and what was happening around him faded until he was drifting in a soft cloud, numb, unthinking.

They have killed me. The thought rose out of the soft clouds of his mind. *They have killed me, and I am already dead.* He drifted further, the pulse of his thoughts slowing until silence filled him.

His eyes opened. The light hurt his eyes, and his temples were hammering. He could see his right forearm, the torn sleeves of his shirt and jacket rolled up to the elbow, the track of needle marks on his skin. There were dried beads of blood above the puncture marks.

How long have I been under? Long enough for the blood to dry hard. The leather cuff on his arm was open. Camberwell must have needed to free it to find a vein. In his drug stupor, Raker had felt none of it: not the cuff loosening or the half dozen additional injections. He flicked his eyes around without moving his head. He could not see the muscled orderly.

Slowly, he tried to move his freed right arm. Pain stabbed into his hand as the dislocated joints of his fingers tried to move. Ribbons of color swam across his sight. For a moment, he thought he would fall back into half-consciousness. The sickly sensation faded, leaving just the raw pain radiating from his hand. He tried again, ready for the pain this time.

His arm moved. A gasp escaped his lips; the effort required was terrible. Apart from the pain, he felt as if he was fighting against his own resisting muscles and nerves. His mind was still pulling itself from the drug dream; he could feel hallucinations and phantom noises waiting just below the surface of his perceptions. He took a breath. He had to do this now. He had been given a chance, a narrow chance to survive.

With a low moan, he moved his right arm across his body until he was touching his left hand. He turned his head so that it was facing to his left, and forced his eyes to focus. The leather cuff was still fastened around his left wrist, the tarnished brass of the buckle glinting dully in the low light. He would need his fingers to open the strap, but with his fingers dislocated he could not close his hand.

"Only way out," he muttered to himself, the words forming heavily in his mouth. He flexed the fingers of his left hand. Carefully, he moved his right hand until the tips of the fingers on his left hand could grip the dislocated fingers on the right. Even brushing the twisted digits was agony. He clamped his mouth shut and gripped the first of his fingers. The pain blossomed to a bright intensity. He wanted to scream but kept his mouth shut. With a sharp jerk, the joints ground and snapped back into alignment. There was a supernova of agony in his body, so intense he did not even feel it as pain. He gripped the next finger and snapped it back into place. He almost blacked out, but after a few panting moments, the pain faded to a sharp ache. Strangely, his head felt clearer, as if the sensation had carved away some of the drug fog encasing his thoughts.

He scrabbled at the buckle holding the strap around his left wrist. His left arm came free and he moved to unfasten his legs. The strap around his left ankle was undone and he was working on the right when there was the noise of a heavy key turning in a lock. The door hinged open.

Raker froze. Camberwell would not be expecting him to be conscious; that gave him a split-second advantage. The heavily muscled orderly pushed through the door with a heavy canvas straitjacket in his arms, his keys still in the door lock. His eyes met Raker's and there was a heartbeat instant of surprise. Raker was already moving. The drugs and pain made his body feel as if it was made of rubber. The buckle came open in his hands and he was standing as Camberwell dropped the straitjacket and brought a fist down toward Raker's face. The blow glanced off Raker's upper arm with enough force to spin him around and send him reeling into the chair. He floundered, his balance wavering as he tried to dodge a second blow that came fast after the first. Raker shoved into Camberwell, pushing forward with all his weight and unsteady strength. The orderly was off balance and half fell back. Raker scrambled for the door, the orderly's hands clutching at his jacket. He stuck an elbow out blindly and felt it hit something. The grasp on Raker's jacket loosened. Raker yanked away from the reaching hands and was out of the cell door. He turned as he crossed the lintel and slammed the metal door shut. The heavy key left in the lock turned with a loud click.

Raker breathed heavily, resting his back against the cell door. From the other side, he could hear Camberwell shouting and beating on the door. A humorless smile flicked across his face. Lemaitre was right: no one would notice someone shouting and screaming in here. He looked around. His vision was still blurred and smudged, and clammy sweat covered his skin. Dirty patches of light fell from light fittings held in the ceiling behind mesh cages. The walls were covered in tiles, stained by runs of rust and mottled by patches of mold. There were openings every few meters, each closed by a rust-flecked metal door. There were no windows, and he could hear the noise of distant dripping water. He guessed he was on a basement level, somewhere underground and half-forgotten in the asylum.

He had to get moving; the corridor looked deserted, but he did not know how long it would be before Camberwell was missed and someone came looking. He turned slowly, steadying himself on the door. The muffled sound of shouting and beating hands still came from inside the cell. There would be doors and gates to get through on the way out. Raker pulled the key out of the lock and hefted the heavy bunch of keys that dangled from the same metal loop.

The dark corridor beckoned him and he began to walk as quickly as he could, his steps clicking on the floor. The passage was long and he passed through pools of light and half shadow. He was panting after a few paces, the receding tide of drugs still lapping at the edge of his perception. Fragments of sound echoed around him: scratching insect sounds and wet dragging noises. He was sure he heard voices from behind some of the locked doors, and shadows twitched out the corners of his eyes.

When he reached the first gate, he had to fumble with the heavy keys to find the right one. The clanking of the lock turning made him think that at any minute he would hear shouts and running feet. No one came for him and he did not see another person, even after he had passed through several more gates and locked doors. For a moment, he wondered if he was still trapped in a drug dream and the half-lit corridors would just go on and on until he woke.

When he found the way out, it was via a staircase that spiraled upward. At the top was a wooden door that he opened a crack. An antiseptic-scented green hall waited beyond and he recognized it as one of those that he had passed through on the way through the asylum hours earlier. He could hear staff moving around just out of sight. Any of them might be part of whatever Lemaitre was doing, but he had no choice—he had to risk that they were ignorant of Lemaitre's nature and plans. It was likely that whatever had been intended for him in the deep, neglected levels of the asylum had been intended to stay secret.

He checked his appearance, refastening buttons and trying to hide the tears in his clothing as best he could. With deliberate nonchalance, he stepped out from the door and began to walk down the corridor. He held himself back from running, focusing his effort on looking unconcerned. He passed orderlies and staff, but most did not spare him more than a glance.

When he reached the stairwell with the painted ceiling, he let out a breath. He was nearly out and it did not seem that Lemaitre had involved more of the staff than the orderly Camberwell. The only risk now was if Lemaitre had asked the staff at the front desk to not allow him to leave.

As he walked down the black and white tiled corridor, his heart started hammering. When he came level with the desk, he smiled at the nurse behind the wooden counter. She looked at him with bored eyes and tapped the book on the wooden surface. He signed out, struggling to stop his hand shaking. She let him out and he kept walking.

Outside, the sky was darkening from blue to bruised purple. The same gatekeeper let him out and pushed the gate shut behind him.

"Not kept in then?" asked the sour-faced man with a dumb grin. Raker glanced back at the looming mass of Arkham Asylum. He thought of the angry, haunted look in the Bradburys' eyes and the phrase that Lemaitre had used: *we have a mutual undertaking.* Raker began to jog down the road toward the darkening horizon.

CHAPTER EIGHTEEN

Jacqueline Fine

French Hill, Arkham

The open-topped car drove through the open gates, gravel crunching beneath its tires, its passengers laughing. Jacqueline was smiling, but it took effort. Her headache and the sense of dread from earlier in the day still lingered, and her worries had grown as the hour to leave for the party had drawn nearer. Neither Walter nor his friends seemed to have noticed, a fact that made her feel all the more like an interloper amongst them. They had all spent hours preparing their costumes for the party. Harry had mixed cocktails from high-end spirits before they'd left his house. "Contraband delights," he had called them. Harry and his wife Margret seemed to pass through life on an effortless bubble of money and easy excitement. Walter seemed caught up in the atmosphere, happily oblivious to her fears. She had laughed and joked, but only sipped at her glass—the heavy taste of spirits had only strengthened the ache at her temples.

Walter gunned the car's engine as they sped up the drive toward Stonegroves beneath the early evening sun, a warm breeze stirring a heavy summer scent from the grass and trees. In front of them, the mansion waited, torches on wrought-iron stands lining the way to the open front doors, the strains of exotic stringed instruments reaching them as the car surged up the rise and onto the open space of gravel in front of the house. The car stopped sharply, occasioning laughter from Margret.

Around them, the chrome, polished wood, and gloss paint of other cars gleamed in the fading light. Jacqueline could see some guests who had arrived just before them walking toward the front door of the house.

The invitation to the party had called it a "Fête of Shadows," and like most parties of the bright young set, it had a theme. There had been black and white parties, where everything from the food to the costumes was pitch black or angel white. Another had taken on the trappings of a circus, with performing animals on display and acrobats spinning in the air above the guests. The plays of Shakespeare, the impersonations of the famous or infamous, medieval chivalry, and a dozen more had all been themes for some of the most infamous gatherings of the rich and beautiful in the last decade. The theme of the Bradburys' party was the occult, the supernatural, and the grotesque. At all such parties, guests added to the spectacle with their costumes.

She could see gowns in a dozen shimmering colors, feathers trailing from headdresses, laughing mouths grinning from beneath jeweled domino masks. Some guests wore no masks but had smothered their bodies in exotic costumes; she saw white-clad Sufis, grey monks, and star-woven magister robes. What she guessed were footmen stood to either side of the portico. Each wore floor-length black robes, wide-brimmed hats, and masks that hid their faces behind bone-white beaks and round eye holes. The trays of welcoming sweetmeats and glasses in their hands were at odds with their unsettling appearance.

Jacqueline stepped out of the car and looked toward the door of the house. Wound in a black, silk dress printed with dragons and golden feathers, her head decorated with a turban of red and black secured with a peacock feather pin, Jacqueline looked the image of a mystic imbued with the hidden knowledge. She wore no mask, but no one could deny she fit the moment.

"Darling, I know I have said so already, but you look positively sublime," said Walter as he got out of the car. Jacqueline smiled with brief pleasure. Walter wore a layered robe of blue silk and coal black velvet embroidered with zodiac symbols and stars. As he looked at Jacqueline, he hooked a mask over his face. It was made of tarnished copper and covered his eyes, turning the upper half of his face into an ugly metal frown above a beaked nose. Looping his arm through Jacqueline's, he turned toward the house with a wide smile.

"Let's go," he said, and they walked toward the mansion.

Not for the first time in Walter's presence, Jacqueline felt as if she was floating forward, the world parting before them like waves in front of a yacht's bow. Just as it was for his friends, for Walter, life was and always had been effortless, the world submitting to him as if charmed. She let the moment take her; for now, she would forget the visions and riddling steps she had traced to this point. The ache in her skull faded and for a moment her world was simple and effortlessly happy.

I can let myself have this moment, she thought. *Just this moment.* They walked through the doors beneath the columned portico. Walter took tapered flutes of drink from the robed and masked servants and handed one to her. Inside the door, it was as if Jacqueline had stepped into another world where sounds, colors, and light warred to dominate her senses. She took a gulp from her glass and let the scene settle over her.

The space beyond was a long, wide entrance hall lined with mirrors, its floor carpeted in red the shade of fresh blood. Chandeliers hung from the ceiling, their crystals replaced by pierced brass shades that reduced their light to a scatter of shadows. Incense burned in copper bowls, filling the air with the smell of the sacred. Gauze covered the windows, turning the summer glare outside into a hazy glow that competed with the hundreds of candles that flickered from shoulder-high iron stands. At the center of the hall, a pyramid of empty glasses rose to a point six feet off the ground, glinting in the candlelight, waiting for black market champagne to cascade down each level. Its presence was a demonstration that those with wealth and influence could choose what laws applied to them.

By Jacqueline's side, Walter was already talking in excited tones to a man dressed in tattered fool's motley, his face hidden by a plain mask of yellow. She saw another guest dressed in the image of some reptilian Egyptian god, his face hidden by an enameled mask of green that jutted out into a fanged snout above his mouth. The god raised a cigarette holder to its mouth and drew in a long breath of smoke. Other guests moved around them in a thronged pageant of costume and finery. It was a shifting mass of glittering fabrics tumbling in shimmering cascades, faces painted in strange symbols, painted masks, and voices raised in laughter and delight.

Jacqueline tugged Walter away from the man in the jester costume.

"Come on, darling," she said as she pulled them deeper into the kaleidoscopic storm of noise and color. "You must introduce me to the Bradburys."

"I suppose I must, only polite thing to do." Walter sighed and shook his head. Jacqueline laughed. "Oh, I know, but Hugo is such a difficult bore. If he is like he used to be, he is probably hiding in a corner away from his guests." Jacqueline frowned. In truth, she did not care about the politeness or etiquette of meeting Hugo Bradbury. She wanted to meet him because he was Vivian Bradbury's brother. He was a connection to the girl whose footsteps Jacqueline was following. She did not like using Walter like this, but she needed to find Vivian Bradbury.

"But they did invite us." She pouted, exaggerating her frown.

"Yes. Okay, you're right." Walter sighed and looked over the press of chattering guests. "He must be here somewhere." They continued to move through the party, gently pushing through crowds, smiling apologies as they passed. They passed mirrors and doorways and tight groups of people clustered around snake charmers, magicians, and fire-eaters. Walter was looking around him, eyes flicking over the crowd. Jacqueline could see lots of servants moving amongst the guests offering trays of delicate food. Unlike the footmen at the front door, these were dressed in monk-like robes of simple grey. Looking into side rooms, she saw people lounging over gilt-framed chairs. In one, she saw a bald man in a black robe who looked too old for the girl draped over him. The man looked bored and the girl over-eager. She listened to snatches of conversations: people telling jokes, gossiping, or making arched comments about other guests' costumes. Some smiled or waved greetings at Walter, others simply turned their eyes to watch them pass.

Jacqueline knew that not everyone who came to these parties was wealthy. Many existed on the periphery, drawn to the light of bright living in a darkening time. Some simply wanted to be part of a set and lived beyond their means to achieve it. Others existed on the money of those they could attract and beguile into giving them a few crumbs from the golden table. As she glided amongst the costumed fops and breathed the incense-soaked air, she felt suddenly out of place.

I am like them, she thought. *A parasite existing in this gold-wrapped world on lies and the wealth of others.* A servant in a grey robe filled her glass as she paused to let Walter exchange pleasantries with a girl dressed as a druidess. She eyed the fizzing drink without taking a sip; she needed to keep a clear head. Somewhere just beyond the horizon, a future of nightmares waited. Here in Arkham was a man who had scattered atrocities across centuries to extend his life, and the only way she had of finding him was to find Vivian Bradbury.

Walter broke away from the druidess girl and they moved on, greeting people, smiling, and exchanging jokes and compliments in a seamless flow. Jacqueline could hear haunting stringed music growing louder as they reached the end of the mirrored hall. Despite her preoccupation, Jacqueline gave a silent gasp as they passed through a wide arch into the Great Hall.

There was no pretension in calling it "the Great Hall"—it was a simple statement of fact. It extended up through the three floors of the mansion to a cupola of glass that showed the darkening sky. Dozens of smoking candelabras burned around the room, filling it with a flickering half-light. Where the hall broke through each floor, an arched gallery encircled the space. Wide stairs led from gallery to gallery, their treads and banisters carved of pale marble. The walls were covered with stucco decorations, and statues in classical dress looked down on all that passed in the hall below. Thick rugs covered most of the wide floor, the hard stone beneath only visible at the edges of the room. From one of the galleries, a band of Middle Eastern musicians played mournful songs on strange wind and string instruments to the beat of hand drums. Jacqueline thought that in the dim light the air seemed to have a vibrating, charged atmosphere of excitement.

Jacqueline struggled against a headache that had suddenly begun to throb behind her eyes as they continued through the crowd. Something about the room was picking at her calm and making her nervous and unsettled. Something inside her wanted to flee screaming from this place, though she did not know why. They moved between clusters of guests, and she smiled without really looking at people. Hugo had stopped to talk to a man dressed in grey. She thought he must be one of the servants. She was trying to tease out what might have set her so on edge when she heard her name and looked up to see Walter looking at her expectantly.

"Jacqueline?" asked Walter. She looked at him, realizing that she had simply been smiling without taking in what was going on around her. Walter lifted a hand and indicated the figure standing next to him. "This is Hugo Bradbury."

The man wore the same grey robes as the servants she had seen moving amongst the guests, but there was nothing submissive about his presence. He was big and had a brute strength that radiated from his blunt face and dark eyes. He offered her a smile that did not reach his eyes and extended a hand. Jacqueline blinked; the pain in her head was building and she was suddenly aware of the close press of people in the Great Hall.

"I am Hugo Bradbury," he said, and she noticed that he had a ring in the shape of two hands clasped together. An amulet with the same design hung around his neck.

"A pleasure to meet you," she said as the ache hammered between her eyes. She reached out and took Hugo Bradbury's offered hand. Her mouth was opening to say something else, but the words never came. The ache in her head shattered into a thousand shards of agony.

She heard herself scream. Her hand felt as if it was burning and the fire was running up her arm. It spread through her, ice cold but at the same time burning hot. Her head felt as if something was scrabbling at the inside of her skull. She convulsed, shaking and juddering where she stood. She was falling, her legs collapsing to spill her onto the floor.

She could feel what was happening but it was as if she was an observer trapped inside her own body. She could sense people around her drawing away, staring in surprise, whispers running through the Great Hall like gusts of wind. All the attention of the hall focused on her; people in the upper galleries had turned to look down at the circle that was forming around her. It was almost as if she could see them all in her mind's eye, the looks of curiosity, Walter's sudden concern, and Hugo Bradbury's confusion.

The voices were becoming louder. She lay on the floor for an instant, her legs folded under her, arms splayed to the sides. Then she stood, unfolding joint by joint with a smooth flow of motion, as if pulled up by a wire. She stood still for a moment and then her eyes opened. Those people near her gasped. Her eyes were rolled back so that they showed only the whites. Her mouth lolled open and something that was not her pulled a voice from the depths of her lungs.

"*The dead are here, and they would like to speak to the living.*" The words rasped out of her in a death rattle, punctuated by sucking breaths. It was not her voice though it used her mouth.

"*A name…,*" she said.

She felt a chill run over her limbs. The chill turned to a sticky nauseous sensation. The crowd was buzzing with excited whispers. They thought it was a show, a performance staged as part of the party, a spectacle to titillate and delight. As a girl, Jacqueline had acted as a medium on stage. She knew all the tricks of such performances, all of the careful misdirection and practiced movements. This was nothing like that. This time it felt real and terrifying. She could feel sweat prickling her skin, could feel the air pressing her close and smothering. Despite the fact that her eyes were rolled back into her skull, she could see everything as it unfolded. The world was dimming, whirling around her even though she was standing still.

"*Solace…*" Something was coming, a presence that was coming to her. She could feel it like the pressure wave that came in front of a storm.

"*Solace…,*" she said again, like a gramophone stuck in the same groove on a record.

"*Solace.*" Her mouth had said the word but it had not come from her. No, the word came from somewhere else, from some*one* else. She felt her hand rise at her side and point at Hugo Bradbury. He looked as if he had been struck by lightning.

"*Why do you pay the blood price, brother?*" her mouth said, her words as brittle as cracking ice. She could hear the crowd around her falling silent, excited whispers fading, laughter dying in throats. Some part of them knew that this was no fashionable outré performance; this was something else, something that touched the soul and made the skin shiver.

"*Brother?*" The voice came again from her lips and the faces of the crowd changed. She saw staring eyes and masked faces and suddenly it was as if she was looking through a glass smeared with blood. The eyes were empty pits, the mouths smiled wide and red, and the masks…the masks were not masks. Over everything she could hear a high, keening, guttural sound like a voice spoken in a thousand muffled cries.

She saw Hugo's face, his dark eyes staring at her with fear. "*Brother*," her mouth said again, "*there is no solace in lies.*"

She saw the man tremble and begin to walk away through the crowd, pushing people out of the way, an expression of anger and fear on his face. They parted before him like a curtain of rotting skin.

Normality snapped back into place around her. Suddenly, she was looking at a sea of shocked people in costumes, their mouths open as they stared at her. From somewhere out of sight in the house, a gale of laugher echoed from where they had not seen what had just happened. Walter was staring at her, a shocked expression on his face, mouth open as if to say something.

Jacqueline spun around, breathing hard, panic rising through her. Everyone was staring at her. She felt like a trapped animal.

There was a knife edge moment, and then someone began to clap. Then more and more began to applaud and people were cheering. For a moment she did not know what to do; they thought what had happened was a part of the entertainment, another spectacle for the Fête of Shadows. Then the habit ingrained long ago on a hundred stages took over. She smiled uncertainly and took a shaky bow. Walter was still next to her, not clapping, but staring at Jacqueline with a look that she could not interpret.

"I am sorry," she said, leaning toward him to speak over the applause. "I do not know quite what happened." He frowned, not saying anything. Unable to think of anything else to do, she extended a hand. Walter looked at the hand as if deciding whether or not to touch it. He took it and gave her a brief worried smile.

People surged close around her, talking at her in a wall of smiles and praise. The sound broke over her in babbling waves. She shook her head trying to clear it, trying to piece together what had just happened. It had not been a vision like she had experienced before. It was as if something had reached into her. Something dead had used her voice, something that had felt dried and desiccated as it wore her skin. And it had used her voice to call Hugo Bradbury "brother." She suddenly felt she could give a name to the voice that had spoken with her mouth.

CHAPTER NINETEEN

Dr. Fields
Merchant District, Arkham

The knife tip at Dr. Fields's back goaded him down the stairs from the shrine room. Behind him, his daughter kept a guiding hand on his shoulder and the knife poised. He felt as if he was walking through a dream; everything seemed unreal. He could not believe what was happening, that his daughter now held a knife a thrust away from his heart. This Hand of Solace had twisted her damaged mind and made her into something unknown and dangerous. What had she become?

"Amelia…," he began, and tried to turn to talk to her. The knife jabbed forward making his back arch and cutting the skin through his clothes.

"Be quiet and walk," said Amelia, her voice cold.

"You won't do this," he said softly. "Amelia, I know you, you are not capable of—" The knife was no longer at his back but at his throat. He could feel the razor edge against his neck. His pulse was beating against the blade, his daughter's mouth by his ear.

"What is a little more suffering, Father? Another death?" she asked. "There is so much already; what is a little more for us to wipe away?" She increased the pressure. He gave a sharp intake of breath and went very still. He knew in that moment that she would do it, and he knew part of what the Hand of Solace had done to her. It had given her the will to kill him. He was silent and still. The pressure behind the knife eased slightly. "Now walk," she said.

He did not argue or resist but let his daughter guide him at knifepoint. They walked slowly down the stairs and he felt the clawed caress on his skin as they passed under the mark above the arch. They emerged into the wide space of the converted loading bay. The light was brighter than in the shrine room and Dr. Fields had to blink for a moment before he could see. The tall loading doors were being pulled open with a loud grinding of un-oiled metal. Two trucks backed through the doors, their black sides unmarked, their rear doors open. People in long grey robes spilled in beside the trucks. He had come to this place while something was in progress, he realized. Something was happening that night and he had walked into the middle of it.

All of the people in the loading area stopped to stare at them as Amelia prodded Dr. Fields into the center of the room. He could see at least twenty people in the room now. They were of all ages: some men in their middle years, some hard-eyed women who could not have been beyond their mid-twenties. All were wearing grey robes, the simple fabric hiding their clothes and bodies. The uniforms unified them—made them one no matter what their physical differences. They were all looking at him with cold eyes.

A cult, the word flicked through his mind. *Not an organization or a society. This is a cult.*

"Take him," his daughter said, and shoved him toward two younger men. They grabbed him, pinning his arms behind his back and holding him with a casual strength that he knew he would not be able to break. "He has been through the cellars," she said, addressing the room. "He has seen too much. He cannot leave." One of the men twisted Dr. Fields's arm and he let out a yelp at the sudden pain.

"Who are you? Why are you here?" asked one of the men, growling in his ear and punctuating his words with sharp twists of Dr. Fields's arm.

"He came for me," said Amelia. "He is my father."

"Your father? How touching." The voice came from somewhere behind Dr. Fields. It was a strong voice, rich with an accent that Dr. Fields could not quite place. It rolled across the room in a mocking purr, and at its sound everyone went still. Dr. Fields heard measured footsteps from behind him, each click of a heel punctuated by the tap of a cane. He could not see who approached, but he could see the eyes of all the others in the room. They were locked to the movement he could not see, like the eyes of prey following the approach of a predator.

A man in white stepped into Dr. Fields's view and smiled at him. The man seemed to shine. The white suit that covered his slim frame hung in tailored perfection, its buttons fastened over an ivory waistcoat and grey cravat. He held a black-shafted walking cane in his right hand, its silver top in the shape of two clasped hands. The man's short, blond hair was combed back in a golden wave above a slim face. Dark eyes glittered from above a smile of perfect teeth. *Beautiful*: that was the word that first came to mind as Dr. Fields looked at him, though the man's eyes made him want to run away and keep running.

"Touching, but foolish," said the man.

"Who are you?" asked Dr. Fields. The men holding him twisted his arm hard and he felt them ready to pull him away. The man raised a slender hand.

"No, let him speak. Do not forget our purpose," said the man, turning to address the room. "This man has suffered as much as any here." He turned back toward Dr. Fields and stepped close, staring into his eyes. "I can see it in his eyes. You have suffered, have you not?" Dr. Fields wanted to look away from those eyes but could not. All he could think was how tired he was, and how he had always tried to do the right thing and it had never been enough. "Yes. I see you have. You have the eyes of one who is dead within."

"Who are you?" asked Dr. Fields again. He had to fight to get the words out, as if he was straining against a force that stilled his tongue.

"I am Joseph Lemaitre," said the man, and turned to face Amelia. "You came here for your daughter? To save her from us?" Lemaitre gave Amelia a smile which she returned with a look of adoration.

"What have you done to her?" asked Dr. Fields, anger giving strength to his voice.

The man shook his head as if saddened by the question. "What have I done?" Lemaitre turned his gaze back on Dr. Fields. "What have *I* done, Dr. Fields? That is right, is it not? You are a doctor, if I remember what Amelia told me."

"Yes, I am a doctor," he stammered, surprised by the question and the knowledge it implied. Lemaitre nodded. There was something unnatural about his movements—they were too refined, too smooth. There was a monstrous quality about him, something cloying and rotten hidden under his silken skin.

"*I* have given her hope, Doctor," said Lemaitre, smiling again at Amelia. "The *world* has given her pain and suffering. The *world* has taken away everything she had. The *world* made her as she is now. I had no part in that."

Dr. Fields felt a stab of anger. "I have read the lies you peddle." He spat the words, unable to keep them inside. "You promise them fantasies."

"You do not see the sickness of the universe that has touched these people?" Lemaitre raised an eyebrow. "No? It has touched you too, hasn't it?" Dr. Fields was still shaking his head. "You know of your daughter's pain. How much else do you not know of what others here have suffered?" Lemaitre walked over to a man who stood by the open doors of one of the trucks. The man had a jowly, middle-aged face, and wore round glasses over nervous eyes; he looked like a clerk slowly aging to retirement. Like all the rest of the people in the loading bay, he wore a simple grey robe.

"This is Peter," said Lemaitre, putting a hand on Peter's shoulder and looking at Dr. Fields. "Peter, tell the doctor why you came to the Hand of Solace."

"I…," the man stuttered. He looked at Lemaitre.

"It is all right, Peter. Tell him." Peter looked back into Lemaitre's eyes for a second, then looked directly at Dr. Fields and began to talk.

"I was on a ship. We came from England. It was winter. It was not a large ship, just for cargo really, but it was all I could afford. No work, see, and we thought…I thought…that I could get work here, start a new life…" A smile drifted across the man's face and his eyes were unfocused as if he was seeing a face in memory. "Mary thought it was a good idea, so we saved." His smile faded and he took a slow suck of breath before continuing. "Ship hit ice just off the coast. It was so cold. I could see the lights along the coast, twinkling in the distance. Mary and the girls…they just vanished. They left me. The cold…it was so cold… I could not hold onto them…" Peter looked away, and Lemaitre raised an eyebrow to Dr. Fields.

"Do you understand yet?" Dr. Fields said nothing, he felt numb inside. "No. Not yet perhaps." The man in white turned to an older man with slouched shoulders and a stubble-covered face with the blotched skin of someone who had been a heavy drinker. "Friedrich, please, for the doctor's understanding." Friedrich bit his lip nervously and looked at Dr. Fields with yellow-stained eyes.

"I had a good job. I laid rail tracks. I laid down steel from here to the Pacific. I had a house, a nice one. I had friends. People smiled at me, said, 'Hi, Freddie.' One day that was all gone. 'We

don't need you,' they said. Just like that. Then no house. Then no
food. Then nothing, and when you got nothing, people don't say
hi no more. Then after awhile, you drift away, and people don't
even see *you* no more. I did nothing wrong and everything of
mine went."

Lemaitre gave Friedrich a reassuring smile and looked again
at Dr. Fields.

"I made the Hand of Solace because of these people, and all
the others like them. I gave them real hope, not vain hope, but
hope built on the knowledge that there are ways to change anything. Is hope such an evil, Doctor?" It took a moment for Dr.
Fields to speak. Hanging in the grip of the two men, he tried to
find a word to hold his scorn. He felt dizzy with the enormity of
what this white devil was implying.

"Monstrous," he spat. Lemaitre shook his handsome head
sorrowfully.

"Monstrous? You say that because your daughter has found a
purpose and a belief that the world can be set right. I gave that to
her. I am not a monster for having done that. This is a world of
cruelty, a world that ruins and rewards life with unequal callousness. That is the monster. All I have done is shown these people
that there is a cure." Lemaitre's radiant presence seemed to grow
as he spoke, and Dr. Fields could see his daughter and the other
cultists hanging on every word. Dr. Fields felt sick. What this
man had done to these vulnerable people, how he'd manipulated
their suffering, was inhuman. How could they not see the jackal
laughing behind this man's words? Dr. Fields shook his head.

"You could understand, Dr. Fields," Lemaitre continued. "I
see that you could. All the things that I can see in your eyes, all of
the suffering you have seen and tried to prevent. Those memories
should let you understand us. How many have you seen die?
How many have you seen drift to the bottom of life to be crushed
under its weight?"

"You know nothing of me," said Dr. Fields. He was trying not to think about the ward full of people shivering to death with fever, of the young mothers dying screaming in childbirth, of the sight of blood coughed onto a handkerchief. He tried not to see it, but it was as if Lemaitre was drawing them out of his memory and parading the past in front of his mind's eye. Why would he not help the people who were dying over and over again in his memory? To Dr. Fields, it felt as if Lemaitre's voice purred in his skull, so soothing, so reasonable.

"I have shown these people that there is hope." Lemaitre had walked to where one of the lead grey boxes sat just inside the back of a truck. He smoothed his hand over the surface of the box as he spoke. "That their suffering can be undone, that there is power in this universe that can put true solace in the hands of men." Dr. Fields shook his head, trying to clear the memories that bubbled on the edge of his thoughts. He thought of his daughter crying for her dead son on the floor of her squalid room, of knives glinting in the light of a match. He thought of what he believed in: scientific theory, medical facts, and the kindness of people to each other. He made himself ask the question that he did not want to know the answer to.

"What power? What hope? Hope that builds a church without a god?"

Lemaitre gave a dry laugh. "There are more things in heaven and earth, Doctor."

"You're a charlatan."

"No, I am like you: a healer of hurt and pain."

"I have seen the knives," shouted Dr. Fields.

"What, these?" asked Lemaitre, and pulled a glittering twelve-inch blade from inside his jacket. "Necessary tools, just as what they must spill is necessary."

"You're insane," said Dr. Fields. He almost felt like laughing with despair. Why could they not see it? Why could all these people, his daughter, not see this man as he did?

"No. No, I am afraid that I am not insane." Lemaitre placed the knife down. The smile was gone and his voice was stripped of its honeyed coating. He looked Dr. Fields straight in the eyes and explained. "I am the man with one eye and you are a citizen of a blind kingdom. The universe is not a god's or man's. Your science, your medicine, is a needle hole through the fabric of the truth." He raised his cane and indicated the people in grey robes watching the exchange. "That is what I have shown them, Dr. Fields; that is what has given them hope."

Dr. Fields looked at his daughter. She was not looking at him, but gazing raptly at Lemaitre. "Amelia, you cannot believe this…"

"You will not persuade her," said Lemaitre. He had taken a silver pocket watch out of his waistcoat and was examining the time. "She knows that if we succeed tonight, you will never have come here, that she will never have lost her family, that she will never have needed to come here. We will remake a past without suffering, Dr. Fields. Can you offer better medicine?" The watch snapped shut and, as if at an unspoken command, the cultists began to move again, fetching and loading crates and bundles into the back of the trucks. He could see the butcher gear piled underneath bundles of shining knives and cleavers. The two grey boxes that he had seen in the cellar sat apart in the back of the trucks. Dr. Fields called to his daughter as she pulled herself into one of the trucks.

"Amelia, whatever he has promised you, it is a lie!"

Lemaitre flicked his hand at the two men holding Dr. Fields and they pulled him toward the open doors of one of the trucks.

"Tonight, Doctor, I will help them take back their destiny from the tides of cruel chance. I will give them the means to re-make history, to undo the hurt they have suffered. And you will see it and know it is the truth. We have an engagement to attend, and I am afraid you have to come with us."

The cultists brought Dr. Fields's hands to his front before binding them with coarse rope, then hefted him into the back of one truck and climbed in after.

Lemaitre vaulted into the back of the truck and looked down at Dr. Fields as the engines growled to life. "You will see the truth."

Dr. Fields was silent. Pressed into his side by his bound arms, he felt the silver dagger and amulet still in his pocket.

CHAPTER TWENTY

Raker

French Hill, Arkham

Raker strode toward the front door of Stonegroves House, his feet crunching on the gravel, flaming torches on iron stands marking his path. Light and laughter spilled from the open windows. People in costumes milling in groups outside the door turned to look at him as he strode toward them. Some shouted greetings or scoffed at his lack of costume. He pushed through them to the front door, disregarding the indignant noises, his mind focused, burning.

He was angry. Questions and unexplained details still boiled at the edge of his mind, but it was his anger that drove him, like a ship cutting through the waves of his thoughts. On his way across town, his rage had stoked like a growing fire. There was an "understanding" between Lemaitre and the Bradburys, that was what he had said. And Lemaitre had killed Vivian because she had found out something about him. Had Vivian been killed to protect that "understanding"? If her mother and brother were complicit in her death, he would find out, and make them pay.

He shoved his way through the door into a glittering sea of

faces and voices, making his way past a pyramid of champagne glasses. A man in grey robes, who Raker thought must be a servant, was pouring champagne into the top glass, the glittering liquid flowing down from glass to glass in a frothing cascade.

Another man in a grey robe tried to grab his arm as he passed, his mouth open to say something. Raker shrugged him off without stopping. He was moving down the long hall of mirrors, his eyes scanning the faces he could see for Helena. He did not want to see Hugo, not yet, not until he had found out what was going on. Between his anger and the hate he had seen in Hugo's eyes earlier, he was not sure he would get any answers from him. More than likely, one of them would end up bleeding on the expensive carpet if they met now.

His eyes passed over face after face, searching, dismissing, and moving on. There was a dim light coming from candles and lights encased in oriental shades. No doubt the intention was to create a mysterious atmosphere, but to Raker it was frustrating. Masks or elaborate makeup hid many of the faces. It was as if the party had swallowed people's identities, blurring faces with half-light and glittering finery. He grabbed a man in a grey robe offering a tray of brimming glasses to a clutch of guests.

Putting his head close to the man's face, he barked his question. "Where is Helena Bradbury?"

The man in the grey robe looked as if he was going to argue, then seemed to think better of it. "I think she's in the study on the second floor, but—"

Raker was already moving away through the crowd, shoving people aside. He entered the vast space of the Great Hall, which extended up to a glass cupola past galleries and landings. He could see the staircases connecting each landing and the wide arch above the start of the first flight just across the room. People filled the floor; most crowded around something that was happening in the center of the room. Excited ripples of conversation washed past him as he worked his way around the edge of the room. Snatches of conversation washed over him as he passed: something about a performance—he could hear the excitement in people's voices—but he was not interested.

He reached the stairs—a wide tongue of marble covered with a thick red carpet—and took the steps three at a time. At the top, he turned to glance back at the people filling the Great Hall. At the center of the crowd, a pale-faced woman in dragon-printed robes and a dark turban was watching the retreating back of a large man in grey robes. The man looked up, his eyes roaming over the heads of those around him. Raker recognized the man an instant before their eyes met. Hugo Bradbury's face hardened with anger and he began pushing through the crowd toward where Raker had paused at the top of the stairs.

Raker began to run, feet hammering on the soft carpet. Corridors and doors led off the landing every few yards. He needed to know where the study was quickly. He saw another servant in grey robes. The man looked at Raker with an expression hovering between hostility and puzzlement.

"The study on this floor, where is it?" barked Raker. He thought for a second that the man was going to resist, but then he pointed back down the corridor he had come from, toward a set of wooden double doors. In his hurry, Raker did not think about the heavy-looking leather bag the man was carrying. He ran to the double doors, pushed them open, and shut them behind him.

The room was tall and well-lit in contrast with the deliberately gloomy party. Wood-paneled walls curved around to high widows through which he could see the last of the sunset settling into black. Gilt scrollwork crawled over the wood paneling, glinting in the golden glow cast from frosted light fittings set just above head height. A marble fireplace covered in high relief scenes from antiquity occupied three yards of the wall to his right. Beyond an expanse of thick carpet was a desk of heavy dark wood. A woman in a grey robe sat looking at the face of a pocket watch that lay on the desk next to an inch deep glass of whiskey. At the sound of the door shutting, she looked up.

"Mr. Raker?" asked Helena Bradbury, the surprise clear in her voice. He had meant to ask her about Lemaitre, to tell her that Vivian had not killed herself, but looking at Helena, he could only think that Vivian died in Arkham Asylum, alone, and a different question came to his lips.

"Why didn't you tell me?" His voice cracked as he spoke.

He could see some of Vivian in the line of her jaw and the color of her eyes. Vivian had always said that her mother was tougher than any man she knew, that she had needed to be strong to keep the family together after Vivian's father had died from a stray bullet in the last days of the Western Front. Now, though, Raker could see the hardness cracking.

"I…," she began, looking back at the watch ticking away on the desk in front of her.

"She's been dead for two months," he shouted. "*Two months!*"

"How did you find out?" she asked.

"That doesn't matter." He walked to the desk, hands thrust into his pockets to stop them shaking with anger. "How could you let me carry on thinking she was still alive?"

"I thought it was for the best, that soon enough, it would not matter." She picked up the glass of whiskey, the glass rattling against her teeth as she took a sip. He wanted to knock it out of her hand.

"It would not matter? How could it *ever* not matter?" He was shaking his head, not able to believe what she was saying. She put the tumbler down and her eyes flicked back to the watch, then up to him.

"Raker, it would be better if you go." Her voice was steady, but he could sense the tension below the control.

"Oh no, I'm not going this time." He put his hands on the

desk leaning in so that his face was only a foot from hers. He wanted her to see the anger in his eyes.

"Raker, it really is best that you leave. We are—"

"Having a party, yes," he snarled. "Your daughter is dead in the ground and you are letting the champagne flow. What do you hope, that it will wash away the past? That you can just carry on?" The whiskey in the glass sloshed and the pocket watch jumped as he slammed his fist onto the desk. His voice became mocking. "The Bradburys are undiminished pillars of society. Tragic what happened to their daughter, but they still throw the best parties."

"We don't expect to just carry on," said Helena quietly. She was fiddling with a silver ring on her right index finger, turning it around and around. Raker caught the image of two hands clasped together worked into the ring. She seemed to make up her mind about something and nodded as if encouraging herself. "We are trying to make things right again."

"By having a party?"

"I cannot explain." She looked at the watch again. "Not to you, not now."

"Why? Expecting someone?" he asked, picking up the watch. It showed two minutes to ten. He tossed it back onto the desk.

"It's…" She gave a humorless laugh. "It's not something I can explain. Please, Raker, just go now, before it is too late." There was something in her voice that made his anger run cold. He had been so angry, so focused on confronting Helena, that his mind had skated over details. He had thought it was obscene that the Bradburys were having a party when their daughter was only recently dead, but why were they doing it? Helena was not entertaining her guests or blotting out the past with laughter and champagne. She was alone, looking at a watch, waiting for something. He thought of the grey robes that the servants downstairs had been wearing, that he had seen Hugo wearing, and that Helena was wearing now.

"Too late for what?" he asked. He remembered the silken words of Lemaitre: *we have a mutual undertaking.* He smiled coldly. "What understanding do you have with Dr. Lemaitre?" It was as if he had slapped her across the face.

"I...," she stammered.

"What is going on here?" He gazed at her and she did not look at him. He saw tears begin to slide down her age-creased cheeks.

"I don't blame you. I have never hidden that I thought you were not suitable for Vivian. But, Raker, I do not blame you."

"What?"

"Hugo does, though. That is why you should go. Something..." She seemed to be struggling with what she was trying to express. "Something necessary is going to happen and Hugo might...might want to use that to hurt you."

"He has lied to you. Lemaitre has lied to you!"

Helena looked at him sharply and her mouth began to form a question. "He—"

The door clicked open behind him. Raker turned. Hugo stood in the door, the hood of his grey robe pulled up to frame his wide-jawed face. He had a gun in his hand and a smile on his face. The gun was pointed directly at Raker.

"Raker," he said, a note of triumph in his voice. He kicked the door shut and took two steps forward, the gun steady in his hand. Raker was frozen where he stood, his eyes locked to the black metal mouth of the gun.

"Hugo, what are you—," began Helena.

"Quiet, Mother. You have said enough." He gave an unpleasant grin. "I listened outside the door after I followed you up here. She might not blame you for what happened to Vivian, but as far as I am concerned, you are as guilty as if you had put the rope around her neck yourself."

"Hugo—," began Raker.

"She was well and happy and beautiful until she met you,"

continued Hugo as if he had not heard Raker. "Then, she went away with you, and when she came back here, she started to fall apart. So, yes, I do blame you."

"Hugo, now is not the time," tried Helena again.

"Oh, I think it is, Mother. You have already told him so much that we can't let him go."

Raker did not move, but inside, his mind was spinning. This was real, the look of determination and glee in Hugo's eyes was real, and the death waiting in the mouth of the pistol pointed at him was real.

"Vivian would not want to see anyone dead," said Raker, his throat paper dry, his eyes following Hugo's gun.

"Don't say what she would want! Don't you dare!" shouted Hugo, and Raker thought he was going to pull the trigger right then. Hugo surged forward, brandishing the gun. "We are undoing the damage you did. We are going to put things back the way they were. And you know what? Even after we have what we need, when we can make Vivian alive again, I think I am still going to leave you dead!"

He is insane, thought Raker, but he could tell that whatever madness had taken Hugo, somehow Helena was also caught up by it. Raker tensed his muscles, shifting his weight onto the balls of his feet, ready to spring.

"The rest of what we have to do tonight I will regret. I really will. But this," smiled Hugo, "this I am going to enjoy." He raised the gun, finger tightening on the trigger.

"Wait!" shouted Helena. Hugo's eyes flicked to her, his trigger finger still for an instant. Raker leapt. Hugo's finger closed as Raker's shoulder hit him in the ribs just below his extended gun arm. Hugo was heavier and stronger, but Raker was fitter and faster. The momentum of his charge pitched Hugo off his feet with a crack of ribs. The gun fired, inches from Raker's head, and suddenly he was struggling in a world of muffled sounds, his ears ringing with the shot. The gun flew out of Hugo's hand as he scrabbled at Raker, pulling him down onto the floor. Raker reached up to where he thought Hugo's face was and grabbed onto something. Hugo yelled in pain and Raker felt a blow whip across his face, hard and powerful, shaking his eyes in his skull. He felt the world turn liquid, his senses blurring. Another blow smacked into his head and his sight turned black. He was on his hands and knees, blood dripping from his shattered nose to be lost in the red carpet.

Hugo was scrabbling away from Raker, getting to his feet. He was between Raker and the door. Raker looked around at the bay windows, at the darkening sky beyond the glass. He saw Hugo grasp something that lay on the carpet. Raker came up off the floor like a sprinter as Hugo turned, the gun in his hand again. Raker felt the bullet score a line of pain across his shoulder as he hit the windows. The glass shattered, edges slicing into his flesh as he dove through. And then he was falling.

He barely had time to tuck into a roll before the dew wet grass of the lawn hit him across the back. The impact shocked through his bones; he felt pain and the sticky wetness of his blood on his fingers as he scrambled to his feet. The sounds of music and laughter drifted over him from the house. A shot rang out behind him and the round thumped into the ground by his foot. He glanced up to see a silhouette at the window he had jumped from. He dove to one side as another round thumped into the ground. He came up onto his feet, his body filled with the stabbing pain of shaken bone and bruised flesh. He hobbled into the darkness, only stopping when he was out of sight of the window Hugo had been firing from.

Crouching in deep shadow by a beech hedge, he panted, his breath coming in short, painful gasps. He thought of what Hugo and Helena had said, and about the watch ticking on Helena's desk, of the phrase "what we have to do tonight," and of Lemaitre, the man who had killed to keep something secret. He had never really cared about anything in his life other than getting what he wanted—that and Vivian. But something about the glee on Hugo's face as he held the gun made him know that he could not walk away. He needed help. Limping, blood drying on his face in the night breeze, he staggered into the dark, toward the gate, toward Arkham.

CHAPTER TWENTY-ONE

Jacqueline Fine

French Hill, Arkham

Jacqueline felt as if she was drowning in noise. People were milling around her, offering compliments, asking who she was and whether she would perform again. She just wanted to scream that it had not been a performance, that it had been real.

Screaming… The sound flared briefly in her mind and faded.

The voice that had come from her mouth had not belonged to her; the words she had said had not been from her. Something else had happened, something had spoken through her. She could still feel the clammy touch of it on the inside of her skin, its dry paper voice in her throat.

People pressed close to her, their animated words a babble of excitement, their faces masks of curiosity and relish. She felt like a bird in a cage, with whispering faces pressed close to the bars. Walter was nowhere to be seen. What was he thinking? She had made a spectacle, embarrassed him, and probably forever broken his trust.

She had to find him, the rest could wait. She tried to push her way through the press of people, but as she moved, so did the wall of faces and questions. Her head was pounding and she felt like screaming.

Screaming. Voices screaming over and over again, calling out for pity, calling out through blood-filled mouths. The bubbling drip of...

...laughter and eager questions. Faces pressed close as she tried to make for the side of the room. Snatches of conversations spun around her, about her:

"...just remarkable..."

"...never seen anything like..."

"...the Eastern Europeans say..."

"...don't believe it for a..."

"...terrifying..."

"...did you see her eyes..."

"...like a scream..."

...screams—half heard half remembered, as if they came from the other side of a dream that couldn't be awoken from...

"...voice. Just incredible..."

"Please," mumbled Jacqueline. She wanted to go somewhere dark and still and quiet. Somewhere the world could reorder itself.

"...quite the best..."

"...miss, would you do me the h..."

"...as to be a trick..."

...screams and blood and a city under a red sun...

"Please." The voices felt like hammer blows. Her head felt like it was going to split open.

"...did you see Hugo's face..."

"...disgraceful..."

"Jacqueline." The voice cut through the babble and she felt a hand on her arm. She turned her head to the speaker and forced her eyes to focus. Walter was looking at her, his mask hanging to one side of his face. His eyes still glittered with an unreadable emotion. Jacqueline nodded. Walter tugged her hand. "Come on, come with me." Walter led her through the crowd and up the stairs, making a path with smiles and reassurances. It was quieter on this floor, there were still guests up here, but they did not crowd her as they had in the Great Hall.

At last, Jacqueline found herself in a quieter corner of a large room. She leaned against a wall and took a ragged breath. People were looking at her, concern and questions in their eyes. Even if these people had not seen what had happened in the Great Hall, she must look ill. She did not know what to think or whether to trust her own thoughts. The only thing that seemed real was the coolness of the surface of the wall she leaned on, and a sense that what had happened minutes before had not ended; it was still there, boiling on the edge of her mind.

She glanced about her. The light was dim, as it had been before, but now shadows seemed to creep over everything, touching them with menace. People were milling around the room, some of them occasionally glancing at her, their eyes hollow behind their masks. The swish of costumes and flicker of candles felt like the twitching of some living thing that filled the floor of the room, its many faces looking, whispering.

"What happened, Jacqueline?" asked Walter, and Jacqueline's attention snapped back to Walter's concerned face.

She tried to focus her attention, to forget the headache throbbing at her temples. The monstrous impressions and thoughts that had been building in her mind faded, and she swallowed. She would have to tell him the truth, at least some of it; there was no way of simply shrugging off what had just happened.

"Walter, I have lied to you. I am not from a good family. My name is not even Jacqueline. I—"

"I know," said Walter quietly.

"What?"

"I know," he said again. She could only stare at him. "Not the details, but enough to know that you are not who you say you are."

"How could you?"

The side of his mouth twitched and he let out a snort.

"You are good, my dear, but not that good. The accent was never quite right, your manner too careful, too learned. Every now and again you would make a slip, know something you should not, or not know something that you should." Jacqueline was shaking; everything was falling apart around her. She realized that she had misunderstood Walter—he wore a mask too: a false face hiding an intelligence that had seen through her sham identity. "Some careful enquiries by a discrete agency turned up a few things before I asked them to stop."

"I'm sorry," she said, her voice shaking, emotion held just below the surface. "I never—"

"It's all right," said Walter. "I have known for quite a long time."

"You knew? But then why did you ask me to marry you?" asked Jacqueline.

"I love you. That is enough." Walter smiled at her and after a moment looked away.

"Thank you," she said quietly.

"You need a drink, I think," said Walter as a servant went past with a silver tray of full champagne glasses. He scooped two glasses off the tray and handed one to Jacqueline. "That was quite a performance."

Jacqueline shook her head. "It wasn't a performance." She took a sip of champagne. It tasted bitter in her mouth.

"It will cause a stir perhaps, but nothing to worry too much about. In fact, people seem quite captivated. I must admit, you did surprise me."

"I surprised me as well," said Jacqueline. She felt heavy and dull, as if her mind was filling with warm fog. The sounds of the guests in the room seemed to be rising and falling as if reaching her through surging water. Walter gave her a long look and took a large gulp from his own glass and made a sour face.

"This stuff is awful. Prohibition is one thing, but I thought they would be able to afford better."

"It was real, Walter," said Jacqueline, putting her hand on his arm. Now that she had someone who knew her secret, she wanted to tell someone about what had been happening to her. "I have been dreaming. I have dreamed terrible things: death and darkness, and places that never were." She paused, swallowing to try and get rid of the bitter taste in her mouth. She looked at Walter, who pinched his lips as if considering what to say.

"You really believe that? It could just be tiredness or a fever."

Jacqueline shook her head slowly. "It means something, Walter. I can't be sure what but…" Her mouth suddenly felt heavy, as if it would not move to form words. She could hear the blood surging in her ears.

…blood—blood dripping onto stone, blood on a knife, a sky the color of blood…

She looked at Walter. He was swaying on the spot, blinking as if to clear his vision. He looked up at Jacqueline as if not seeing her, the half full champagne glass tumbling from his hands. Then he fell, the silken robes of his costume rippling around him as he collapsed.

Jacqueline felt strength drain out if her, her legs going weak as she staggered over to Walter. She blinked; her vision was going red as if the dim light was from the glow of a furnace. Walter lay on the floor, his limbs twitching, his eyes closed, spit foaming on his lips.

There was a yell from nearby, then another, and a shout. Jacqueline turned her eyes to see people dropping to the floor, glasses shattering. She could not stand up, her knees felt like rubber.

This was different from the visions—this was something else. There was a chemical edge to the feeling, a slowly spreading numbness. She remembered a rare visit to a dentist as a child: the smell of the chemicals and the smiling face of the dentist as he looked down at her while he anesthetized her—*in a moment you won't feel a thing*. The echo of that chemical numbness filled her mouth. Jacqueline looked at the champagne bubbling in her glass. She thought of the bitter taste in her mouth, of Walter's face as he'd tasted it. *In a moment you won't feel a thing.*

She heard the thumps of people falling around her, more and more falling like corn before the scythe. Some people were laughing, thinking that some grand entertainment had begun. Jacqueline's legs gave way and she slid to the ground, the side of her face pressing into the carpet. Spilled champagne bubbled in a puddle around her. The laughter was turning to screaming. Then the screaming faded to silence.

Jacqueline fought to keep her eyes open, to stay conscious. Cold numbness was spreading through her. She blinked, her eyes watering with the effort. Figures in grey robes moved amongst the unconscious guests. A man in the costume of an orthodox priest stood alone, shocked to stillness as he looked down at the carpet of people around him. He looked young, no more than twenty-one perhaps. His mouth gaped open with shock as he looked around. A figure in a grey robe walked up to him. The man dressed as a priest looked up at the hooded figure, his face all puzzlement. The grey-robed man brought a heavy wooden baton up and crashed it into the man's face, spinning him around, crushing bones, and sending a spray of blood through the air. The guest fell with a sickening thud. The figure hit him twice more, hard, each blow wet and heavy.

Jacqueline wanted to vomit. The numbness was flooding into her mind; she could not see clearly, spots of color ran in front of her eyes. She blinked, and saw a city under a red sky, and blood flowing across a stone floor. She blinked again, saw the mirrored hall, but now it was as if she looked through glass smeared with blood. She saw the unconscious guests twitching on the floor, and remembered the words that had come from her mouth, but were not hers: "*Why do you pay the blood price, brother?*"

Her vision began to narrow to a corridor of darkness. The

images that she could now see blurred into the smudged colors of a waking dream. But somehow she knew this was no vision of the future but of the present; what she saw was happening now as if to show her that she stood at the tipping point between past and future.

This is the beginning, she thought. *This is what Lemaitre planned, and I have failed.* As if in answer to her thought, she saw a door open at the end of the dream corridor. A figure stepped through the door. He wore white and had a face that was beautiful. The man looked around at a sea of people silent and unmoving at his feet. He smiled. Jacqueline started to scream, but the sound was swallowed as darkness enfolded her.

Part Two

The Blood Price

Chapter Twenty-Two

Dr. Fields
French Hill, Arkham

The truck halted and the doors swung open, revealing the front of a huge, white stone mansion glittering under the silver light of a summer moon. Lemaitre gave Dr. Fields a reptilian smile and jumped down from the back of the truck. Amelia followed, keeping close to Lemaitre as if she was his aide. Lanterns and burning torches cast flickering light across the white stone surface of the mansion. Dr. Fields stepped down from the back of the truck, his bound hands making his movements awkward. As his feet touched the gravel, he looked around and saw rows and rows of cars parked around them, their bonnets gleaming. He wondered where they had come and why. They had not driven for more than twenty minutes. *We must still be in Arkham*, he thought, *or very close to it.*

Lemaitre and Amelia were striding away from him toward a pillared portico and an open door into the mansion. Around him, the grey-robed cultists moved, unloading the vans of the knives, butcher gear, boxes, and other equipment. He heard the heavy metallic clunk of cocking weapons and looked around to see cultists hefting drum-fed submachine guns. His eyes lingered on the glinting gun-metal and the narrow muzzles; he still could not quite believe what was happening. The armed cultists did not look at him, but moved toward the house with focused determination.

The muscled pair guarding him shoved him toward the door and he did not resist; his only chance was to stay close to Amelia no matter what. He had to find a way to shake her out of this madness. He did not know why they had brought him, but perhaps leaving him was too much of a risk. For him, it was another chance to find a way of breaking Lemaitre's hold on her.

The dagger was still in his pocket, wrapped in velvet with the green stone amulet. Perhaps he could reach it if they let go of his arms, but then again his hands were still bound. The cultists behind him shoved him again and he nearly stumbled on the step leading up to the door. Regaining his feet, he kept his face impassive, not giving them the satisfaction of a reaction, and stepped through the front door of the mansion. What he saw beyond made him feel like vomiting.

The space was a long hall, dimly lit and still, the light from dozens and dozens of candles glinting from mirrors. Swathes of thick fabric hung from the ceiling, creating a shadow-filled space. The lights hanging from the ceiling and jutting from the walls were hidden behind oriental paper shades or pierced metal coverings. Scented smoke curled from braziers atop black iron stands. It looked as if the inside of the mansion had been dressed for a play, one perhaps featuring the tales of *Arabian Nights* or Faust's pact with the Devil. Somewhere in the distance, a gramophone piped out band music. Lemaitre was standing a few feet inside the door looking around, a satisfied smile on his handsome face. Hand of Solace cultists gathered around him, waiting.

But it was what he saw at Lemaitre's feet that made bile rise in his throat. Unmoving people carpeted the floor. Dr. Fields heard a low moaning noise, like the noise a person might make in sleep as a dream turned into a nightmare. The people were wearing outlandish costumes, their limbs tangled amongst each other, an occasional twitch of fingers or spasm saying that they were not dead. Spilled drinks stained the fabric of costumes and dribbled over exposed skin, and the smell of champagne filled the air. Combined with the smell of incense from pierced brass braziers that stood at the edges of the hall, it gave the scene the feeling of some Bacchic temple to excess. Thirty-some people lay before Lemaitre, insensible and defenseless, and the man in white nodded, satisfied.

"Go through the house," said Lemaitre, flicking his pale hand toward the far end of the mirrored hall. "Find any that have not succumbed to the sedatives." He looked around into the faces of those nearest him. "Kill any that are not unconscious." He flicked a hand over the carpet of people. "We cannot risk anyone getting away." Some of the cultists nodded and began to move down the corridor, treading on people as if they were not there. Most carried submachine guns, others, long-handled batons of wood.

Lemaitre flicked a glance at Dr. Fields. "Give the good doctor some room for a moment, I am sure he will want to appreciate the beginning of our work, and I am sure he will not be going anywhere." The two men holding Dr. Fields let go of his arms. He looked around, trying to avoid Lemaitre's eyes as he felt him watching his reactions.

It must have been a party, thought Dr. Fields, *and the guests were drugged.* He looked at a champagne glass that had fallen and rolled to near where he stood, some dregs of golden liquid still caught in its curved side. He bent down. The rough hemp loops of rope drew tight around his wrists so that he had to clasp his hands together to his front. He dipped the tip of a finger into the liquid and brought it up to his mouth. He flicked his tongue over the smear of liquid, tasting the alcohol and the bitter undertone of another substance beneath it. The drug had been in the drink, which meant that this party had been set up to put hundreds of defenseless living people into the power of Lemaitre and his deluded cult. Anger boiled through him and he shot a disgusted look at Lemaitre. Lemaitre caught Dr. Fields's eyes and his dark eyes flickered with pleasure at the doctor's disgust.

He had seen that look in Lemaitre's eyes before. That cruel amusement had flickered in them as they'd bumped and rattled away from the House of Solace in the back of the truck. A dozen grey-robed cultists had been crammed into the windowless space, sitting on the floor or on their equipment, not speaking, faces grim. The closed cargo trailer had smelled of machine grease and been lit by a paraffin lamp that hung from the roof on a wire loop.

"You still do not understand me, do you, Doctor?" Lemaitre had asked, his face fading in and out of shadow as the lamp swayed with the motion of the truck. Dr. Fields had stayed quiet, not wanting to give Lemaitre the satisfaction of playing along with his word games. "You see, there are powers beyond what we see and touch every day, powers and beings that make our achievements look like those of children. These powers can cut through the mundane laws that we think bind us; they can allow the miraculous to be real." Dr. Fields had shaken his head and looked away. Lemaitre had carried on, his voice still calm and reasonable.

"I do not need to convince you, Doctor—you will see soon enough, and know that what I say is true." Dr. Fields had curled his lip and given a disgusted snort. Lemaitre had simply smiled. "You see, what I have promised these people, is that I will help them use these powers to return to them all that they have lost. Tonight is the first step."

"With guns and knives?" Dr. Fields had blurted out his disgust, overcoming his determined silence.

"The power of which I speak has a price. If all goes as we intend, then any harm we inflict will be set right along with all of the other suffering we will undo."

"And you are doing this, using this power, to help these people?"

"Of course; why else would I be doing this?" Dr. Fields had thought he'd seen a glitter of humor in Lemaitre's eyes at that moment.

As he gazed into them in the hallway of the mansion, he thought he saw it there again. Already the exchange in the truck seemed like it had taken place in another time. No matter if he believed Lemaitre's insane theories, the Hand of Solace did, and they were about to do something monstrous because of that belief.

"You, go down to the gate. Make sure our man is there to turn away any visitors. Then come back to me for your next duty," said Lemaitre to a woman with a gun, who nodded and left by the front door.

"Clear a path through this," said Lemaitre, flicking his hand at the hallway full of unconscious bodies. A few grey-robed cultists moved to obey, picking up people like sacks of grain and tossing them to the side, piling them in heaps to the sides of the hallway, clearing a path of ground. They had not questioned, had not needed anything but Lemaitre's words, to treat living people like debris to be cleared from a road. Again, Dr. Fields thought he could feel a compelling quality to Lemaitre's words, a force that pulled at him to believe and obey them. He glanced at the face of his daughter, who stood by Lemaitre's side. She cradled a submachine gun in her arms and the sight jolted him back to sharp, painful awareness.

There was a scream in the distance, and the staccato bark of muffled gunfire, then another yell, closer but out of sight, the sound of running feet, and then the bark of a gun.

"Go and make sure that nothing is missed, my dear," said Lemaitre, nodding to Amelia. She gave a defiant look toward her father and strode off down the path between unconscious bodies. Lemaitre flicked his fingers in the direction of Dr. Fields and strong hands gripped him again, pushing him forward in Lemaitre's wake. They moved down the cleared hallway, the sounds of violence growling in the distance as the Hand of Solace secured the mansion. Somewhere, the gramophone playing band music was winding down, the muffled music distorting like the cries of the damned.

As they passed the piles of unconscious people, Dr. Fields kept his eyes on Lemaitre's back; he did not want to look at the people piled like cordwood to either side. He thought about what Lemaitre had said about there being a price for power. He had to do something, but he did not know what or how. This was no illness with a diagnosis, treatment, and cure. It was madness and callousness in a form that he had never encountered before. He felt helpless in its path. It was the same feeling that had come to him when his wife had died, when he had stood in the ward during the pandemic, and when he had heard of the death of his grandchild. This, though, was no uncaring force of nature; it was man-made, calculated, and deliberate.

In front of Dr. Fields, the mirrored hall came to an end and he could see that the space beyond opened out. Lemaitre had stopped at the edge of this space and was looking around with an appraising look, his hands in his pockets, as relaxed as if he was a tourist appreciating the space for its aesthetic merit. Unconscious bodies covered the floor around him, candles on iron stands casting flickering light across them.

"Greetings," said Lemaitre, and for a moment Dr. Fields did not know who he was speaking to. Then, he noticed two figures walking down a flight of wide steps beneath an arch that led up to what must have been the next floor of the mansion. One was a man with a wide, blunt head, and dark, slicked back hair. He looked flushed with anger or excitement. The other figure was a thin woman in late middle age with curled, grey hair and a narrow, worried face. Both wore the grey robes of the Hand of Solace, and silver clasped hand amulets hung around their necks. They stopped at the bottom of the stairs and made a brief bow to Lemaitre, their hands clasped in front of their faces.

"This is Hugo and Helena Bradbury, Doctor. They are our hosts tonight," said Lemaitre as if making introductions at a dinner party. He turned back to the pair. "Things seem to have gone as planned. You have served our purpose superbly." Dr. Fields could feel the subtle tones in the accented voice, insidious and compelling. The two figures straightened and exchanged a glance. "Is there something wrong?" asked Lemaitre.

"There might be a complication," said the big man, glancing at the grey-haired woman, who was avoiding his gaze.

"Yes?" asked Lemaitre, an edge of danger beneath the soft tone.

"Someone might have gotten away before the mansion was secured," said the big man. Dr. Fields had the impression that he was picking his words with care. Lemaitre hissed.

"Do they know what is happening here?" he asked.

The woman shook her head. "No, not really. It's just one man and he has not seen…" She looked around at the carpet of unconscious guests as if seeing them for the first time. "He has not seen all this."

Lemaitre nodded. "We have someone at the gate—if he goes that way, he will be stopped." He smiled. "It is of no real consequence; as you can see, we have another complication that we acquired before coming here." He indicated Dr. Fields. "Dr. Fields is Amelia's father who was concerned for her, and is now my conversational companion. Is that not right, Doctor?"

Dr. Fields did not reply, but looked at the Bradburys. He had heard of the Bradburys—a wealthy family of the best stock. *They must be the owners of this house; they must have hosted this party and lured the people here who are now lying on the floor at their feet.*

How can they not see the madness in this man? How can they follow him and his horrific fantasies?

Lemaitre seemed not to notice or care about Dr. Fields's silence. Turning back to the Bradburys, his tone was commanding. "This complication of yours does mean that we will have to progress the ritual with haste."

From behind them, more cultists entered the room, clearing space amongst the unconscious people for the strange, dull grey boxes they had brought from the House of Solace. Others cleared side tables, sweeping away lamps and decorations in a clatter of breaking glass and china. On the tables, they began to lay out knives, meat hooks, and cleavers in neat rows of glinting metal.

"Good," said Lemaitre, waving his hand across the floor. "We need the floor completely clear. Pull up the rugs; we need the bare stones." The grey-robed figures nodded in agreement and began to clear the Great Hall. They dragged and tossed bodies to the sides of the room, exposing a growing area of richly patterned rugs. Through this growing space, Lemaitre wandered, nodding, a pleased look on his face. The rugs were peeled back, exposing a floor of rough white stone. Lemaitre walked across it, tapping his silver-topped cane in places and breathing deeply as if savoring the scent of a wine.

"Yes, yes," he murmured, then flicked a command at the Bradburys. "Bring me charcoal." They bobbed in assent, but he was already walking away from them toward where Dr. Fields stood at the side of the room, flanked by his two minders. He took off his jacket and undid his grey silk cravat, handing both along with his cane to one of the cultists, and began to roll up the sleeves of his white Egyptian cotton shirt. Dr. Fields glanced at him and saw that Lemaitre was looking back at him, an amused curve to his lips.

"You want to know, don't you?" asked Lemaitre.

Dr. Fields shook his head. "I don't want to know anything that you might tell me."

Lemaitre gave a laugh. "That is a bold thing to say; you don't know what I might have to tell. I have seen many things, and I understand more of this universe than any who has lived in the last thousand years." He finished rolling up his sleeves and stood with his hands loose and relaxed at his sides. "And the thing is, you *do* want to know. You want to know the reasons that have led you to this moment." He half turned away as Hugo Bradbury brought him a black stick of charcoal. "You want to know what might have convinced your daughter, what it is that I could have shown these people that made them follow me."

Dr. Fields said nothing and tried to return the young man's look with indifference. The man was right: he wanted to understand, to find something to hang some kind of rational explanation on. The man was toying with him, though, like a cat with its food, and Dr. Fields was damned if he was going to give him the satisfaction.

"Yes?" asked Lemaitre, raising an eyebrow. "You are a strong man, Doctor; stronger than your daughter sees, stronger than most credit. Yes?" Lemaitre raised the stick of charcoal like a conductor's baton. "No matter, you do not need to say anything. I will answer your need and then we will see." He walked to the center of the room, the heels of his patent leather shoes clicking.

"There is a lot in names. Is that not so, Doctor?" Lemaitre bent down, running his hands over the stone floor. "This grand house is called Stonegroves. *Stonegroves.* People hear that name and do not understand where it comes from, what it implies." He patted the stone in emphasis. "Stones once stood here, long ago, before the language we speak had begun to be formed. They stood at a place where the veil between this world and many others is thin." He began to trace lines on the floor, marking the white stone with confident strokes of the charcoal. "This sounds like fantasy, but it is a truth older than your medicine, than science, than human life itself." The marks began to form patterns. Dr. Fields felt his eyes following the formation of every mark and intersection. He felt giddy, as if the air was becoming hot and close.

"The stones are gone, but their roots and the power of this place, this spot, is not." Lemaitre was moving faster and faster, his hands black with charcoal dust, and on the stone floor, a pattern grew and grew in curving lines. "The Bradburys acquired this place, and I have done a great deal to obtain their cooperation in this undertaking." With a final flourish, Lemaitre made a last mark and stood up. The pattern drawn in charcoal made Dr. Fields's head ache to look at it.

Lemaitre nodded to the cultists at the side of the room and said, "Prepare the first offering." The grey-robed men and women lifted the unconscious bodies of the party guests and carried them out onto the charcoal-patterned floor. Dr. Fields felt his fingers twitching inside his bindings. He did not need to imagine what was happening, or guess at what the Hand of Solace needed the guests of the party for. They needed a sacrifice, they needed blood.

Carried by head and foot, a dozen unconscious people were placed at different angles around the pattern Lemaitre had drawn on the floor. The cultists arranged their limbs in line with marks drawn on the floor, so that the drugged bodies became part of the pattern. Dr. Fields saw two cultists place a girl along the edge of the pattern closest to him. She could not have been more than twenty-one, her red hair spilling around her pale face, the white folds of her dress marked by smears of charcoal from the floor.

Lemaitre came to stand by Dr. Fields, wiping his hands on a cloth.

"This will take a little time, Doctor. There are several stages before you will see your first glimpse of what is possible." To one side of the room, Dr. Fields could see that the cultists were pulling leather aprons on over their robes and flexing their hands into thick hide gauntlets. The knives and cleavers waited on the sideboards. Dr. Fields tried not to think of all the warm, unconscious, but still living, people heaped like wood for the furnace throughout the house. One of the cultists, an older woman with a pinched face and glasses that made her look like a school teacher, was the first to lift a long knife and heft it.

"Incredible, is it not, Doctor? What ordinary people will do for hope?" asked Lemaitre, as if exchanging an observation with a friend.

"Why are you telling me this? Why are you making me see this?" asked Dr. Fields, his voice shaking as other members of the Hand of Solace picked up knives and cleavers. A group off to the side picked up heavy meat hooks and waited, ready to clear the space for a fresh offering.

"Why?" Lemaitre leaned in close to Dr. Fields, so close that he could smell expensive cologne and feel his dry breath as he whispered. "Because it pleases me to watch your hope die, Doctor." Lemaitre smiled, and Dr. Fields closed his eyes as the first cultists walked into the pattern of charcoal and flesh and put a knife to a throat.

CHAPTER TWENTY-THREE

Raker
Easttown, Arkham

Raker was deciding which would get him further: a lie or the truth.

The interrogation room was small and stank of sweat and cigarettes. The walls were a sickly tint of sepia under the yellow light of the unshaded bulb hanging by a wire from the ceiling. The young officer at the front had brought him back as soon as he had started saying the word *murder*. Now the young officer, a gangly youth he gathered was called Ed, and a fat, older deputy, who had not given his name, were looking at him. There was a wary look in the older man's eyes, and Raker could tell that the dried blood on his face and torn clothes were already causing assumptions to be formed in the lawman's mind. The younger man just looked terrified.

"So, Mr. Raker," drawled the fat deputy. "What is this about murder?"

Raker let out a sigh; he needed to speak to the sheriff, not to this pair of lackeys. He thought about what answer would get him to the sheriff fastest, and decided on the truth.

"Someone tried to kill me," he said slowly, looking steadily at the fat deputy. "And I think that a lot of other people might be murdered." The deputy raised an eyebrow.

Raker closed his eyes and ran his hands over his face; he could feel the scabbing cuts and smears of dried blood under his fingers. Pain was spreading up the side of his body where he had hit the grass when he'd jumped from the mansion window, and he could feel bruises spreading in a dull ache under his shirt. He felt exhausted. He had scrabbled through the darkness of the Stonegroves estate for at least an hour, avoiding paths and the main drive, waiting for a shot at his back that never came. He had thought of going back through the front gate, but he was sure that the Bradburys would have sent someone to watch it. So he had scaled a wall and stumbled down darkened roads into town.

For a moment, he'd thought about walking away, finding a way out of Arkham, a way back to a normal world of comfortable assumptions and easy choices. Then he'd thought of the look in Hugo's eyes, and the echo of sorrowful determination in Helena's words: *something necessary*. Something that people would die for. He had limped up the steps into the police station not knowing what he would say. He did not like the cops, and so far in his life, the feeling had been mutual, but he could see no other option. The gunmen from Boston were still out there somewhere scenting for his blood, and whatever Lemaitre and the Bradburys had planned felt big and tinged by madness. He needed help, and in a town stalked by enemies, the cops were his only chance of getting that help. It was a slim chance.

It was not until he'd reached the steps of Arkham's police station that he'd considered what he looked like or what he was going to say. In the dim light seeping from the police station windows, he had looked at himself—his suit streaked with mud and blood, torn from wrestling with Hugo, his face and hands still weeping blood from glass cuts. He looked like what he was: a guy from the other side of the tracks on the wrong side of town, or worse, a vagabond in stained and stolen clothes. What would he say? Even if they didn't believe that Hugo Bradbury had tried to kill him, they would make enquiries. Most likely they would think he was trying to pin something on Hugo. That last possibility was the way things seemed to be turning out.

The wooden table in front of him creaked as the deputy leaned on it. Raker looked up from his hands at the face of the fat man. He could smell the stink of the man's dinner on his breath. They had not thrown him out on the street, at least—a firm voice and a demand to see the sheriff had been enough to get him a seat in this small room answering dull questions.

"Who was it who tried to kill you?" rumbled the deputy with the double chins.

"Hugo Bradbury, up at Stonegroves, just on the edge of town."

The deputy snorted. "That right, is it? Tried to kill you?"

"Yes, that's right," said Raker, trying to keep his voice even. Tiredness and pain were hammering at the edge of his thoughts, eating his patience. "He tried to kill me, and there are a lot of other people up at that mansion—" The deputy snorted again, standing up from the table and half turning away. "He said that there would be deaths tonight."

"Yeah?" The fat deputy chuckled. "Hugo Bradbury—one of the best turned out men in this city—said that there would be deaths." He turned to the young officer, jerking a thumb at Raker. "Throw him out, Ed; we don't need the boss to hear this moonshine."

"I am on the level."

"Sure, why not? You look like a respectable guy after all." The deputy smiled. "What I do know is that the Bradburys are some of the most respected people to come to these parts. So why don't we drop this story." He grinned, and at the sight of those crooked, stained teeth, Raker's patience broke.

"Listen." Raker came to his feet without thinking, his hands slamming onto the table. The atmosphere changed in an instant.

The fat deputy moved surprisingly fast, his hands coming up to grip Raker by the hair. His face slammed into the surface of the table hard. Half dazed, he felt his bruised muscles tear as his arms were wrenched behind him and he heard the snick of handcuffs locking around his wrists. A hand hauled him up and dumped him back on the chair. His nose was bleeding again, the blood running down to add fresh stains to his shirt.

"Stay sat down, son," growled the deputy from behind him. "I think we've heard enough from you. No need for a phone call. You just sit there till morning, then you can get on your way out of town." The fat deputy returned to his seat across from Raker and leaned forward on the table.

"People are going to—"

"I am giving you a chance, son. A chance—you get me? Last night, someone went running out of Hibb's Roadhouse with a couple of hoods after him. Gunshots were fired. The guy they were after sounds a lot like you. So, when I tell you that I am giving you a chance, take it."

"I am telling you the truth," said Raker, forcing his voice to be calm. "I am telling you that tomorrow there will be a lot of people dead and if you want to take the risk that I am wrong, go ahead. Just remember that if I'm not lying about this, how bad it will get if people find out that you knew and could have stopped it. There are a lot of important people up at that house; do you really *not* want to be sure that they aren't about to be killed?"

The fat deputy let out a skeptical grunt but Raker could see the calculations going on behind his eyes. He stood up and walked over to the door.

"Ed, stay here and make sure he doesn't smash the place up. I'm going to see if the boss wants to hear this." He gave Raker a humorless grin and pulled the door shut after him.

Raker looked up at the young officer, who was looking back at Raker with wide-eyed intensity. The officer was almost a kid, gangly and tall, with short hair and a long nose above a weak chin. Raker tried a grin. The kid just kept staring, and then he took a step forward. There was something in that step, a purpose, a decision taken, that made Raker feel cold. The kid, Ed, was pulling a baton from his belt, his long-fingered hands holding it with a slight tremble.

"I am sorry," he said, and took another step.

"Ed, look, I don't know what your buddy told you to do, but—"

"It's not him. He doesn't know," said Ed, his voice squeaking with tension. "It's for Ma. In the end, in the end… You can't tell them…" Raker saw the ring—the loop of silver, the clasping hands—as the officer took two faster steps and looped the baton under Raker's chin, pulling it across his throat. Raker tried to yell as the hard wood bit into his windpipe but all that came out was a rattling gurgle. He could see the thin, rat-like face of the officer looking down at him. "I am sorry," he moaned. "I can't let you talk to Sheriff Engle." The boy's thin fingers were flexing on the dark wood of the baton. "You tried to wreck the place, I had to restrain you, that's what I'll say." Raker's vision was darkening at the edges, his lungs burning as he thrashed for air. "Won't matter soon anyway," gasped the officer, straining with the effort. "So long as no one knows, it can all be set right."

Raker felt the darkness coming like the mouth of a tunnel before a rushing train. Then, over the rushing sound of oncoming oblivion, he heard a door open and a shout. He could not see. The pain was receding, turning into soft, enfolding darkness. Something released, and he felt someone shaking him. It felt like it was happening far away. Then he was back in the nicotine-stained room, coughing bile onto the floor from where he somehow still sat in the chair, gasping for air. He could feel hands on his back, steadying him. There was shouting and the sounds of a struggle off out of sight.

"If you're coughing, that means you're alive," said a voice from above him. Raker looked up into a wide face and a pair of hard, grey eyes. A stainless white shirt covered the man's broad chest and gut, the sleeves rolled neatly to the elbow above thick forearms. A metal star was pinned above the heart. "You wanted to talk to me, then one of my officers—a kid I've known for close on fifteen years—tries to choke you to death before you can." The man's voice was a low rumble seasoned by cigarettes and time. "That means that whatever you got to say, I am going to listen to, so you better start telling me something to explain all this."

"There is something going on up at the Stonegroves mansion tonight," began Raker, feeling the bruised muscles of his neck and jaw twinge as he spoke. Sheriff Engle nodded, measuring what Raker said against his own facts.

"Yeah, a party. This about contraband? Is that what you were going to tell me?"

Raker shook his head. He wanted to move his arms, but they were still manacled behind his back.

"This is about something else, I don't know what, but—"

The sheriff cut through him. "You're the guy who was mixed up with their daughter, aren't you?"

Raker looked up at him sharply. "Yes. How did you know?"

"Word gets around, especially in a place like Arkham, especially if it is about the new rich people who just bought a big house."

"I came here to find her," said Raker.

"You say Hugo Bradbury tried to kill you?" The sheriff tilted his head to the side, his eyes holding steady on Raker. "You sure that this is not about you and the brother of your dead girl?"

Raker felt his face tighten. *Dead girl*; the phrase rang cold in his head.

"An argument between me and the brother of 'my dead girl' made your officer try to kill me?" He spat the words. "I don't know what's going on, but it's not a party up at that house." He paused and swallowed. Sheriff Engle was still looking at him, weighing truth against possible lies. "They said that there would be more deaths tonight, that they would be necessary. They had rings and broaches in the shape of clasped hands. Your officer wears one just like it."

"The Hand of Solace," muttered Engle.

"What?" asked Raker.

"The Hand of Solace," said Engle, nodding. "It's a charitable organization, a fellowship of comfort or some such. They have a meeting house down in the Merchant District. Ed went to them after his mother died. They seemed to help him."

Raker snorted. "They are intending to do something terrible, and there is a doctor from the asylum involved. A man called Lemaitre. I got the sense that…" The sentence trailed away as his thoughts formed into words.

"What?" asked Engle.

"I got the sense that it was something that they believed in; something made them sound like they were talking about religion, or something occult."

Sheriff Engle said nothing for a moment and then went to the door of the room. "Something occult," he muttered, rolling the word around his mouth as he opened the door and called to the men waiting outside. "Get everyone you can—shotguns, side arms—get them here in the next half hour. I don't care if you have to tip them out of bed. And get the wagon out." There were murmurs of assent and the sheriff closed the door. He walked over to Raker and reached down behind him. There was a click and the cuffs around his wrists fell away.

"I am going to trust you, Mr. Raker," said the sheriff, looking down at Raker.

"Thank you."

"You prove my trust wrong, and I will be a force of wrath." The statement was flat without the pretense or need of a threatening tone. Raker nodded, massaging his wrists. "You're coming with me up to that house, and I must say, I hope to almighty God that you are wrong."

"You going to ask that officer of yours any questions? If he is part of this group, this occult—"

"No time. Remember, Mr. Raker: if you are right, we have no time." A stony expression had set hard across the sheriff's features. Raker had seen that look in men he had known who had come back from the Great War. They looked like that when they remembered.

"Why are you sure I am on the level now?" asked Raker, standing up and trying to ignore the pain that shot through him as he moved.

"It's because I can't take the risk, Mr. Raker," said the sheriff, a faraway look in his eyes. "That is why I am going up to that house. Because you look like a liar through and through, but I can't take the chance. Not again."

Raker frowned. "Again?"

Sheriff Engle seemed to ignore the question, and went and opened the door.

"What was the word you used, Mr. Raker? That there was 'something *occult*' about it?"

Raker stepped through the door after the sheriff. "Yes."

The sheriff nodded, not looking at Raker as he walked down the corridor toward the front of the station and the sounds of his officers preparing weapons.

"That's why? I say that one word and no more questions?"

The Sheriff of the City of Arkham did not answer.

CHAPTER TWENTY-FOUR

Jacqueline Fine
French Hill, Arkham

Jacqueline woke to the feeling of hands dragging her by the ankles. She bumped across the ground like a sack of corn pulled across a granary floor. Everything was dull and cold, her sensations coming to her in incomplete, distorted parts. At first, all she could feel were the fingers locked around her ankles and the uneven surface she was being pulled over. She tried to move her limbs but found that they were unresponsive and numb. Sound came back, and she heard the dragging rustle of her clothes and the occasional grunt of effort from whoever was dragging her. There was an overwhelming smell of different perfumes and spilled alcohol souring as it dried. Her sight was the last sense to return, and when she slowly opened her eyelids, she had to swallow a scream.

She was on her side, being dragged over a carpet of still people, her body bumping over heads and limbs. She pushed away her instinct to scream and thrash and began to think coldly and quickly. She remembered the bitter taste of the drugged champagne and people dropping around her. There had been people in grey robes, and the man in white. Then the distant, red, warm hints of her visions swam across her mind. The future she had feared was here and now, insistent, terrifying, and real. This would not end well; it would end in blood.

Keeping her eyelids barely open, Jacqueline angled her eyes to look at the person dragging her. The light was dim, but she could see a figure in a grey robe—a thick chin and wide mouth visible beneath a heavy hood. The mouth grimaced with effort, a pink tongue flicking over stained and crooked teeth. She guessed by the tone of the breathing and the look of the mouth and hands that the figure was a man. He was strong—she could feel it in his grip. There were no sounds of anyone else. There might be others that she could not see, but she had to take the risk. She tried the muscles in her hands, moving a finger a fraction of an inch. She had some control over her body again, but whether it was enough, she did not know. She could feel that she still had one shoe on, the right one. That was good. She waited until the figure dragging her grimaced as he had to use extra effort to get her over a hump of flesh.

Jacqueline kicked forward as the grey figure tugged her legs. The momentum pulled the toe of Jacqueline's shoe into the figure's groin. The figure yelled, releasing Jacqueline's ankles and folding over. She scrambled to her feet, feeling the sluggishness of her movements. The man in grey looked up at her as she stepped forward and brought her knee up into his stomach. She put all of the lessons taught to her by necessity and years as a woman surviving on the edge of life into the blow. The man let out a gasp of air and reeled back. Jacqueline could now see that they were in a corridor, just outside a door beyond which she could see unmoving people stacked in a tangle. She glanced behind her and saw a long-stemmed lamp sitting on a marble-topped side table. Two fast steps and she had the lamp in her hands, its cord trailing behind her.

There was a roar from behind and a hand seized her hair. She twisted in the man's grip, ignoring the pain as hair ripped from her scalp. She hit the man in the mouth with the base of the lamp, shattering his teeth in a phlegmy spray of blood. The hand let go of her hair. Without a pause, she raised the lamp and brought it down onto his head with a crunch. Suddenly, the man in the grey robe was twitching at her feet. Blood was seeping through his hood. Jacqueline let out a shaking breath.

She felt the beginnings of panic on the edge of her thoughts forming in a storm of fears and questions. *What is happening? Why? Oh Lord, these people might still be alive. Where is Walter? He must be here? Where was I being taken? What would have happened if…*

Calm. Jacqueline clamped the word over her feelings, strangling off the panic like an iron hand around a throat. She had to be calm. She closed her eyes for a second, forcing her thoughts into cold focus.

She opened her eyes and looked around her, searching for information. She was midway down a long corridor that she could not remember walking down when she was conscious. So she had been moved after she'd blacked out. The dim lighting from covered lamps and candles with the sumptuous carpet and wood-paneled walls told her that this was still Stonegroves. She looked at her wrist watch and found its face had been shattered. There was a window just behind her; the curtains were open and the glass reflected her face back at her when she stepped up to it to look out. It was pitch black outside, which meant at least that it was still night and whatever was happening had not been happening for long. Pressing her face against the glass, she looked out into the night—if she'd been moved to the ground floor, this could be a way out. Blinking against the reflection, she saw darkness filling the space in front and below the window. Somewhere below, the lanterns hanging from the trees leading to the mansion still shone. Jacqueline cursed to herself; she was on an upper floor, and climbing down the outside in the dark was a fast way to the grave. Besides, Walter must still be inside the house. If she could find him, they could both get out. If not, then she would have to get out and find help.

Stepping back into the room, she looked at the heaped bodies of the other guests, costumes and limbs tangled, makeup smeared down faces that looked as if they were asleep. Bending down, she checked the pulse of one and found it was strong. They were alive then; all these people were alive.

But why? Why had they been drugged? The accounts she had read in the university library rose in her thoughts, accounts of massacres and slaughter that followed the man called Lemaitre like a trail of blood. *He is here*, she thought. *Here in this house, creating another bloody mark on the pages of history.* She began to shake the woman whose pulse she had taken. The woman's head lolled from side to side, her eyes still shut.

...blood dripping on white stone...

She gasped, blinking as her eyes stung. She felt nauseous. Panic began to flair in her again, taking the form of half-thoughts and images: Walter lying as if asleep as a second smile in his throat pulsed his life away, beside him dozens and dozens more, all the same, all dying without waking... She could feel herself begin to shake as she looked across the room: at least thirty people. There had been more people than this at the party, many more. Where were they?

She forced herself to stillness and calm again. Whoever the people in grey were, they had made this happen. She wanted to find Walter—instead of continuing to imagine the worst—but the house was vast and Lemaitre's minions seemed to have taken swift and complete control. She could try and find him, but it was most likely only she who would be found. She bit her lip, looking at the dark night outside the window. She had to think calmly and rationally. She would have to find a way out of this house to get help. It was the best chance of stopping what was happening and saving Walter. The front door and hall would be too risky, but there would be servant entrances and side doors. Jacqueline pulled her hands away from the woman and stood up.

Now that she had decided what to do, she moved quickly. She hauled the body of the grey-robed man out of the corridor into the room, hoping that the trail of blood from his head would be lost in the thick weave of the rugs. She checked the man's pockets, but found nothing but a thin fold of soiled bills and an amulet in the shape of clasped hands. The image of a similar amulet around Hugo Bradbury's neck floated into her mind. This was his house, he had been the host of the party, and he was one of these people in grey. His sister had discovered that Lemaitre was still alive and living in Arkham. She was dead and her brother now seemed connected to what the sorcerer was doing. What could that mean? With a shiver, she shook off the thought.

Back on her feet, she moved out of the room and down the corridor. Keeping close to the edge, she moved as fast as she dared, glancing around corners, ready to duck into the shadows. She saw no one; it was as if noise and people had drained away from these parts of the house.

After several turns, the corridor came to an end in a narrow set of stairs behind a velvet curtain. The stairs led down and for a moment she considered retracing her steps, but then she remembered the man in grey she had left bleeding from a cracked skull. He had been taking her somewhere when she had come around. When he failed to come back, someone would come looking. She began to walk down the stairs, glancing behind her at every step. At the bottom of the staircase was another thick red velvet curtain. Pressing herself to the wall beside it, she opened the curtain a finger's width.

She could see a wide balcony, its floor covered by dark rugs, white and gilt railings breaking the view of a wide space beyond. Opening the gap in the curtain wider, Jacqueline glanced left and right. There were no signs of people or their recent presence, just the balcony extending until it curved around out of sight. She opened the curtain and slipped through, ducking into a half crouch. She guessed that this was a gallery on one of the upper floors that looked down into the Great Hall. While there was no one on this floor, she still wanted to stay hidden from anyone lower down who might look up.

Now that she was beyond the curtain, she could hear low noises drifting up from the space below the balustrade. There was a mingled murmur of sounds: the clinking of metal against metal, the occasional soft ripping noise, and a low rhythmical chanting. Still crouched, she moved to the balustrade and looked down into the Great Hall below. The light was low, and at first, she could only see indistinct brown shapes moving against a glossy black floor. Around the darker edges of the room, the shadows seemed to shift and move as if she was looking through a heat haze.

A circle of grey-robed figures ringed the Great Hall. They stood, faces hidden by cowls, chanting a discordant dirge that made Jacqueline's skin crawl. Within the circle was an open space of wood so black and polished that it looked like black glass. A design of white spiraling lines crawled over the glossy surface, each part weaving with another to make angles and shapes that were difficult to look at directly. Even trying made Jacqueline feel dizzy and bile rise in her throat.

Then, Lemaitre, the man in white, the man circled in a grainy photograph by a dead girl, stepped out where she could see him. With the tip of his finger, he drew another line in white on the dark floor. No, not drew, smeared, the substance of the black surface trailing from his fingers as he stood up. With a sickening feeling, she realized what she was looking at. Congealing blood covered the floor. The white marks were where scratches through the sticky layer revealed the white stone beneath. She was looking at the spilled life blood of many, *many* people glistening under the flickering candlelight. She wanted to vomit, to look away, but she could not. Her eyes would not move from the scene below. Her head was suddenly full of pain that vibrated like the sound of a drum. A hot, greasy atmosphere smothered her. Sweat prickled her skin. It was as if she was standing by the open door of a furnace.

The tempo of the chanting changed. The man in white raised a hand to someone out of sight, beckoning. Two figures, their faces covered in drying gore, stepped out. An unconscious man hung between them. Jacqueline caught sight of the serene, unconscious face of the man as the figures placed him to one side of the center. There was suddenly a knife in one of the robed figure's hand, its edge dark and matted with stains. She could still see a smear of billiard chalk on the unconscious man's hands. The knife came down. She turned away with a grunt of effort. Sweat clung to her skin and she was panting.

She knew now, knew what fate she had avoided by waking as she was dragged from storeroom to slaughter hall. *Sacrifice*, the word felt like a hole through her skull from which her sanity poured. Human sacrifice and ritual. On the stage, she had learned the panoply of superstition, had a passing understanding of some beliefs that underpinned what some notorious figures were calling "magic." This was not that puzzled set of rules and formulae, this was blood and death.

She moved back from the balustrade. Going back to the stairs, she twitched aside the red curtain and before she knew it, she was running down the spiral staircase, breathing in gasps, her feet hammering down the steps. There had to be a way out. She would not die in a pool of dried blood under candlelight. Her previous calm had vanished. All that was left was the need to get away, to find a door out of the nightmare.

The bottom of the spiral stairs opened into a wide corridor, its walls plain white, its floor covered in worn terracotta tiles. Simple, unadorned doors led off to either side and Jacqueline frantically tried each in turn. Some were locked, others opened into pantries or unlit rooms that smelled of soap and linen. None had another door that might lead outside. With each turn of the corridor and each locked or exit-less room, Jacqueline felt her panic rise. She was running between now, rattling handles, barging open doors. Every moment, she felt she could feel fate drawing around her, consigning her to bloody oblivion.

Then, a door handle turned and she staggered into a room larger than any she had found. It was long and the light from the corridor behind her glinted off copper pots hanging from the ceiling. A series of three long tables extended down the center of the room, their marble tops gleaming. Beyond them, Jacqueline could see the dark outlines of windows and between them a door.

She took a step, not letting herself hope. Then she was running across the tiled floor, past gleaming copper pots and a row of black iron stoves. Her hand scrabbled at the door handle. It turned and she tugged, but the door was locked firm.

A voice came out of the shadows and she froze were she stood.

"Please," it said.

Jacqueline stood frozen, her hand locked around the door handle.

"Please," came the voice again, a little louder, and she looked toward the dark corner where the voice had come from. There was a scraping noise and a hand appeared at the edge of the light spilling from the open door at the other end of the kitchen. Voices were screaming inside Jacqueline's head telling her to run. Then the face and shoulders of a young man with dark hair slid into view. He dragged himself across the floor with one hand, the other tucked in an odd position against his side. His face beneath his dark hair was very pale, and there were dark stains on his dress shirt and hands.

"Please help me," he said, trying to pull himself closer to Jacqueline. She took a hesitant step toward him, looking at him in the half-light. She saw the blood. It covered his shirt in dried stiff blotches and glistened fresh under his left hand. Breath was coming out of him in wet whistles.

"I...," she began, not knowing what to say.

"They shot me," he said, then gave a cough that splattered dark liquid at her feet. All the control Jacqueline had forced on herself earlier had evaporated; she wanted to hammer down the door, to get away from this man who was dying at her feet. But she could not look away from the blood oozing in slow pulses between the man's fingers.

"I...I can't help you now," she said, thinking of the people she had left unconscious, heaped like firewood upstairs. She was powerless and wanted only to run and forget. She turned back to the door, gripping the door handle again. The man's hand gripped her ankle, his grip cold but strong.

"Please...," he said, his voice a bubbling whisper. "They shot me; they shot me when I tried to get out. Please..." But Jacqueline did not hear the rest of the dying man's plea. A figure had stepped into the room, its shadow thrown out in front of it by the light from the corridor. Jacqueline could see a gun glinting in the shadowy figure's hands. He had seen her and she had nowhere to run.

CHAPTER TWENTY-FIVE

Dr. Fields
French Hill, Arkham

He had not looked, but the sounds had been enough. Held between his minders Dr. Fields held his face in his hands and the room around him had been painted in sounds: soft sounds, slithering sounds, sharp cutting whispers and splashes. There was also the smell, a rank smell of exposed guts and spilled blood. Behind his closed eyes, Dr. Fields had felt those sounds like knives cutting into his soul. He had heard figures moving about him, assembling, and then the chanting had begun. It was low and rhythmic, made up of guttural syllables that human mouths were not intended to form. The sound built in waves and after awhile he could not tell where sensations began or ended, whether he tasted it in his nose, or felt the smell of blood behind his eyes.

Disbelief surfaced and resurfaced through his thoughts; his daughter was a part of this. It was a fact that burned him, his thoughts constantly returning to it through the horror. He understood her loss—had felt it in himself—but he could not understand the inhuman madness that she was helping to create.

"There are people who believe that evil enters the soul through the eyes," said a nearby voice, its tones rounded by a rich accent. It had an amused lilt to it and Dr. Fields could feel Lemaitre smiling without having to see it. "Come, open your eyes. You wish to understand why anyone would do this, do you not?" When Dr. Fields did not respond he continued. "This is the moment, Doctor. The universe is about to show its true face. If you see it, you will understand why someone like your daughter can dip her hands in so much blood and still hope." Dr. Fields did not move. He would not give the monstrous man the satisfaction of acknowledgement. He felt the other man's breath as he leaned close to him; it smelled cold and dead. Wrapped in his pocket, the stone amulet was so hot that he could feel it through the fabric. Beyond the sound of Lemaitre's voice, the droning chant rose and fell.

"You will listen to me and I will show you everything, my friend. You are my confessor, a man of compassion, reason, and science, a priest of these times. I am glad my servant did not consume you when it followed you to the boarding house." Dr. Fields thought of the shadow spreading under the door and the frost forming on the walls of the little, dark room, so recent yet so long ago. "Your daughter suggested I dispose of you, said that you had been asking questions, and when we glimpsed you trying to get into our little rite, I agreed something needed to be done."

Lies. He is lying. But the thought faded and died as if it was too weak to survive.

Lemaitre gave a low, mirthless chuckle. "I am glad it failed. If it had not, we would not be able to talk, no? There is little that gives me pleasure or sadness anymore. There was once a time when the sight of blood would thrill me, when I would feel joy at the power I had wrestled from the universe. Ashes, Doctor, ashes is all I taste now; there is no pleasure or fear left to me. My confession to you is my last pleasure, to make someone else understand what I want."

Strong hands touched Dr. Fields's own hands, which were still pressed against his shut eyes, and firmly pulled them down. "You will hear me, Doctor," whispered Lemaitre, "and you will see what I show you. You will not deny me this last pleasure." The razor edge rose in his voice. "You will not, or I will cut out your daughter's eyes and you can listen to her screams."

Dr. Fields opened his eyes.

Lemaitre stood in front of him, the light of candles flickering in the dark surfaces of his eyes. By his side stood Amelia; she did not look at him, but he could read the defiance in her stance. She still wore the grey robe with the clasped amulet at her throat. He glanced down and saw the red stains on her robes and hands and looked back up. She had seen him look and was glaring back at him. Behind his daughter, Dr. Fields could see that the Hand of Solace had formed a rough ring around an exposed part of the floor. They chanted and swayed, their faces and hands hidden beneath their grey robes. The space at the center of the chanting circle was mottled and dark with blood drying and clotting in a red brown slick. To the side, guarded by a cluster of figures, were the lead grey boxes he had first seen in the basement of the House of Solace. Dim light flickered from the candles and ornamental lamps prepared for the Bradburys' party. The space above the open floor flickered and blurred as if he was looking through a heat haze. He felt like he was in a temple to an ancient and hungering god. The smell was like fresh meat and offal. For a second he flinched, sure that he had felt something sharp running over his skin and a warm breath brushing the back of his neck, but there was no one near him, just Lemaitre smiling like a snake from a few feet away.

"Good," said Lemaitre, as he turned away from Dr. Fields. "Helena, Hugo," he called, flicking his hand like a king summoning servants. "It is time: place the first artifact at the center." Two figures in grey pulled back their hoods and Dr. Fields recognized the bull-like man's face and the hard, thin features of the older woman. They were the ones who owned this house, the ones Lemaitre had introduced as the Bradburys. They had hosted this murderous party.

Hugo and Helena moved one of the two dull grey cube boxes that the Hand of Solace had brought with them to the side of the room. Gripping the box between them, they moved through their chanting comrades onto the blood-soaked circle of floor.

"It is hard to believe now, Doctor," began Lemaitre in a low tone, "but in centuries past, what you are about to see would have been said to be an artifact of sorcery, a fragment of something forged by gods or demons. When I first encountered such things, it was the only way I could understand them." Lemaitre smiled as if enjoying a conversation with a close friend. "Since then, I have watched the rise of science and what you call technology. I wonder which would be a better description for this thing: sorcery or technology."

Hugo and Helena had placed the box on the floor and worked the top off. Each had put on thick leather gauntlets and now reached inside the grey box as if they were pulling something from a furnace. Dr. Fields's eyes stayed locked on the box, waiting to see what would emerge. Lemaitre was right, he wanted to know.

The object that came from the box was small but heavy—it took both Helena and Hugo to lift it. It was a three-sided pyramid no more than two palms wide and the same high. It looked to be fashioned from a glinting, sea green stone or metal. Twisted gold protrusions jutted from its surfaces at odd angles. As soon as it was out of the box, Dr. Fields felt the hairs on his skin rise. He could taste the charged air on his tongue. A high-pitched hum filled his ears like a finger running around the edge of a glass. Slowly, the Bradburys set the pyramidal object on the blood-soaked ground and backed away.

"Though analogies are limited, you might think of that as a knife. It cuts through this time and place to another," Lemaitre explained as if he was a professor explaining to an apt pupil.

"Once that is accomplished, it acts like an anchor: keeping this place, and the place we must go, bound together."

Dr. Fields did not want to be drawn by the man's explanations, but he felt the question come from his mouth before he could stop it. "'The place we must go'?"

Lemaitre nodded at the question. "Yes. That is why we are doing this: to go to a world that exists beyond the skin of this world."

"Lies," said Dr. Fields, but he felt the hollowness of the word and could not take his eyes from the open bloody circle and the glinting pyramid. He tried to swallow, but found that his throat was too dry. Something was changing in the Great Hall. The atmosphere had shifted in a way that touched every sense: an electric caress, a smell and taste of ozone, a sound like a tuning fork, shapes crawling at the edge of sight.

"Do you feel it yet?" asked Lemaitre. "Do you feel the truth, Doctor? I have not offered these people solace in lies. You can feel the truth in this moment, can't you?" The chanting changed, becoming higher and higher. The grip of his minders seemed to increase in sympathetic pressure. Dr. Fields looked away from the rippling haze at the center of the room. He looked at the people chanting, their mouths straining to make the sounds of the rising discordant chorus. Some had thrown their heads back as they shouted their words into the thickening air. He could see the flesh of their cheeks straining as their mouths opened wider and wider. Their eyes were rolling in their heads, the panic evident in their eyes as the chant grew and grew in volume. But they were not chanting, the chant was running through them like flood water through a culvert. They were no longer chanting, but screaming. Blood was running from the cultists' eyes, red tears that fell onto an already blood-stained floor. Some fell to the floor and were still. Others stood juddering as if they were being electrocuted. Dr. Fields felt the hot, iron taste of blood in his mouth. The air around him felt close and warm, like the touch of raw meat. He wanted to move, to run, to close his eyes and scream to drown out the noise.

Lemaitre stepped in front of Dr. Fields and Amelia and traced a flaming red sign in the air that hung above them, burning as if he had branded reality with his touch. Dr. Fields felt the heat of the red sign. It squirmed in front of his eyes.

With a brief nod at Amelia, Lemaitre stepped out onto the bloody floor, muttering as he picked his way across. The words he muttered were little more than whispers that should have been lost in the cacophony, but Dr. Fields could hear every jagged syllable. The sounds might have been words, but if they were, they were not created for human lips. The pale skin around Lemaitre's mouth cracked and split as he spoke. The blood that coated the stone floor was bubbling, forming dark clots that rose from the ground. There was a sound in the air like the grating of broken glass edges. The air was pressing closer and closer, pressure building with every passing instant.

Lemaitre touched the top of the pyramid at the center of the circle. A jagged line of light sprung from it and hung in the air like an arc of frozen lightning. For the length of a heartbeat it remained still, burning its image on Dr. Fields's retinas. Then it split open with a shower of light and a sound like ripping skin. The glowing split spread, forming a ragged hole. It was like the eye of a turning storm, its center a spinning tunnel. He could not guess at its dimension, or even if it had one. Dr. Fields could barely look at it and when he did, it changed with his every blink: a tunnel mouth framed by a halo of green light, a black sphere in which stars glinted, a bleeding fissure like a wound in the flesh of reality. *No, not a wound or a sphere*, he thought. *It's a gate, a gate to the impossible.* A wind blew from it that smelled of ash and rusted iron.

Lemaitre stood in front of the gate, his hands loose at his sides, face tilted up as if at the light of the sun. He was still, an unmoving point at the center of a spreading storm. Green light poured out of the gate, twisting as it spread as if it were a living liquid. Some amongst the Hand of Solace were on their knees, their vomit mingling with the blood on the stone floor. Others shook where they stood, their muscles racked by spasms as if they were puppets jerked by wire.

"He cares nothing for any of you," cried Dr. Fields, shouting at his daughter over the noise of the unearthly wind coming from the gate. "You see now: he uses you."

"There would always be a price, Father," said Amelia, not looking at him. "We all knew that. In the end, we will be able to set all of it right, even this."

"He…," began Dr. Fields, but his voice died in his throat.

Moving shapes like the shadows of strange, multi-limbed beasts were forming on the torn edges of the gate from the streamers of glowing energy that flapped there. On the edge of his sight, someone screamed and screamed and was suddenly quiet.

Lemaitre turned and looked at them. His perfect face was spoiled with wounds where his pale skin appeared to have split, and dark veins could be seen underneath its surface. His eyes glittered with triumph. He raised a hand and pointed through the shifting form of the gate.

"The truth!" shouted Lemaitre. "Do you believe I lie now?"

CHAPTER TWENTY-SIX

Raker

French Hill, Arkham

The police wagon stopped in front of the gateway to the Stone-groves estate. The night was clear and the distant lights of the mansion glittered between the still leaves of the trees. Beyond the gate, the gravel drive stretched away, pale under the starlight until the darkness under the trees swallowed it. Unlike when Raker had visited earlier that day, the wrought-iron gates were shut.

"Guess no one is going to open the gate for us," said Sheriff Engle. He sat with his shotgun across his knees, his bulk wedged between Raker and the right-hand door. The inside of the wagon smelled of motor oil and nervous men pressed together. The other wagon would be behind them, half a dozen in each, all with shotguns and enough ammunition to fight a war. Raker hoped it would not be needed, but if it was, that it would be enough.

A man in the uniform of a footman stepped out of the small door next to the main gates. Raker felt the sheriff stiffen next to him, his hand going to the trigger of the side-by-side. The footman walked up to the front of the wagon, a puzzled smile on his face. He wore a long-tailed coat in black, dark pants, and black shoes polished to a mirror finish. Silver buttons down the front of his grey waistcoat reflected the glare of the headlights. His eyes looked a little red, and he had the slightly bleary look of someone just woken from an uncomfortable sleep.

"Hello, can I help you?" asked the footman, raising his hand to shield his eyes from the headlights. Sheriff Engle grunted and opened the door to get out of the cab. Raker's hand went out and caught his arm.

"The Bradburys would have had to get their staff involved, or replaced them," he hissed. Sheriff Engle gave him a blunt look.

"What do you want me to do? Shoot him where he stands?" growled the sheriff, and shrugged off Raker's hand. There was a murmur of laughter from the officers sitting in the dark behind Raker. That the sheriff had come out in force still surprised Raker, but now that he was here, he wanted to get into the house as quickly as possible. This part of him wondered if shooting now and attending to the niceties later might not be the better plan. The sheriff hefted the side-by-side shotgun and stepped out onto the gravel turning circle in front of the gate.

"Evening," said Engle, standing next to the open cab door, the shotgun held loose by his side. "Sheriff's Department. We had some reports of disturbance up at the house." The footman shook his head politely, hand still raised against the headlights. Raker suddenly felt the skin on his arms prickle and a cold feeling in his stomach. There was something that he had seen as the footman shook his head—something that his eyes had caught, but his brain had not grasped.

"There is a party, sir," the footman said, smiling. "A big one, mind you."

Engle nodded at the footman. "Yeah, I know about that. The matter we are here on is a bit more serious than that."

The footman's smile fluttered. "What is the matter, Sheriff?"

"I would prefer to talk to Mrs. Bradbury or her son about

that," said Engle, pointing at the closed gate. "And I would like to have a look up at the house."

The footman looked pointedly at the two black police wagons, their engines running, waiting. "You have brought quite a posse, sir," said the footman, stepping back out of the beams of the headlights. "I don't think Mrs. Bradbury would appreciate her party being disrupted, sir. If you can come back in the morning—"

"I am not coming back in the morning, son," growled Engle. "Now open the gates." Raker saw the footman's face freeze, the smile and polite air solidifying into a mask.

"You got a warrant, Sheriff?" asked the footman, his voice's courtesy wrapped in ice.

"Open the gate," said Engle, and flicked his hand at the lead police wagon. Two officers pulled themselves out of the back. One was the butter-bellied deputy who had questioned Raker, his stomach shaking under his shirt as he walked to the front of the wagon.

"Mrs. Bradbury has three judges at her party—greeted them myself. You want to bust in on them without a warrant?" asked the footman, backing toward the gate, hands dropping to his sides. This time Raker caught it: the glint of a heavy ring on the man's right index finger. He thought of the ring on the finger of the young officer who had tried to kill him, and the ring on Helena's finger.

"Get out of my way or open the gate," said Engle, and the fat deputy took a step toward the footman.

Raker opened his mouth, the warning rising out of his throat.

A gun roared. The fat deputy was falling, his thick legs folding under him, breath wheezing out of him. Raker saw the dark metal of a handgun in the footman's hand as the man dove through the small door to the side of the gate. Sheriff Engle brought his shotgun up and there was a concussive boom as both barrels spoke. In the wagon there was an instant of numb stillness, then chaos.

Men were spilling from the wagons, guns clutched in their hands. A shot smacked into the windshield a foot from Raker, glass shards showering him. There was another boom. Raker had ducked below the level of the windshield. He could hear shouting and the sporadic cracks of weapons firing. He wanted a gun in his hand.

Glancing through the shattered windshield, he saw Sheriff Engle advancing on the small door beside the gate. The shotgun's breach was open and the lawman was loading fat cartridges with the casual air of a man walking through the woods. The small door slammed shut a second before the sheriff brought the shotgun up and blew a hole in it. The door sagged on its hinges. An officer ran up past Engle and put his boot into the splintered wood of the door. Raker saw the shape of the footman beyond the wrought-iron lattice work of the gate a second before a shot flared in the gloom.

Sheriff Engle was turning when the bullet hit him and spun him to the gravel. Shots boomed out from the officers clustered around the wagon, bullets whizzing blindly into the dark. Raker was out of the cab and running to Engle's sprawled body before he considered what he was doing. Rounds buzzed passed his head, smacking into the gravel around him. He dropped next to Engle.

There was blood on the pale gravel. The sheriff was slumped on his face. Raker rolled him over. Blood had spread over his front from a wound punched through the meat of his right shoulder. Raker could see the ragged lips of the wound through the hole in the shirt. He had seen a few gunshot wounds before and this one did not look good. The sheriff groaned. Another bullet smacked into the gravel, showering Raker with stone fragments. He looked up and saw the figure just to the inside of the gate, shielded from the guns of the officers by the wall. The shotgun lay at Engle's side, the breach open, a single shell already loaded. Raker took a heartbeat to decide.

He scooped the gun up, snapped the breach shut, and fired.

The roar filled his ears and the gun spat an orange flare into the night. For a moment he did not know if he had hit true, or if the gunman's next shot would send him into the afterlife. A thick noise filled his ears, and he realized that he was staring down the barrel of the shotgun into the silent dark. He let the barrel drop.

Officers were moving past him, kicking through the side door, hauling open the heavy gates. At his side, Sheriff Engle stirred, rolling so that he was sitting, hand clamped over his bloody shoulder. Two officers came over and hauled him to his feet between them. The skin of his face was the pale white of ground ash, and Raker saw him grit his teeth as he stood. He looked up at Raker.

"Guess this is final proof that you meant what you said." He winced and Raker noticed blood seeping from between his fingers.

"What—," began Raker, but the sheriff cut through the question.

"I am going up to the house, Mr. Raker. That's what I am going to do." He nodded to the gun still in Raker's hands. "And I will have that back." Raker passed the shotgun over, noticing the effort with which the sheriff gripped the stock. "Thank you," he said, nodding to one of the officers. "Give Mr. Raker a weapon, and a badge." He looked back at Raker as he thumbed shells into the shotgun's breach. "Consider yourself deputized under the authority of the Sheriff of Arkham."

Raker stared at the .45 and the bronze star that a thin-faced officer put into his hands.

"You know how to use one of these?" asked the officer. Raker nodded, and pinned the badge awkwardly to the breast of his soiled grey suit. The gun was heavy in his hand, reassuring and familiar in its dead weight and feel. His mind kept returning to the figure of the footman at the end of the shotgun barrel as he pulled the trigger. He thought about going to look, his feet taking two steps toward the fold of darkness that concealed the dead footman. A strange numb sensation like a sleeper waking from a dream had crept over him; no matter where he went, blood seemed to follow him.

Behind him the engines of the wagons growled as their drivers revved them. Officers were climbing back in. The pale-faced figure of Sheriff Engle was lowering himself into the space next to one of the drivers. A bandage of ripped shirt tied around his arm and shoulder, he winced as he moved. Two officers had moved the body of the deputy who had taken the first shot. A sheet of grey canvas covered the unmoving mound of his body, and his two colleagues stood over it like a guard while the rest got back into the wagons.

Raker walked back to the wagon and pulled himself into the cab next to Engle. Fragments of glass from the shattered windshield crunched in the foot well under his feet. Engle looked at Raker and gave a curt nod of acknowledgement, then turned his head to the officer at the wheel.

"Take us up, Freddie, fast as this thing can do. All the way to the house, and don't stop for anything."

"Sir," acknowledged the officer with a curt nod, and the wagon surged forward through the gate.

The drive beyond was lit only by stars and moonlight filtering through the leaves of the avenue of trees. Dark pools of shadow and silvered patches of ground caught in starlight slid past them. In front of them, the lights of the mansion shone electric orange behind the trunks and branches of the trees. The air streaming in through the broken windshield smelled of dew settling on grass after a hot day. The sound of the wagon's engine was a constant growl, but beyond that it was silent. No sounds of distant laughter on the still night air, no strains of music reaching out from the mansion. Raker felt the contrast with his earlier arrival at the party as a crawling dread. There was something tomb-like about the absence of noise. Part of him, despite the murderous footman and his encounter with Helena and Hugo, had hoped that they would arrive to find he was wrong. The silence and stillness denied him that hope.

The wagon turned the final bend in the driveway and they had a clear view of the mansion in front of them. The pale stone was the color of the skin of a drowned man. Lights burned in its windows and bright paper lanterns hanging from the trees glimmered. Cars were parked in front of the house, unmoved from where Raker had seen them before.

They were within three hundred yards when it happened. There was a flash of dry lightning, bright and silent, stabbing down out of a cloudless night sky. It struck the center of the house. For a moment it remained frozen in the air, like a vertical crack in a furnace that burned with the fury of the sun. Raker and every policeman in the two wagons raised their hands to shield their eyes. Then the light became red, the frozen lightning bolt spreading outward like a widening mouth, tinting the sky and ground the color of rust and blood.

The lead wagon swerved, the driver half-blinded by the light. Raker could still see the lightning bolt as a luminous line across his vision, burned onto his retinas. The sky above the house had shifted to the color of a bruise, the stars sliding across it in impossible directions. Around them, shadows shifted their dimensions, elongating in ways that were not possible. Raker felt the world around him twist, felt his sense of depth and perspective flip as if he was looking at an optical illusion. The trees around him extended to an infinite height into a sky that vanished to a distant point far above. The house appeared to be in the distance and curving all around him at the same time. The wagon was racing toward the house and getting no closer. Senses became confused: he smelled the color of the stars that moved across the sky, darting like fireflies, tasted the blade-edged texture of shadows. It was as if they were driving through a land of dreams that their human senses could not grasp.

Then, the world snapped back into place like a twisted sheet of metal returning to true. Raker sat in a juddering police wagon racing toward a pale stone mansion. For a second, Raker could only feel that something was still not right; then, the officer driving the wagon screamed. It was the scream of a mind imploding under the weight of violated reality.

The stars were gone. The mansion and trees glittered under starlight from a hollow black sky with no stars. The wagon began to slew across the road again, its wheels bumping and skidding. The shadows around them suddenly boiled and flowed like oil. Things with wings the color of midnight were folding out of the shadows around them. Raker screamed in horror and warning as something with claws and clusters of dead star eyes landed on the front of the wagon.

CHAPTER TWENTY-SEVEN

Jacqueline Fine
French Hill, Arkham

Luck saved Jacqueline from the first bullet. A jet of flame stabbed from the gun in the hand of the shadowed figure in the kitchen doorway. There was a sound like a gong as it hit a copper pan hanging from the ceiling. Jacqueline had ducked at the shot and dropped to the floor, the long marble-topped counter between her and the gunman. She made to crawl around the counter to better cover and found that the dying man's hand was still clamped around her ankle.

"Please…," he murmured. The life was fading from his face, his skin death pale. Jacqueline did not answer, but yanked her leg out of his grip. She could hear fast steps coming closer across the tiled floor. She had no time for dying men, not if she did not want to suffer the same fate.

Keeping low to the ground, she scurried around the side of the counter, keeping it between her and the gunman. His shadow moved across the polished copper of the pans hanging above. She could hear his sharp breaths as he moved past her on the other side of the counter. Suddenly, the sound of footsteps stopped.

She could hear the swish of cloth, could almost see him moving, slowly turning, looking for where she had gone. He could not be more than a yard away. She pressed herself close to the counter, the worn wood of its drawers smooth against her skin. She heard a low, bubbling groan from the bleeding man on the floor, but if the gunman heard it, he did not stop—previous victims were not his concern.

Moving one limb at a time, she began to edge toward the lit doorway into the rest of the house. A shadow loomed above her, the glint of gunmetal so close she could almost touch it. She did not think, but came off the tiled floor in a single movement of uncoiling muscle. The gun roared thunder and fire again but she was already past the muzzle, fingers clawing at eyes and skin. The gunman screamed as she gripped blindly and ripped at his face. She did not know what she was doing, she was just pouring her fear and fury into every movement. With a snarl, the man shoved her back with all his strength. She reeled back, her feet scrabbling for grip on the tiles as she fell. The floor hit her hard, pain shooting across her back, lights dancing in front of her eyes. The gun came up, light reflecting from the dead circle of the muzzle, death poised on a trigger pull.

There was a cry of surprise and the gun jerked up, firing into the ceiling. The gunman turned, half falling as the dying man on the floor behind him grabbed the long hem of his robe and pulled. Jacqueline came off the floor. The gun glinted close to her and she grabbed at it, gripping it in both hands, and slamming it into the edge of the marble-topped counter until the gun came free in her hands. The man fell to the floor, his breath leaving him with a grunt. She stamped down blindly on his body, felt her feet impact into flesh and bone. Jacqueline bent down and hammered the pistol into the side of the man's head. He went still.

It was suddenly quiet in the dark kitchen. Jacqueline could only hear her own heavy breaths and the pounding of blood in her ears. She looked down at the gun clutched in her hand and the unmoving man in grey robes at her feet. She needed to get out. Perhaps she could shoot the lock off the kitchen door. Moving into the light coming from the doorway at the other end of the kitchen, she snapped open the breach of the pistol and spilled the shells into her hand, looking to see how many still had their copper-sheathed tips. None. That wild shot into the ceiling had been the gunman's last.

She went and began to search the gunman, looking for bullets, but finding only a few coins and a photograph of a woman smiling out of a creased and faded print. The man was old, she realized, perhaps fifty, with a kindly face and greying hair. He looked like a shopkeeper, the kind of man who would smile and wish you a good day as he bagged your groceries. She shook herself, remembering the gun she had taken from his hand. He might have once been something else, but here and now he was a killer. She felt the thick weave of the man's grey robe in her fingers: perhaps there was another way.

With quick movements, she stripped the heavy grey robe from the unconscious man and slipped it over her head. It covered the patterned silk of her gown and reduced her to a shape of ruffled grey. The man also had an amulet of polished metal in the shape of two hands clasped together. Jacqueline took this as well and hung it over her head. With the robe's hood pulled over her head she would look like any of the other grey-robed figures in the mansion. As long as no one saw her face and recognized her as not being one of them, she might slip through the corridors and rooms of the mansion and find a way out.

She turned to leave the kitchen and heard a gurgling whimper at her back. The young man was still alive. She turned back; he did not look up at her, his head lolling on his chest, his hands fallen loose on his lap. Blood seeped from the wound in his chest, its flow weak. The effort of tangling the gunman to save her had spent him. He turned his eyes up to look at her, a froth of blood and saliva dribbling from the side of his mouth. He made a gurgling noise that might have been a word, and tried to shift himself toward her. Jacqueline looked back at him, tears tingling at the corners of her eyes.

"I am sorry," she said, and turned away, walking out of the kitchen without looking back.

She found her way to the spiral staircase that had led her down to the servant's area and climbed them again. Once she was on the next floor up she would circle around, avoiding the central area and its blood ritual. She would look for other doors, or open windows close to the ground. If she met another of the murderous grey cultists she would trust in her disguise and act as if she belonged. Years of creating a false persona for herself had taught her that it was all posture and the attitude one walked with, but she hoped that she would not need to test those skills.

It happened without warning or build up. She had left the spiral stairs and was walking down a silent corridor lined with heavy framed pictures lit by electric lamps that curled from the wall above them. There was a sensation of heat and static charge running over Jacqueline's skin. The corridor in front of her seemed to stretch so that it was extending to a vanishing point. The light from the electric lamps was pulsing as if in rhythm with a vast and terrible heartbeat. Jacqueline staggered, her mind flooding with images and sensations that vibrated through her. She heard a noise like ripping skin and a storm of screaming and babbling. The walls around her seemed to fade to grey gauze and she saw a vast hole, its edges impossible to look at. It seemed to be getting closer and farther away at the same time, and beyond she could see a red sun dying in a bruised sky. A hole to another world; she knew it without thinking or knowing why, as if her soul felt the truth.

She blinked and found herself on her hands and knees, the corridor returned to physical reality around her. The lights were still pulsing between gloom and brightness and she could still hear the sound of a wind of screams howling in her head. She did not want to look up to see her reality twisting around her, did not want to feel the howl of the dead on the wind blowing from another world. She wanted to beat her head until it stopped. She balled her fists and felt the thick softness of the carpet in her fingers. The floor beneath her hands was real. She pushed herself to her feet and made herself look. The corridor was there, real and firm. The screams of a wounded reality still ringing in her mind, she began to walk again.

It was after several more corridors and many minutes that she turned a corner and saw the figure on the ground. She had not looked in any of the rooms she had passed, had not opened any doors to see what might be behind them. The thought of the pile of bodies they had dragged her from, and the mute appeal of the dying man on the kitchen floor, kept her from looking. The figure was a man, slim under silken blue and black robes, a burnished metal mask hanging to the side of his face. He lay at the side of the corridor, curls of his golden hair bright against the thick red carpet. His arms were reaching out in front of him as if he had been crawling. Jacqueline did not need to pull the hair away from the face to recognize him: it was Walter. She bent down and put a hand on his back. Under her fingers, she felt a shallow rise and fall of breath.

He's alive, she thought, relief flooding through her. Perhaps he had come around and tried to crawl to safety, and then fallen back into the numbing clutches of the sedatives used to drug them. Jacqueline pulled her hand away. She could not carry Walter—if she tried to take him both their chances of escape and survival were less—but if she left Walter his chances became nothing. She shook him, but his eyes stayed closed and his body limp.

She sat back on her knees and closed her eyes. She was finding it hard to think clearly. The wrongness of things in this house pressed on her mind, emanating from the center of it like heat from a fire. The visions she had experienced, the things she had seen that these grey-robed fanatics were prepared to do: all of it told her to run. If she tried to help Walter, she would most likely never live to try and forget, but if she did leave him here she would have to spend the rest of her life never forgetting this night. She thought of the ritual in the Great Hall. She had seen blood on the white stone floor, so thick it covered it almost edge to edge. The life of people who had been laughing hours before had been drained away. *The blood price*—those were the words that had come through her and she had spoken to Hugo Bradbury—*the blood price*.

Jacqueline opened her eyes and looked at Walter, blond hair spilling over a pale cheek. She stood up, making sure that the hood of her stolen robe still covered her face, and gripped Walter under the arms. With a grunt of effort, she began to pull him down the corridor. If she could find a way to get out, then she would have saved at least one person; she would not pay a larger blood price than she already had.

Jacqueline had dragged Walter only twenty yards when a figure in grey rounded the corner.

CHAPTER TWENTY-EIGHT

Dr. Fields
French Hill, Arkham

The presence of the gate came close to leaving Dr. Fields shaking on the bloody floor. It hung in the air, its lowest point a hand's width from the ground. It drew the eye and at the same time repelled all attempts to look at it directly. It radiated a warm charged aura, and around it a shimmering haze overwhelmed the features of the Great Hall. Reality was unraveling, breaking and reforming. Paint and plaster flaked from the walls as if aging centuries in seconds. Sources of light cast shadow rather than light, the dark spreading from candles and lamps in long pools. Where there should have been shadows there was flickering light. The wooden frames of pictures and furniture rotted and crumbled to dust. Vases and sculptures fell to shatter on the floor only to reform. Flowers and plants broke their pots as they grew and spread, creating thickets of glossy, unnatural green in the dead light spilling from the gate.

For many of Lemaitre's followers, the impossibility of the gate broke their minds on the spot. Some stood still, staring at it, swaying as if they were trees stirred by a wind, their eyes weeping red

tears. Some tore at their skin, their screams and whimpers a disso-
nant chorus. Others just collapsed to the floor. Whether they were
unconscious or dead, Dr. Fields could not tell. The two minding
Dr. Fields kept a loose hold on his arms, but he could hear one
moaning quietly and the other one's hands were shaking.

Lemaitre seemed utterly unmoved by the fate of those who
had helped him. He did not look at them, but beckoned to the
few who seemed to have clung to a shred of their sanity.

"Listen!" Lemaitre shouted. There were perhaps a dozen whose
faces turned to listen. Dr. Fields noticed that the bull-like Hugo
Bradbury and his mother were among those who were still standing. "We are close to success, so close. A price has been paid and
more will have to be paid. Do not forget that no matter what the
cost, we will be able to set everything right, but only if we succeed."
Some of the grey-robed and blood-stained few nodded. Most of
them just looked numb, as if they were walking in a dream.

"We need to take sacrifices with us, so that we can pay the
final price." He looked at Helena and Hugo Bradbury. Helena
was wiping a thick trickle of blood that was running from her
nose. "Helena, make sure that those of the fellowship are gathering the last of your guests to take with us. Once the last of us
are through, you must stop anything or anyone from interfering
with the device." He indicated the pyramid beneath the gate.
"You," he pointed at three cultists, "bring the second device.
Amelia, stay close to me."

Dr. Fields felt those last words like a knife thrust. *Why did Lemaitre need Amelia? What use had he yet to put her to?* As if he heard
his thoughts, Lemaitre turned and walked toward Dr. Fields, the
casual smile still on his face. He stepped very close, so close that
Dr. Fields could smell the expensive scent of his cologne.

"And you, Doctor," he said in a conspiratorial voice, "you will
stay here, and wait for me." Dr. Fields wanted to slam his fists
into that pale face. "You have been a good confessor, and so I

will leave you with a last thought. You can contemplate it until I return." The sorcerer smiled and Dr. Fields saw that the skin around his mouth was split, cracked like that of a dried cadaver. "It is not the power of immortals or gods that I want; I already have that. It is something else that I want, something lost to me. In a way, I am like your daughter, like all of my Hand of Solace. I have lost something, and getting it back is all I want." He leaned closer still so that only the doctor could hear his whisper.

"Your part in this, Doctor, is nothing. Nothing. Except that when I return, this face I wear will not be suitable to walk through the world. Yours will suit me quite well, I think." Dr. Fields wanted to say something, to shout defiance, but he found he could not. Terror had silenced him. "Goodbye, Doctor, until we meet for the last time."

Lemaitre turned away and with a gesture to his surviving followers he turned and walked into the gate. For a moment, it seemed as if he was just walking across the Great Hall. Then it looked as if he was walking in place, as if he was caught in a loop of time, repeating the same steps over and over, getting nowhere. His glowing silhouette lingered in the air like a shadow burned onto a wall.

Others followed Lemaitre, some dragging unconscious guests, others grunting as they carried the second dull grey box. Still held by the two cultists, Dr. Fields looked across to Amelia. She had one of the unused, silver-bladed daggers he had seen in the House of Solace. The light glittered off the blade as she checked it and slid it back into its sheath. Their eyes met. There was a cold surety in her eyes, and at that moment he realized that he had never known her. There was an iron hard coldness in her that was more than grief, more than fanaticism created by Lemaitre. She was a stranger, and always had been. He opened his mouth, a last appeal forming in his throat. Amelia turned away from him and strode into the waiting gate to disappear into another world.

Dr. Fields stood for a moment, the look on his daughter's face worse than the mind-warping dimensions of the gate. Then he realized that the grip of the men holding him had slackened. He glanced around and saw the Bradburys had left the hall, perhaps to get away from the maddening sight of the gate, or to perform the tasks given them by Lemaitre. Of the living cultists that remained, some were trying to help those who tore at themselves or howled in terror. His hands were still bound in front of him but his legs were free; he had an opportunity.

He had never been strong, and the last time he had fought had been as a child in the playground. Putting all his weight into it, Dr. Fields rammed his elbow into the gut of the man behind him. He was lucky and the man was unprepared. The man folded, his head coming down and his grip breaking. The other man reacted, but too slowly. Dr. Fields twisted out of the cultist's fingers, half falling to the blood-soaked floor. He felt the leather soles of his shoes scrabble on the slick stone. The cultist he had elbowed was upright again and surging toward Dr. Fields. He managed to stand up and dodge the man's grasping hands, fear and adrenaline overcoming age and straining muscle. He turned and ran toward the gate.

Other cultists in the Great Hall were looking around. In front of him, the gate seemed to beckon to him, pulling his eyes and thoughts to it. Amelia lay on the other side of that gate with Lemaitre. In that moment, Dr. Fields felt hate like never before. He wanted to punish that white devil that had smiled and said that he offered hope to his daughter. Dr. Fields ran toward the shimmering gate to another world.

Behind him, the cultists who had been guarding him ran after him. One of the cultists had a gun. There was a dull crack, and a bullet hit the floor a foot away from Dr. Fields. He was close to the gate, so close that he could feel the edges of it like oil on his skin. There was something inside the kaleidoscopic vortex of the gate: a view of dead cities and glittering stars, swirling as if seen through a rippling heat haze.

A hand gripped his hair and yanked him back at the same moment as the gun fired again. Dr. Fields tumbled backward and the bullet smacked into the pyramidal device beneath the gate. There was a sound like a bell struck by lightning. The gate twisted and distorted, squirming like the mouth of a wounded animal. A sound like a thousand sheets of glass shattering filled the air. Dr. Fields was on the floor, scrabbling in blood, as hands tried to grip him. He was face up, looking into the gate. He saw something inside the gate, something moving like a huge sea creature gliding past a porthole. He did not have enough air in his lungs, nor the time to scream.

The gate billowed outward. To Dr. Fields, it looked like a thunderhead expanding up toward the high ceiling and outward to the edge of the hall. Green light edged the cloud, and its center was the color of night. A formless mass of black congealed liquid poured from the gate, the air around it sizzling as if burned by its presence. The black mass hit the ground with a wet thump, oozing across the ground, the stone and blood burning under its bulk. The air reeked of burnt sugar and rotting meat. The formless mass spread and elongated, its tar-like surface shifting and writhing. Long fronds of black tentacles pushed from the glistening surface. Shapes that might have been hands split from their tips, reaching, touching, burning. The formless creature expanded and grew, filling the space in front of the gate, towering over the few people that remained alive.

One cultist looked at it and screamed continually, unable to look away, unable to run, as the black ooze flowed over him, burning and dissolving. The cultist struggling with Dr. Fields released him and tried to turn as a tentacle flicked toward him. It brushed his face and he screamed and screamed until his skull dissolved and collapsed. Dr. Fields pulled himself to his feet and ducked out of the way as a wet, half-formed claw scraped the stone floor where he had been. He tried not to look directly at the creature, but he could hear its bulk moving with an acidic hiss of burning and dissolving matter.

The creature grew, its bulk bloating and spreading in a viscous wave. Dr. Fields ran back to the edge of the hall. The nearest doorway out of the Great Hall was over twenty yards away but he could make it if he was lucky. The creature rose up from the floor, the substance of its body foaming with a sound like boiling molasses as it formed a snake-like body. A mouth formed in the glossy black bulk, liquid drizzling from vast jaws. It roared.

Dr. Fields felt as if his brain was vibrating, as if the noise was penetrating his thoughts, flooding him with despair. He was lost; there was nothing. All he knew, all he thought was true, was a lie, was an insignificant flicker on the edge of an uncaring and monstrous universe. Then he thought of the cold iron in the eyes of his daughter, and the mocking face of Lemaitre.

He steadied himself, took one long breath, and ran toward the gate. The creature seemed to sense him and began to move, half-formed limbs pulling it across the floor. He ran in a circle, arcing past the creature toward the gate that still pulsed and fluxed behind it. His breath was coming in gasps, his old muscles felt as if needles were stabbing them, but his eyes stayed fixed on the gate. Behind him, the creature boiled toward him like a living wave, extending limbs and tentacles, stretching and reaching. Dr. Fields felt the edge of the gate touch his skin, felt it coat his skin in static. His eyes saw bright light, shifting colors, the swirl of dying galaxies. A thin, black tentacle unfurled toward his back, its tip almost brushing the stained fabric of his jacket. He took another step and vanished.

CHAPTER TWENTY-NINE

Raker

French Hill, Arkham

The creature tore the head off the officer behind the wheel. Blood sprayed across Raker's face. Beside him, Engle was trying to bring the shotgun up, his wounded arm slack and numb. The sheriff was swearing, mixing obscenities and prayers. The wagon hurtled forward. Air was rushing past the creature into the wagon with a tainted smell like ashes.

The creature on the hood of the wagon had a long, humanoid body of charcoal black flesh. Multifaceted eyes glittered at Raker from a face framed by polished chitin. Ragged wings sprung from its back, seeming at once solid and nothing more than shadow and suggestion. It was a nightmare, a thing that swooped through the darkness of dreams to make the dreamer wake unable to breathe and with a fading memory of terror. It reached toward Raker, claws glittering at the end of an arm with too many joints. Raker did not have a chance to raise his own gun. The wagon swerved, its front wheels digging into soft earth at the side of the drive, the rears spinning in gravel. The claws were an inch from Raker's throat when the wagon flipped over.

Raker felt the world turn, experiencing an instant of weightlessness. Then the world collapsed in the sound of splitting metal. The wagon pivoted over the front fender and came down on the box-like compartment at the back. Those inside did not have a chance to scream before the impact crushed them. Momentum plowed the wagon farther through the ground, ripping up mud and cutting a scar through the grass before it came to a halt.

In the crumpled remains of the cab, Raker tried to open his eyes and found that he could not. His world was sightless, filled with a dull ringing and the dim feeling of injuries numbed by shock. He was upside down, legs in the air, caught in something that felt jagged and hard. Something warm was dripping down his face. The ringing noise was fading and he could hear the pitiful noises of those still alive in the rear compartment, and the gurgling of hot oil dripping from the engine. There was a sound of screeching breaks, gun shots, and shouts. And there was something else, too—a sound like the flap of tattered wings through still air.

He had to move. Working his right hand out from under him, Raker reached up and felt his face. It was wet and sticky, and he could feel the places where glass had lacerated it. He wiped across his eyes, blinking until his lids ungummed and he could see. Everything around him was a close, pressed in world made visible only by what he guessed were the headlights of the second wagon. He blinked more, letting his eyes adjust. He could hear gunfire. It was close by; no, it was very close. He twisted, trying to untangle his body from the crumpled cab, hoping that his legs were not broken. The warm fuel was still dripping on him. There was a hot smell like grease dropped onto a hot cooking plate. He twisted harder, panic rising in his throat. Something moaned near him. The liquid was dripping faster, running down him. He could taste its flammable reek. With a muscle-wrenching yank, his legs came free from the wreckage above him. The moan came again, louder. He twisted his head around and saw the bulky form of Sheriff Engle jammed next to the crushed door. Through the shattered side window beyond the sheriff, he could see a muzzle flash. Shapes with wings moved and slid through the air, swooping down in frozen instants as the guns of the other officers fired.

The fuel fumes were thick around him. He squirmed forward, shifting until he was lying half across the semiconscious sheriff, his feet toward the door. Gritting his teeth, he stamped into the door panel, felt his feet slam into something solid, pulled them back, and kicked again. The door gave but still held shut. The sheriff shifted next to him. He could almost feel the heat of the engine. In his mind he could see the dripping oil sizzling as it hit hot metal. The next kick pushed the door outward in a scream of metal. Raker shifted toward it and turned to grab the sheriff. The wounded man's hand fastened on his reaching arm. There was a warning in that grip. Raker saw the sheriff's eyes glittering in the half-light, focused beyond Raker, out of the open side door.

Something was next to the door of the overturned wagon. Raker suddenly felt its greasy presence, its ashen scent blotting out the petrol stink. He turned and saw a pair of clawed, reverse-jointed limbs just beyond the door he had kicked open, between him and safety. A talon scraped on the side of the wagon. It bent down until its head filled the open door. Raker thought he heard a rattling sound come from the creature, like a snarling chuckle. It looked at him with rows of multifaceted eyes. There was a noise so loud that Raker thought the wagon had exploded. The creature fell away from the door, black liquid oozing from its head. It gave a wild, hooting cry that made Raker want to scream. There was another booming roar from next to him and the thing was blown from its feet in a spray of chitin and ichor.

Raker twisted around, half-deafened. Sheriff Engle was still pointing the barrels of his shotgun at the creature on the floor. Half dead and bleeding, the sheriff had kept his hand gripped around his weapon as the wagon spun through the air. The older man looked at Raker, his face half-hidden in shadow.

"Move. Move now," he rasped. Raker's awareness snapped back; suddenly the smell of petrol and oil was all around him. There was a soft noise like a sharp breath, and flame filled the wagon. The space around him was suddenly flowing with thick runnels of liquid fire. Raker screamed as the heat washed over him. He reached out and gripped the sheriff's hand where it still gripped the empty shotgun. Viscous fire was falling around him, on him. The sheriff gave a weak shake of his head. Raker ignored it and heaved. The fire was getting hotter, eating fuel and the wood of the police wagon's frame. The sheriff's body shifted slightly. Raker heaved again, felt some give, and pulled harder. Something white hot and burning splashed on his face. He was nearly out of the cab: half of his body was outside and the sheriff was nearly free. Bunching muscles that had already been ripped and battered many times, he gave one last heave. The sheriff came free of the wreckage. They both collapsed on the grass as the fire closed around the wagon like a beast closing its jaws.

There was a sound of feet running across the soft ground and Raker brought his head up to see a clutch of three officers running forward, silhouetted in the headlight beams of the other wagon. There had been more than three in the other wagon, he was sure. Two ran to the burning wreck of the wagon, but could approach no closer to the intense heat than a few feet. The third ran over to where Raker and Sheriff Engle lay on the grass. In the flickering firelight, Raker saw that the officer was one of the younger men he had seen earlier; he looked fit and tough but there was a hollow look in his face that reminded him of the patients in Arkham Asylum. He stopped, looking down at his blood-and-fire-stained sheriff barely conscious on the ground. He looked as if he did not know what to do next. Raker was not in the mood for hesitancy.

"Those creatures: where are they?" he snapped. The officer

looked at him. "Where are they?" asked Raker again, his voice louder. The officer blinked as if moving his mind around a thought he did not want to have.

"They…," his voice shook slightly. "Some we shot down, I think. The others just went."

"Just went?" asked Raker.

"Yes, sir," said the officer, his tone respectful as if anyone who could keep their nerve after what had happened was someone you called "sir." "They…," began the officer, and Raker thought of a child trying to describe something it did not like and did not understand. "There are only three of us left," finished the officer. Raker did not ask what he meant; that fact said enough.

The other two officers were approaching. Their faces showed the same signs of numb disbelief at what they had seen and that they had survived. There would be no other survivors from the first wagon—it was a petrol-fueled funeral pyre for all those who had ridden in it. Raker pulled himself to his feet. Pain shot through him, his body a mass of cuts, bruises, burns, and torn muscles. He looked toward the mansion, its pale stone shining in the starlight no more than three hundred yards away. He looked back at the officers and the barely conscious form of Sheriff Engle.

"He is going to need some help…a doctor." The officers looked at him, listening to the authority in his voice. "If there are any others, find them, get them back to town." One of the officers glanced toward the first wagon that still burned. Raker looked at him and shook his head. "No one else is coming out of that." He pointed at Engle. "Help your boss." Two of them bent down and lifted the sheriff between them. Blood covered Engle's chest and head, and burns glistened on exposed skin, but he was breathing. The officers carried him back to the second wagon, his feet dragging along the ground.

Raker glanced around as he followed the clutch of lawmen. There were shapes on the grass, hidden by the dark. Whether they were the bodies of officers or the remains of something else, he could not tell, and did not want to know. They put Engle in the back of the wagon and one of the officers climbed in after him. The other two went around to the front to climb into the cab.

Raker stood where he was, looking toward the house. The night was very still, and he thought he could feel a texture to that stillness, something out of place and unnatural about it. The house itself seemed to be indistinct around its edges, as if its substance was bleeding off into the night. He had a feeling that the quiet around them did not mark an end to whatever was happening; it was only a temporary respite. The shadows were shifting around them, repositioning in increments like waves drawing back before surging forward.

"Sir?" It was the voice of the officer who had gotten into the back of the wagon with the unconscious sheriff. The officer was leaning out of the back of the wagon, hand on the handle of the open door, ready to pull it shut. He was perhaps only a few years younger than Raker, but for a moment Raker felt like an old man looking at a youth. The man's eyes were wide, his hands had an unsteady twitch about them, and his face had a strained desperation to it.

These men are on the edge of hysteria.

The wagon's engine grumbled back to life. "Sir, you should get in. We need to get back to town, get help, and…," the man trailed off.

And what indeed, thought Raker, not moving toward the wagon. They wanted to be gone from here, from this place. They had no plan, no direction other than fleeing, leaving their dead friends and colleagues on the grass. It was not cowardly; it was the instinct for survival. *Understandable*, thought Raker, *given what this officer of a quaint, New England town has seen and done tonight. How will he cope in the years to come?* Would it become something they would not talk about unless it was just them and the liquor had been flowing a long time? The question of what they had seen tonight and why nine men they had known had died would run through these men's lives like cracks through marble. Would they find the answer to that question at the bottom of a bottle or the end of a gun? In the end it didn't matter; it was not a future Raker would choose, nor one he expected to see.

"May I have your gun?" he asked the officer. The man looked confused.

"Sir…," he began, but Raker gently cut him off.

"The sheriff deputized me before we came up here." He pointed to the metal star on the pocket of his ragged jacket. "This is all about what is going on up at that house, and it isn't over."

"We've got to get the sheriff to a hospital. Come back with more men when it's light," blurted the officer. He looked desperate, as if Raker was suggesting he put his hand into a fire.

"I know," said Raker, and he did. There was no way he would get these men up to the house. They were broken and he could not say why he was willing to go on, to go further into this hole to madness. "I know, but I am going up there." He held out his hand, palm up. "I think I might get further with your gun if you can spare it." The officer looked at Raker with an expression of fear mingled with disbelief and admiration. He pulled his revolver from his holster and put it into Raker's hand. His hand shaking, he pulled a handful of cartridges out, the brass of the casings bright in the light of the burning wagon.

"You might…," he began, then licked his lips not looking Raker in the eyes. "You might need these, too." Raker took the cartridges and poured them into his jacket pocket.

"Thank you," he said. The officer nodded and pulled the wagon's rear door shut. It pulled away, turning back toward the town, surging toward a normal world of petty crimes and comforting familiarity. Raker did not watch it go; he hefted the revolver, double-checked the cartridges, and began to walk toward the house.

CHAPTER THIRTY

Jacqueline Fine

French Hill, Arkham

Jacqueline went still as the figure in grey came toward her. She still had ahold of Walter under the arms, his unconscious weight pulling on her suddenly still muscles. The figure walked toward her with slow steps. She guessed it was a man by the walk and the body shape under the grey folds of the robe. Walter was heavy in her hands. The man in the grey robe was closer, no more than five steps away over the thick, red carpet. There was no way that she could escape carrying Walter—she doubted she would get more than three steps. She noticed the grey stubble on the man's chin that projected from the hood which kept the rest of the face in shadow. *There must be eyes in that dark space*, she thought, *eyes looking at me, judging*. The man was within two paces and she realized that she had left it too late to run. There was no way out of this situation.

"Heavy, eh?" asked the man, his voice a low rumble from within his hood. It was a friendly, even comforting voice. Under different circumstances, it would have suggested an offer for help with heavy groceries, or lifting a wheeled cot down a flight of stairs. Jacqueline did not reply, but watched as the man reached down and took hold of Walter's ankles. He lifted them easily so that Walter was suspended between Jacqueline and the man.

"This one to go through to Lemaitre?" asked the man, looking up at Jacqueline, his face visible. He was in his mid-years, with unshaven jowls, eyes set wide above a broad mouth. He gave her a small smile. He looked like a kind man, the type of man who would help clear snow from the porch in winter, or lend you more than a few bucks if you were short. The smile made Jacqueline shiver inside her skin. It was the smile of a kind man offering to help carry a powerless human being to slaughter.

Assuming silence as assent, the man began to pull Walter, glancing at Jacqueline when she paused. Her mind was a blur of confused thoughts and fears. If she did not move in an instant, the man would realize something was wrong. She could not pull Walter out of his grip. Even if she did, how far would she get dragging his unconscious body? She could let go of Walter, of course: drop him and run. The man would be caught by surprise and she would have a head start. It might work, she might get away. She could do it…

"Something wrong?" asked the man. Jacqueline could see his eyes glittering out of the shadow of his hood. She swallowed, ready to turn her back and run as fast as she could. Walter twitched in her grasp as if something in a dream had made him grip to stop himself from falling. She looked down at Walter's face and remembered the man bleeding on the floor of the kitchen. "This one's coming around," growled the man. "We best get him down to the Great Hall. If Lemaitre needs more meat for the gate we had best not keep him waiting." He tugged again. Jacqueline knew that she had no choice. She yielded to the tug and she and the hooded cultist moved down the corridor, carrying Walter toward an unknown fate.

Jacqueline tried to think of a way out of the situation. Her eyes darted around her and at the man who was backing away from her, glancing behind him to see where he was going. She had until they reached the Great Hall to find an opportunity to get away. If she had a chance, she could attack him, but it had to be when he would not see it coming. Shuffling forward, Walter heavy in her hands, she watched and tried to keep her fear from overwhelming her with every step they took.

They were turning a corner when Walter twitched again and murmured half-formed words. The hooded man was looking behind him and lost his grip on one of Walter's ankles. He cursed, reaching down to grip the ankle again. Walter's weight sagged toward the floor. Jacqueline did not pause. She dropped Walter the short distance to the carpeted floor and leapt at the man, putting all her weight into her shoulder. She hit him in the face as he looked up. Already off balance, the impact knocked him onto his back. Blood was running down his face from his mashed nose. Jacqueline was already stamping and kicking him as he tried to get up, grunting with the effort, fear giving her blows power. He was strong, though, and on the third kick his hand gripped her ankle and pulled her off her feet.

As she hit the ground, the man was already behind her, gripping her hair, a big hand clamped around her neck. He squeezed. Jacqueline felt the muscles in her neck strain against his grip, felt the panic flood her as she could not breathe. She thrashed, her limbs flailing. She could feel the man sucking breaths as he squeezed harder. Her eyes bulged. She saw Walter on the floor two paces away. Walter was moving, pulling himself to his feet like someone pulling themselves out of a mire of mud. Walter staggered, looking at Jacqueline locked in the hooded man's killing grip. He blinked as if clearing his eyes and continued to stare at her. Then he screamed. He screamed like a person waking from a dream to find the dark thing from his nightmares beside the bed. He screamed and ran, and through her panic, Jacqueline realized that Walter had run in the direction they had been carrying him.

Jacqueline could feel darkness pressing on the edge of her vision. She reached up and tried to pull the hand away from her throat. The world she could see was getting darker and darker. The man's face loomed above her, blood dripping onto her cheek from his broken nose. He was grimacing, gritting his teeth with effort. She saw his eyes glint with reflected light. Her hand stabbed up at his face. Her fingers rammed into his eyes, and now he screamed. The hand around her throat came loose and she fell to her knees, gasping for air. The hooded man was clutching his face with one hand, staggering and making a whimpering noise.

Without waiting to see if he was blind or not, Jacqueline came off the floor and ran. Still sucking air, she ran down the corridor in the direction Walter had fled. There were no sounds of pursuit behind her, but she still ran. Walter had fled toward the Great Hall, toward the madness and killing.

Jacqueline twisted around corners, passing exquisite paintings, marble statues, and decorated vases. There was a warm, close feeling in the air that got more intense the closer she got to the Great Hall. With every step, the corridors and passages became darker, the electric lights burned out or sparking in their brass fittings. In the gloom, it looked as if the white paint had begun to peel from the walls. There was a stench like sour milk and engine oil that became stronger and stronger with every stride. She turned a corner and saw an arched doorway and beyond, the shifting darkness of the Great Hall, its edges lit by green-tinged pulses of light that came from something in the center of the room. Something she could not see.

Walter was in front of her, moving toward the door and the light, half limping half running as if his feet could not find proper balance. Jacqueline felt suddenly sick, as if a wracking fever had been poured into her body. Her mind filled with a thousand images, flitting from one to another so fast that she could not grasp them. A high-pitched ringing filled her ears; she felt as if needles were being pushed into her temples. She blinked as patches of color and light flowed across her eyes.

A few paces in front of Jacqueline, Walter had gone through the door into the Great Hall. He was standing in the pulsing light that washed across him, turning his pale skin and hair to the color of a rotting corpse. He staggered forward as if blind to the light or what cast it. Jacqueline moved after him, forcing her legs to move even though her head was swimming. She stepped into the Great Hall, using the stone of the arched doorway to support her. The hall looked as if it had been burnt and then dowsed in water. The walls were scorched clean, bare stones of the building exposed like white bones showing through charred flesh. The floor was not bloody but covered in a filmy residue. Puddles of lumpy, viscous liquid dotted the floor. There were no candles, no lights burning; the only illumination came from the green-tinged light of the shifting hole that hung above the floor.

Jacqueline looked at the glowing green shape and felt a warm wind blowing across her face. Through it, she could see a landscape of black stone and red dust under bruise-colored thunder clouds.

It's like looking through a window into another world. She took a step toward it, staring, wanting to be close to it, to see more clearly. A warm numbness had replaced the pain and fever in her head. The Great Hall faded around her, its features and sounds draining away like water soaking into dry earth. She felt her feet move forward, felt the edges of the glowing gate to another place caress her skin. She wanted to look closer, to be closer, as if something were pulling on a hook embedded deep in her mind and soul. She took another step.

Walter screamed and Jacqueline blinked. The gate was in front of her, its strange shifting edges almost touching her outstretched hand. The image beyond the gate had gone and all she could see was a shifting haze of glowing energy. Jacqueline turned and saw why Walter had screamed. Something black, like hot tar, was oozing up out of cracks in the stone floor and out of the holes in the walls. Its surface shifted with an oily sheen that hissed and smoked. It pooled together, its gelatinous mass surging up from the floor, growing until it was a black wall encircling them, pressing in toward them. A stink like sulfur, petrol, and spoiled milk filled her nose, making her gag and cough.

Walter was on the floor, shaking, his eyes wide, and his legs pulled to his chest. The liquid black wall rippled toward him, extending tendrils and stalks that looked like hands with too many fingers. Walter did not move. Jacqueline took two fast steps and grabbed his arm and pulled. The reaching limbs and tendrils snapped out, lashing at the spot where Walter had been. Jacqueline pulled Walter to his feet; he was as slack as a puppet with its strings cut. They stood in a closing circle of glossy black liquid that broke and shifted like the crest of a wave frozen on the edge of the shore. Jacqueline took a step back and felt the electric, hot presence of the gate behind her. The formless wall crashed forward like a wave released by a dam, extending tentacles reaching for them.

Jacqueline did not even think. Gripping Walter, she turned and pulled them both through the gate. As she felt the gate fold around her, she felt something tug on them and heard the sizzle of dissolving flesh.

Part Three

The Mount of Dead Gods

CHAPTER THIRTY-ONE

Dr. Fields
Another Time

There was dust under his hands. He could feel its fine texture as he flexed his fingers. He lay face down, eyes closed, his shallow breaths sucking dry air that tasted of iron. For a moment, he was not sure who, or where, he was. Perhaps he had had an accident. Perhaps he had fallen while walking the cliffs above Kingsport. Perhaps he lay on the sand at the bottom of the grey cliffs, a pile of broken limbs and blood, clinging onto life, while the tide inched closer. Had he gone out for a walk? Had he even been in Kingsport?

He tried to move, to roll over, but it was as if his body was disconnected from his will. A thick, prickling sensation filled his limbs; he could feel but not move. No, he could move his fingers, he could blink and breathe.

I have severed the nerves in my spine, he thought. *The fall has broken my back, I will never be able to do more than blink and breathe. I will spend the rest of my life being wheeled around in a bath chair by Amelia.*

Amelia.

It was as if a sealed door had opened in his mind, flooding him with memories: *Amelia, the Hand of Solace, and Lemaitre smiling as he walked through the glowing gate. The gate.* The prickling sensation in his limbs vanished and his mouth filled with bile. He coughed, choking on the acid taste. He had gone through the gate after Lemaitre. He could remember it now, the feeling of stepping between worlds, as if he was being folded like a rag, his body stretching along dimensions he did not understand. A torrent of images had passed before his eyes: great cities by glittering lakes beneath alien stars, the emerald depths of a city that dreamed beneath the waves, a tower rising out of sight into a bright sky. All of them had overlapped and blurred while sounds and sensations beat on his senses in a chaotic storm. His mind had felt as if it was being split and reassembled, broken into pieces that could not comprehend what he was experiencing. He had not been able to scream because sound did not exist. This had lasted for an instant and for an age longer than the lifetime of stars. It had ended and he had woken in the dust.

Pain crept over his body. He tried to move his arms and found that he could. He realized his hands must have come unbound during his trip through the gate. He pushed himself to his hands and knees, and vomited with the effort. The yellow bile splattered down from his mouth, hanging in strings from his short beard. He wiped his left sleeve across his mouth, smearing the soiled fabric. He took a deep breath, tried to lift himself further, felt his stomach turn, and vomited again in dry spasms.

I have to move. Amelia had come through the gate, Lemaitre too, and some of his remaining followers. They had come to find the Obsidian Key, he was sure. He did not care for prophecies or dark legend, but they did, and that was why they had come here. That was what had given his daughter false hope.

I have to find her. If I don't, what will happen to her?

He blinked, trying to get a hold on something real and solid.

He looked at the dirt beneath his hands. Fine red dust and shards of dark grey stone covered the ground. It was hard and unyielding. He took a breath and brought his feet up under him. Every muscle ached and his head throbbed. His mouth a grimace of effort, he pushed himself upright. He swayed and almost fell. He staggered a few steps, breathing hard, eyes screwed shut against the shooting pain in his temples.

He opened his eyes. The ocher light of a feeble sun strained across a dry landscape of dust and sharp rock shards. A mountain rose in front of him, its jagged tip pointing at a sky the color of bruised skin. The mountain was the color of rust and dried blood. For a moment Dr. Fields thought there was a forest of bare trees covering the mountainside. Then he realized that they were not trees but statues, thousands upon thousands of statues chiseled out of dark grey stone. They covered the mountain and spilled onto the plain at its foot. The closest statue stood listing to one side half a mile from where he stood. He guessed the statue must be at least fifty feet tall, a towering, vaguely humanoid figure marking the beginning of a host of others. Even from far away he could see dust-filled winds had pitted and weathered its features so that he could only make out hints of limbs and the worn suggestions of a snarling face. Looking past the first statue he could see a road of broken stone twisting up the mountainside through the forest of statues.

"A dead land, under a dying sun," he murmured to himself, wondering whether he had once read that phrase or if this place had created it in his mind. He turned to look for the gate through which he had come. A dead plain of dust folded into low hills as it extended away from him to a horizon that was lost in a sickly haze. He blinked; he had expected to see a glowing green wound in the air, a visible gate like the one that had opened above the bloody floor of Stonegroves's Great Hall. But there was nothing, just the dead plain and the haze-blotted distance that seemed to draw his eye no matter where he looked.

It took him several moments to notice the dark, pyramidal object placed amongst the dust. The anchor, as Lemaitre had called it. It sat on the ground no more than twenty paces from where he stood. Squinting at it, he could see that the red dust had formed concentric ripples around it, like frozen ripples in a pond or iron filings shaped into neat arcs by an electrostatic charge. He walked toward the device. There was a low, ringing hum and the air smelled of ozone. He was about to step closer still when he noticed that the air above the device was shifting like a heat haze. The gate was there, but here it was like a rippling sheet of water through which he could see the red plain of dust stretching away to the murky horizon. Glancing around, he saw the dull grey box that had held the device, empty and discarded amongst a tangled pattern of footprints.

He made to turn back toward the mountain, when something flickered across the heat haze curtain of the gate. His head snapped around and he stared. There was something there, something coming toward him out of the rippling patch of air. At first it was just a dark form, blurred and coalescing like a mirage thrown up out of a desert's heat. As he watched, it became more defined: a dark silhouette of a person walking toward him down an invisible tunnel, getting closer and closer. He found that he was not afraid. It was as if something had switched, or perhaps broken inside him. After all he had seen, he found himself resigned to the possibilities of this new, unkind universe.

The silhouette was close enough now that Dr. Fields could see that it had no depth or texture beyond the ragged edges of its two dimensional shape. But it bulged around the waist, things flopping and hanging down that were in the wrong place for a human's arms. It moved with limping, labored steps. It drew closer until it was shimmering in the air above him, like a flickering shadow cast upon an invisible screen. There was a noise like tearing silk, an acrid smell like electricity and iron, and something fell to the dust with a cry.

Dr. Fields looked down and his jaw hardened with anger. He had been wrong. What had come through the gate was indeed human, but there were two humans that now lay in a tangle of limbs at his feet. A man in a costume robe of blue and black lay face down, not moving, his golden blond hair spilling around his head. The other person was moving, struggling under the weight of the unmoving man who had fallen on top of her. The girl had dark hair, and a sharp, pretty face. She looked as if she was caught between panic and the need to vomit. She wore grey robes. She had not yet noticed him standing still a few feet away.

He had never hurt anyone in his life, had never wanted to. In the nightmare chaos of the mansion, he had felt only fear and revulsion at what was happening. The bloodletting and the impossibility of what was happening had overwhelmed him, allowing him no room for anger. Desperation and disbelief had been all he had felt. Now, in the quiet of this dead plain, with only the sound of the dry wind around him, he felt rage. It was a cold feeling, like ice hardening in his blood. So much blood and death and suffering, and all to bring a cult of the desperate here, to this dead place. It was all because of Lemaitre; he had made people like the girl in grey an impossible promise that had turned them into monsters. But they had chosen to believe that promise, they had done the killing, and they were responsible for the uncertain fate of his daughter. They shared responsibility for everything that had happened.

Dr. Fields looked at the rocks that littered the ground. Some were the size of a fist, flat and jagged-edged. Brought down on a skull it would kill. Dr. Fields began to bend, reaching for a stone. The struggling girl looked around sharply at the movement. There was something desperate in her eyes. It was not the look of a fanatic, or a killer.

"Help me, help me please!" she cried, looking back to the unconscious man whose body was trapping her. "Please, help me. I think it reached him." She was crying. Dr. Fields moved his fingers away from the stone. "I think…," the girl in grey's voice trailed away as Dr. Fields moved closer and saw what had happened to the blond-haired man. Black, viscous liquid had splattered his face and right shoulder. It had burned through his flesh and exposed the white bone of the skull underneath. The man was not moving.

He may be dead already, thought Dr. Fields. He looked at the girl in grey, and saw that she was not struggling to get away from the unconscious man but shaking him, as if trying to wake him from sleep. He did not know why, but that gesture briefly over-rode his suspicions. Dr. Fields bent down, the stained and dirty knees of his suit pressing into the red dust. He reached toward the man, but the girl caught his wrist. She was surprisingly strong.

"I am a doctor," he said, looking steadily into her eyes. "I can help." She let go of his hand, and nodded.

He leaned forward and put two fingers up under the blond man's jaw, being careful not to touch the hissing patches of burnt flesh. He waited, feeling for the beat of a pulse however faint. There was one, a low, unsteady beat. He reached out and put a hand on the girl in grey's arm. She went still and looked up at him. He gave a weak smile. Her dark eyes met his, and an understanding passed between them.

"He is very weak, and may die if his wounds become infect-ed." He gripped the man under the arms, and pulled him off the girl as gently as he could.

Carefully, he helped the girl to her feet. She stood looking down at the still form of the man in the dirt.

"He will live?" she asked.

"Perhaps. He needs hospital treatment to give him a good chance, but he might recover."

She closed her eyes. Dr. Fields could almost feel the anger and pain burning behind her eyelids. She was tall and her movements fluid and precise, as if she was a dancer or actress used to controlling her every muscle. She had a thin face, grubby with dirt and what looked like dry smears of blood, framed by a tangle of dark hair. She was beautiful in a sharp sort of way, and there was a glitter of intelligence in her eyes. He still did not know who she was, or if he could trust her.

"Who are you?"

The girl looked up at him, her eyes scanning his face, assessing, judging.

"My name is Jacqueline," she said.

"You were at the party, at the mansion?" he asked, watching her face for a reaction or a sign of if he could trust her or not.

"Yes, I was a guest." A strange look passed over Jacqueline's face. She looked down at the blond-haired man on the ground between them. "Walter, he…brought me as a guest."

"You survived what they are doing?"

She nodded, not looking at him.

"How?"

She shook her head, eyes still fixed on the man at her feet.

"Luck," she said. She glanced up at him, and must have seen the hard judgment in his eyes.

"You are wearing grey, Jacqueline," he said. She looked down at herself then up at him, a flicker of fear in her eyes.

"I am not one of them," she said, her voice suddenly filled with panic. He kept his face still and pointed at the unconscious man on the ground between them.

"But you are here, and you are alive and dressed like the people who I saw commit murder." He could see panic on her pale face, her eyes flicking from side to side as she searched for an explanation. Then she went still and looked up at him. There was anger in her eyes.

"Who are you?" she snarled. "And why are *you* alive if you are not one of them?"

"I am a doctor; my name is Fields," he said, ignoring her anger.

She curled her lip, defiance and doubt in every line of her face. "And why should I answer you, Dr. Fields? Why should I not doubt you?"

"I—," he began to answer, but she cut through him.

"You are here, wherever here is, and you came through that, that door, and you are alive."

He nodded. "I am here to try and save someone," he said, his voice quieter.

"Oh, and you want me to explain this." She gripped the rough, grey fabric of her robe. "But I should just accept that you are a doctor who came to save someone."

"I am," he said.

"And I am not one of them." She let out a long breath. "I cannot prove it to you, and you cannot prove to me that you are telling the truth."

He looked at her, at the defiance and steel in her eyes. *She is strong*, he thought, *stronger than me.*

"So we have a choice: we can trust each other or…" She left the word hanging.

He paused; she was right. He felt the ache and tiredness in his body, the dull throb in his head. He was suddenly very tired. *I cannot rest, not yet.* He wanted to believe the girl; he wanted to not be alone in this nightmare.

"All right," he said, nodding slowly. "I am sorry about your friend. He was your friend, wasn't he?"

The girl called Jacqueline bit her lip. "He is my fiancé." She looked directly at him. "There were drugs in the champagne. They drugged all the guests so that they could murder them." She sounded as if she could still not quite believe it.

Dr. Fields nodded. "Yes, the people who owned the house, and hosted the party. They were part of it." He shook his head and ran a hand across his face. "'Bradbury' I think was their name. They are part of the Hand of Solace."

"The—," she began to ask, but Dr. Fields answered before she could finish.

"The Hand of Solace—they are the ones who did this. They

murdered to create a way to get here." He waved his hand to encompass the rust-colored landscape. "They believe…" He paused and took a breath. "They have been *made* to believe that there is something here that can help their suffering."

"Something to help their *suffering*?" asked Jacqueline incredulously.

"Yes," said Dr. Fields. "They are all people who have suffered very much. Too much." He glanced at Jacqueline. "My daughter is one of them."

"But you said—"

"I am not one of them." He held her gaze and measured his words out slowly. "I am here because of my daughter. She has been lied to, they all have." Jacqueline was shaking her head. "What she has done—what all of them have done—is monstrous. But they have done it because they have been lied to." He thought of the beautiful, unnaturally young face of the man called Lemaitre. "There is a man, called Lemaitre. He lied to them, gave them an impossible dream that the past could be rewritten."

"The white angel," said Jacqueline softly, as if naming a memory.

"What?"

"Lemaitre. The man in white." She looked at him. "I saw him in the mansion." There was something else she was not saying, he could sense it.

"Yes, he was there. He has knowledge, knowledge of—"

"Sorcery," said Jacqueline.

Dr. Fields nodded. He had seen things in the last few hours of his long life that had undone his understanding of the foundations of the universe, but he had shied away from naming this new understanding.

"Yes," he said, glancing back at the shimmering gate hanging above the strange pyramidal object. "Sorcery."

"What they were doing, the killing, it was to open a way to here?"

"I believe so," said Dr. Fields. "They seek something called 'the Obsidian Key.' It must be here. Or at least, Lemaitre believes it is here."

"And where is *here*?" asked Jacqueline, looking around at the desolation.

"I do not know," said Dr. Fields, following Jacqueline's wandering gaze.

"But they are here? Your daughter and Lemaitre?"

"Yes, they must be."

"Where?"

Dr. Fields did not reply, but let his eyes scan across the land between them and the mountain. He could see the beginnings of a road of broken stone no more than fifty paces away. Following its direction, he could see where it snaked up the mountainside under the gaze of countless statues.

"There." He pointed toward the road and the mountain.

"How do you know?"

"Because that mountain is the only thing here," he said softly.

Jacqueline nodded. Dr. Fields looked down at the man still lying on the ground at his feet.

"Your friend," he said, "you should take him back through—he needs a hospital."

Jacqueline looked at him and he caught the tear in her eye. "Will he survive here for awhile?"

"Yes. For awhile, but it is a risk. Every hour wasted increases the likelihood of infection." He looked directly into her eyes. "You should go back, and take him with you."

"I can't...not yet," she said. The tears were rolling down her cheeks, cutting through the skim of red dust on her skin.

"You must."

"No. I can't. Someone has to end this."

CHAPTER THIRTY-TWO

Raker
French Hill, Arkham

Raker walked toward the pale house under the reaching shadows of trees. The gun was heavy in his hand and the night was quiet around him. There were no sounds of nocturnal birds, no rippling chirps of cicadas, only the gravel crunching under his feet. He did not look beyond the trees. The light was pale and thin, as if it was diluted moonlight or starlight. In front of him, only a few more steps away, the house waited. Its white stone walls almost seemed to glow in the silver light. It looked more real than anything else around it, but somehow out of place, as if it was another house from a different time occupying the same place on the margin of reality. The more he looked at it, the more it seemed larger and older than the times he had seen it before.

He shifted his grip on the gun the officer had given him, its weight and the feeling of the greased metal in his hand reassuring. He paused for a moment and considered how he was going to proceed. If Lemaitre and his followers were still alive, they might be guarding the obvious entrances. But the house looked quiet, almost dead.

He walked around the side of the building, looking for other ways in that were less likely to be watched. Edging his way around the corner of a wing he saw a set of French windows that opened onto a veranda bounded by worn statues of nymphs. The windows were closed, the inside of the house hidden in darkness behind the panes of glass.

He moved toward the French windows, careful to keep out of the direct line of sight of anyone who might be looking out into the garden. When he was next to the windows, he peered inside. There were no curtains drawn across the windows, but the inside was so dark that he could see nothing. He swallowed. Images of grey-robed gunmen waiting just inside the window flickered across his mind. Slowly, he reached for the wrought-iron handle halfway up the window frame. The metal was cold against his palm as he turned the handle. There was a click, and with a gentle tug the left half of the windows opened toward him. He held his breath.

There was no gun shot, or shout from the dark. Raker let out his breath and pulled the window open fully. He straightened and looked into the darkness inside the house as he was stepping through it. It was not empty. A figure was standing inches from him, shrouded and still. He stepped back, shock and terror making the blood ring in his ears. The figure turned on the spot and showed him its face. It had no eyes and its face was a pale mask of skin. Raker had an impression of a robe, mottled with dark stains, hanging from a bone thin frame. Its hand grabbed his throat and pulled him through the door. A stench filled Raker's nose and mouth. It was like the smell of a flooded grave, of flesh that had bloated and split in sea water. Cold spread through him as the fingers dug into his neck. The figure lifted him from the ground and threw him across the room. He fell hard and felt the breath leave his chest in a rush. It was near pitch black; he could see nothing and only heard the swish of the figure's robes as it came for him. Raker had time to blink before the figure was on him; its hands tried to pull at his head to expose the soft flesh of his throat. The dead flesh stink filled his lungs as he tried to breathe. The gun was still in his hand, he realized. He brought it up, pointing it blindly into the space where he thought the figure should be, and pulled the trigger.

There was a flare of light from the muzzle and an echoing roar. In the flash, he saw the figure falling toward him, its mouth wide in its dead and eyeless face. And beyond it there was something that filled him with the cold panic of a trapped animal. There were dozens of other figures, figures with pale, dead faces, standing still and shrouded in stained robes and tatters of evening wear.

Then darkness returned, the image just a glowing smear on his retina. The hands holding him released and he heard something fall to the floor. The stink of cordite had blotted out the grave smell of the thing. He scrambled to his feet, ready to feel cold hands reaching for him out of the darkness. None came. He waited for a second, his heart hammering. He felt in his breast pocket with his left hand, keeping the gun raised in his right. The matches were there in his pocket, next to his cigarettes. He pulled them out, fumbled the box open, and struck a match head on the grip of the gun. The sulfurous light flared around him.

There were no dead figures standing at the edge of the match light. He looked around; his eyes trying to absorb some detail from the gloom. There were heaps on the floor covered with a layer of grey dust so thick that he could not tell what they were. Where the light reached the walls he could see crumbling strips of wallpaper peeling like flaking skin. It was as if he stood in a house left to rot in silence for decades. The light of the match vanished as it burned out. After a second, he saw the low, moonlit glow from the windows he had come through.

Carefully, moving one foot at a time, he moved back toward the French windows. They were closed, as if the dead figure had pulled the door quietly closed after pulling him through. He stepped up to the glass; a thin layer of grime covered the surface, blurring his view. Moving his face so that it was almost pressed against the glass, he tried to look out. The thought struck him that this was how the dead thing must have stood in the dark, waiting for him to open the door.

It took him a moment to discern anything beyond the filthy glass. Slowly, an image resolved itself, as if forming out of a haze. The world he saw through the glass was different from how it had been only moments before. The light outside was still the silvered glow of moonlight, but now it fell across a landscape of rolling dunes of ash. Twisted, burnt trees clawed at a starless sky. There were no statues clustered around a paved veranda, no leafed trees swaying in the wind of a July night. He was looking across a withered, alien land.

Raker realized that his hands were shaking. More than anything he had seen this strange night, this was somehow the worst. He let out a breath and noticed that it fogged in the dead moonlight coming through the glass. His hands were cold and he realized that he was shivering. He let out another shaking breath and watched it sheen the grimy glass with a layer of ice.

How can this be? He had come through these doors only moments before, pulled from the warm air of summer by a dead hand.

Warmth, he thought, *a beautiful summer night, alive and warm.* This land beyond the glass, this empty room, seemed like cold remains left to freeze and turn to dust in the dark. It seemed as if years, centuries even, had passed for the house and the world outside. In the time it had taken him to fire his gun and strike a match, time had raced ahead.

He was so cold; he could feel the heat of his body leaching away into the freezing air. He wrapped his arms around himself and felt his legs fold as they bled strength. He leaned against the frame of the door, his breath becoming shallower, and his shivers becoming weaker.

Had he really stepped through these doors only a moment before? *No*, he thought, *no, it was a long time ago, an eon ago.* He had just forgotten how long he had been here. He felt his eyes flutter shut and the death cold reach toward the slowing beat of his heart.

There were bright lights beyond his closed eyelids. It was warm. No, not just warm, *hot*. His eyes snapped open. He was crouching by the side of a set of French windows, the red velvet of the open curtains soft against his cheek. Light burned from electric bulbs held in brass fittings on the walls. Striped burgundy and ivory wallpaper sat smooth across the surface of every wall. He smelled the blood before he looked. People, and the remains of people, were heaped on the floor in a glossy red tangle of limbs. The smell was warm and rank. He felt his stomach rise as he pulled himself to his feet and staggered toward the open door that led to the rest of the house. The carpet squelched under his steps.

He reached the door as the man in grey staggered through it from the corridor beyond. Raker did not have time to raise his gun before the man fell against him. Raker could see dark stains on the man's robes. He tried to throw him off but the man held on.

"Help me," the man in grey gurgled, looking up at Raker. And Raker saw that the man was blind, his eyes and face melting as if doused in acid.

He blinked and the world was different again when he opened his eyes.

The room and the corridor beyond crawled with shadows thrown by electric lights that flickered and sparked in their fittings. The man in grey was a slumped pile of formless flesh and burnt fabric at his feet. He looked over his shoulder into the room where a second before there had been fresh and bloody corpses. They were there, but they had begun to bloat and rot as if they had been lying there for weeks. He gagged at the reek coming from them. He could see now that some must have been guests at the party, dressed in costume and evening wear. Others wore grey robes, stained by blood and the juices of their corruption. He looked at the windows and saw the moonlight falling through them in a silver sheet of light. The lights had stopped flickering.

He found that he was staring at the moonlight, unable to remember what he had just been thinking. He blinked and shook his head. The world was different once more. How had he gotten here? It was quiet and still; there were no bodies on the floor, no dust. There was something he had to do, some reason he had come here, but he could not remember what it was. Was this his house? He looked around at the patches of wall lit by the glow of gas lights set in glass shades high on the wall. He shook his head. No, no, it was not his house, and something was wrong, something was very wrong. He just could not grasp what it was.

He brought his hand up to his face, felt something heavy in it, something metal. There was a gun in his hand, a revolver. He saw the scratch on its textured grip where he had struck a match. Reasons and memories burst into his mind. He remembered the figure pulling him through a dark door, the bitter cold, the land of dead ash, and the corpses bloating with rot. It could not be more than a few minutes since he had been outside, opening the windows, looking into the house. He looked around himself. What he saw seemed wrong—the color of the walls and furnishings the wrong age and style, and the lights he had seen in the house before had been electric not gas. It was as if the house was changing around him, shunting backward and forward along the rails of time. A dull, throbbing pain started to beat behind his eyes, and his skin felt clammy. He felt as if he did not fit, as if his body was rebelling against where it found itself.

He needed to find the source of what was happening here. Whatever Hugo and Helena Bradbury had set in motion, it needed to be stopped. He would get to the center of the house and work outward until he found them.

He began to move down the corridor toward were he thought the center of the house must be. The corridors were silent apart from the hiss of gas in the lights and the creak of polished boards under his feet. He glanced into side passages and open doors as he went, seeing dark wooden furniture, faded velvet curtains closed over windows, and the occasional pile of logs burning dull red in fireplaces. After a few turns and doorways, he had lost track of where he thought he was in the house. More than once he thought he passed the same place twice.

It was as he was turning a corner that the lights faded, plunging him into gloom. He was caged in darkness, unable to see anything. The hiss of the gas lights had gone, replaced with ringing silence. He was reaching for his matches again when a voice spoke from behind him.

"I knew you would come back," it croaked, sounding like the rustle of dry leaves. He felt the cold creep over him, the ice touch in the air sucking the heat from him. He turned slowly. The figure stood two paces behind him, lit in a cold glow. It was old, old and thin and clothed in grey rags, wisps of white hair hanging from a face that was thin and shrunken. "This is your fault, it was always your fault," it hissed. Raker could hear the menace in the figure's words. He tried to raise the gun but could not; his limbs had become weak and his strength was draining from him. He was cold again, so cold.

"I have done—"

"You have done too much, Raker," said the figure as it stepped forward with a lurching, spindle-limbed gait. "I should have killed you when I first saw you that day."

Raker looked up at the hard, dark eyes in the sagging face. He recognized them through the wasted flesh and wrinkled skin. The muscles and the broad chest had gone, withered and crumpled so that the man's tall frame bent and stooped, the bones of his arms visible under the paper-thin skin.

"Hugo?" he gasped. The cold was like needles stabbing into his muscles.

"Yes," growled Hugo, and took a step closer. "You could not leave her alone, Raker. You killed my sister through despair, and you undid all we were trying to do." Hugo reached out toward Raker; he could feel the chill spreading from Hugo's hand. He felt weak, so weak, and cold. He dropped to his knees, swaying.

"You ruined all the good we were trying to do, all the things we would have put right," hissed Hugo, raising Raker's chin with thin fingers. Raker could see the glitter of a shard of mirror in the fingers of Hugo's other hand. "You came back, though." Hugo smiled. "You came back after all this time, and now there is nowhere to run." Raker could not move. There was only the cold, and the razor edge of the mirror on his throat. He felt his eyelids flutter.

At least I will not feel it, he thought.

His eyes snapped open. Bright sunlight was falling on his face through the trusses of an unfinished roof above him. He was on his knees in a corridor. There was no sign of Hugo, just a feeling as if a sliver of ice had traced a line over his neck. He got to his feet. The corridor walls were bare, unrendered brick. The boards at his feet were unpolished fresh timber and trailed away to an open space where he could see rafters and the half-tiled floor of the level below. There was a smell of drying mortar and brick dust on the cool breeze.

There was a shadow on the floor in front of him, its edges blurred as if cast by a flickering light. It was the outline of a man, reaching out to him, blurred fingers reaching across the floorboards.

The world blinked and electric lights were pulsing around him. There was screaming and a fetid stink like sour milk and ozone. Pulses of light reflected from the mirrors lining the walls, the cold marble fireplace, and the polished expanse of a wooden desk. He stood in the same study that he had confronted the Bradburys in at the start of this madness. Lurid green light filled the space beyond the open door to the rest of the house. Tendrils of mist-like energy followed from the opening like reaching tentacles.

Standing a foot away from Raker was Hugo Bradbury. He was not old or withered by the passage of time, but splattered in drying blood, his face held in a serene expression that made Raker freeze where he stood. He smiled when he saw Raker, as if he had been waiting. It was a smile like a crack running though a pane of glass. Hugo's eyes glittered in the ethereal light pouring from the arch at his back.

"Raker," he purred, licking his lips. It was an almost childish voice, pleased at being given a treat. Raker looked into the eyes above the broad smile, and saw that madness had eaten whatever had been Hugo Bradbury.

Raker half turned to run, but saw the light glitter on the cleaver as it cut. His arm came up to try and shield the blow, but Hugo had thrust out his other hand and had him by the throat. With a twist, he sent Raker crashing against a heavy framed mirror. Without a pause, Hugo was on him, pinning Raker to the wall, his left forearm across Raker's chest. Hugo brought the cleaver's edge against the soft flesh of Raker's neck. It was a delicate movement, slow, as if Hugo was savoring the moment before he sawed open Raker's neck. Hugo was gurgling to himself, his tongue slowly licking his lips.

Raker felt a raw stab of anger. He was going to die here at the hands of a madman playing out a grudge. Hugo tensed.

There was a noise like thunder and Raker felt warm, wet liquid splatter his face and gush down his chest.

CHAPTER THIRTY-THREE

Jacqueline Fine

Another Time

The dead gods looked down on them as they trod the road. Many were so worn and weathered that they were little more than pillars of pitted stone. On others, Jacqueline could make out features, and a few still held their shape as if carved only a few days before. Some had human faces, others snarled in the likeness of beasts. Here and there she noticed a form that she thought she recognized from books on ancient history of the world: a jackal-headed man holding a set of balances; a half man half sea serpent leaning on a trident, his beard falling like crashing waves over a muscular chest; a winged woman in a spilling robe, her face turned away from them. But there were many more that she did not recognize. Inhuman forms squatting atop stone plinths carved with rune-like marks that made her eyes sting when she looked at them: a fat toad-like thing with membranous wings and a domed head covered with squid-like tentacles; an androgynous human wrapped in thorns; a tall figure defined only by its swaths of tattered robes carved from yellow alabaster. There were tens of thousands of them looking down from the mountain at the dead land.

All her life, Jacqueline had felt the truth that human life and perception were a comforting lie. Now, she walked in a place that proved she had been right, that she had seen what others did not. Under the eyes of these forgotten gods, she wished she had been wrong.

As they passed deeper into the forest of statues, the stone figures whispered to her. It had begun as they'd walked closer to the mountain, like a rising tide, growing nearer and stronger with every step. She had tried not to listen, but the noise had pressed itself into her thoughts, insistent and demanding. It was a constant murmured chorus of names: *Yog-Shothoth, Artemis, Nurgahothes, Cthuga, Basatan, Nodens, Glaaki, Freya, Hestia, Cthulhu, Eth, T'hash, Zatariel, Eris, Harpocrates, Mordiggian, Bel, Dionisus, Azathoh, Set, Nyarlathotep, Pan, Tiamat Ithaqua, Merrow, Venus, Nurgal, Tsathoggua, Erebus, Oden, Hogethshen'sur'ashen, Isham, Cyaegha, Tchar, Shamdan, Hastur, Bast, Orion, Shurgarhet, Horus, Baal, Atlach-Nacha, Velacannor, Yig, Chaugnar Faugn, Peor, Apollo, Vulcan, Shudde M'ell, Abhoth, Shub-Niggurath, Ithaqua, Hypnos, Daoloth, Tulzscha, Hecate, Phrengartol, Hades, Dagon…*

On and on the babble went, whispering in her mind like claws and feathers caressing the inside of her skull. It had taken all her will to concentrate on what Dr. Fields was saying.

"They have been used," he said.

Jacqueline did not reply. She was not sure if she trusted him. He had thought she was one of them, one of what he called "the Hand of Solace." The look in his eyes as he had looked down on her had held something cold in it—a fanatic cruelty that had reminded her of a loyal dog beaten to madness.

He paused to take a breath of the dead, dry air. "Lemaitre used them to get here. He twisted their grief until they became his slaves."

Jacqueline looked at him, an old man, tall and thin, his dark suit stained by blood and dust.

He ran a hand across his mouth and coughed. "It's not their fault," he said, glancing at Jacqueline with bright blue eyes.

He is trying to persuade me, she thought, *or perhaps himself.*

They had talked as they approached the mountain. He had spoken quickly, as if releasing a stream of thoughts he had kept dammed up inside. He had talked about Lemaitre, the Hand of Solace, and the thing they sought, the so-called "Obsidian Key." But more than anything he had talked about his daughter, the daughter who had joined the murderous cult to try and regain a lost life. She had felt his need for her understanding, the pauses and glances judging her reaction. She could not give him that understanding; she could not help thinking of Walter lying half dead in the dust. Keeping her face expressionless and her eyes on the uneven surface of the road, she walked on up the mountain.

"Can you see them?" she asked, cutting through whatever he had been going to say. "They must be at the top if they were ahead of us." She was looking up to where the road snaked on the mountainside above them to the mountain's summit. He stopped by her side and shielded his eyes from the bruised light that came from the sky.

"No, but they must have been on the path ahead of us," he said.

"Must they?" Her acid tone made him glance at her. They had caught a glimpse of a cluster of grey-clad figures moving in the distance over an hour ago. Since then, they had been following the road on the assumption that Lemaitre and his remaining followers were climbing the mountain to wherever the road led. "There are dozens of side paths leading to the bases of statues, or who knows where." She flicked a hand at where a dusty path split from the main road to vanish amongst the tangle of carved stone. There were ruined or dilapidated stone buildings dotted here and there amongst the statues. Some looked like little more than roofed shrines fallen to disuse, others seemed to be entrances to chambers beneath the mountain surface.

He pursed his lips, not looking directly at her. "I think I saw something moving on the path above us, about five minutes ago."

"Why didn't you say something?"

"I…" He paused and looked at her with that same imploring look in his eye that she had seen when he'd talked about his daughter. "I was not sure it was them."

She glanced around her, her eyes flicking between the shadows that pooled at the statues' feet. The whispering voices in her head seemed to get louder.

"It must have been them," he said. Jacqueline felt the dry wind blowing across the hairs that had risen on her skin. "We have not seen anyone else here; it must have been them." She did not reply.

There was a sound like the peal of a distant bell. It echoed and distorted on the stone of the statues, flitting on the wind. She twisted around, trying to discern where it had come from. Jacqueline had been trying not to think about where this place was, but it was as if the sound broke a barrier in her mind. The statues of numberless gods, the road of broken stones that must have been built by something or someone, the entrances to fanes dotted amongst the forest of statues. This was a place of pilgrimage set adrift far from the time that she knew.

"Did you hear that?" asked Dr. Fields in a dry whisper.

"Yes," she said, her eyes scanning the road above and below them. "There are other…" Her voice trailed away for a moment. "…there are other pilgrims here besides Lemaitre and your daughter."

"What could…," he began, but his voice died in his throat. Above them, the road curved and disappeared around a thicket of statues. Around that corner, shapes moved.

"Quick," hissed Jacqueline, grabbing Dr. Fields's arm and tugging him to the side of the road. They crouched in the shadow of a statue that had fallen so that it leaned against one of its fellows like a drunk on the shoulder of a friend.

The shapes that came around the corner were twice as tall as men, hunched and swathed in trailing robes of dusty yellow that covered their bodies and hid their faces. There were six of them, and they moved with relentless, slow power, their bulks cracking the grey stone road under their stride. Each bore an object of tarnished bronze: an octagonal rod covered in flowing letters, an amphora, a tablet worked with geometrical patterns. The figure at the front of the procession held a bell which it struck with a jade scepter. The noise vibrated through the air, echoing through the statues. The giant figures passed slowly, not noticing, or not caring, about the two humans pressed into the shadows by the side of the road.

Jacqueline watched them pass, unable to take her eyes from the flowing folds of the robes that hid the creatures' forms. She wondered at whether it was muscle or something else that surged under the yellow cloth. Her eyes fixed in fascination, she almost missed the last figure in the procession: a small figure, no taller than a child, made smaller by the size of the figures that had passed before it. It wore yellow robes like those of the creatures it followed, but its face was visible, and it leaned on a bronze staff topped with an eight-pointed jade star. Its face was thin and long, the flesh very pale and smooth, like unbaked china clay. It had no mouth, as if a sculptor had not finished his work and had left the clay to wait for features.

Just as Jacqueline realized that she was staring, it stopped and turned its head to look at her. She felt a surge of fear and beside her Dr. Fields let out a moan. Its eyes were blue, as bright as the sun glittering from the sea. They fixed on Jacqueline's eyes. It was still, so still that it might have been one of the statues that surrounded them.

There is no solace here, wanderer. Jacqueline felt the voice in her head and gasped. It spoke in a voice made of snatches of speech stolen from a lifetime of memory. The drunken lilt of her father, the clear sing-song tones of a jazz singer she had known once, her own tear-soaked whisper after her mother died.

"Stop," moaned Jacqueline. Beside her, Dr. Fields looked at her, his eyes full of fear.

I give you this one thing, wanderer. The voice hissed in her mind. *Turn back now; leave this place to the dead gods. This is a path of ashes.*

Jacqueline felt as if the statues around her faded, and the sky dimmed until she was staring at the figure on the road across a dark expanse. The words echoed in her mind.

Why do you say this? she said, and realized that she had not opened her mouth. The figure with no mouth turned its head to look up at the summit waiting a few hundred paces above them.

It begins, it said in a voice like a thousand last breaths.

She blinked and the statues and the yellow light of the dead world flicked back into place. She started forward, but the figure on the road was gone, and the sound of the gong echoed through the air like a fading memory. She thought of the dreams she had had when she first came to Arkham, of the image of blood and a man in white, of a shadowy figure in the distance moving closer. *Wanderer.* She remembered that word coming from her own mouth in her dreams, her own voice shouting warnings to her. She could turn back. Perhaps she should turn back. Then she looked up toward the top of the mountain and realized she could not.

"Save us," gasped Dr. Fields. The yellow sky had faded to black, darkness spread from the mountain peak like ink spreading through water. In a heartbeat, the view in front of her changed. The statues covering the mountain seemed carved not of stone but of ice that glittered with a twilight gleam. There was no sun, only a diffused half-light that made the suddenly crystalline statues crawl with thorn-like shadows. She began to run toward the peak, scrabbling over the broken stone of the road. Lemaitre's quest for immortality across the centuries had led to this time

and this place. All that had come before was just the terrible over-
ture to what she had seen would happen if he succeeded and
returned to Arkham.

The mountaintop grew closer with every frantic stride she
took. She did not look behind her to see if the doctor was following. She was panting, the blood hammering through her body,
her mind filled with half-remembered images of a shadow figure
coming closer and closer in half-remembered dreams. This was
the last chance, the fulcrum point of a narrowing future.

Jacqueline came over the crest of the mountaintop at a run.
She stumbled to a halt, her will stolen by what waited for her
there.

"No," she gasped. Behind her, she could hear the wheezing
steps of the doctor.

The temple sat under the bruising sky as if waiting for them.
Cupped in a bowl of broken stone, it was made of polished and
gleaming black granite. Thick pillars as wide as the arm span of
a man, and as tall as great trees, framed a doorway that disappeared into the rock wall of the mountain. Each pillar crawled
with markings, the edges of the carvings catching the light. In
front of the pillars, steps descended into a wide, paved plateau
that separated Jacqueline from the waiting door. But it was what
lay in front of the temple that made Jacqueline stop.

The ground in front of the steps was a smooth expanse of white
stone. Wide plinths rose from the stone floor every few paces.
Dead and bleeding people lay on the flat tops of the plinths. Some
were the unconscious party guests brought through no doubt for
just this purpose. Beside them, on a score of the white stone
blocks, the remainder of the Hand of Solace writhed as they died,
their blood dribbling down the white stone. Dark shapes, like
animate smoke, coiled over them as they held the death wounds
in their bellies. More and more of the snake-like shadows flowed
up from the ground as she watched. A sound rang through the

air, a low keening on the edge of hearing that made Jacqueline think of the calls of carrion feasting on a carcass.

"Another blood price," whispered Jacqueline to herself, seeing the knives that some of the dead and dying still held in their hands. The Hand of Solace had paid the price for Lemaitre again, and as they died, not one made a sound. She could see no sign of Lemaitre.

There was a cry from just behind her and Jacqueline turned to see Dr. Fields. His face was deathly pale under the dust that coated his skin and ragged suit. His blue eyes were wide as he looked at the scene before the temple, his mouth working silently as if pleading to a deaf god.

"No, no, she can't be," he moaned, and ran forward. Jacqueline reached for him to pull him back, but he was already beyond her reach.

"Wait!" she shouted to him, but he did not stop.

He ran between each bloody block of stone looking down into the red-smeared faces of those that lay on them. Jacqueline muttered a curse and ran after him. Shadow shapes flicked around them, curling around the dying like leaches, or fish stripping flesh from a fresh carcass. The air was filled with the keening cry. Jacqueline paused to pick up a heavy-bladed knife from the hands of one of the dead cultists. The handle was sticky with fresh blood, but she needed a weapon.

The doctor ran from plinth to plinth looking into face after face. Jacqueline could feel the future pressing against her mind, getting stronger with each step. The dreams, the visions of blood, of dark silhouettes against storm-lit skies, all seemed to be spiraling around her as if she stood at the center of a whirlwind.

She heard a cry. The doctor had reached the end of the rows of plinths. He was on his knees, a figure in grey crumpled on the ground in front of him. It was a girl; she lay face down, her thin body wrapped in grey, feet bare, dirty blond hair falling around her head. There was no blood, but there was a stillness about the figure that made Jacqueline want to shout to the doctor not to turn her over.

Dr. Fields was reaching down to the still figure when Jacqueline reached his side.

"Don't," she said.

She could see the dread in his eyes as his hand touched the shoulder of his daughter.

"Amelia," he whispered. "Amelia, it's your father." Jacqueline gasped as the figure on the ground stirred. Dr. Fields let out a shuddering breath. "You are alive." He smiled, tears running down his cheeks in dusty runnels.

The figure on the floor pulled itself up until it stood, face turned away from them. There was something wrong; Jacqueline could feel it as an electric charge across her skin. She reached down to shake the doctor, who still knelt on the floor looking up at his daughter.

"Amelia?" he asked, a note of uncertainty in his voice.

The figure did not reply. The doctor stood and reached out a hand to the hair that fell over the hunched shoulders. The figure turned slowly and looked at them. She had no eyes. Dr. Fields stood frozen, his hand still stretched out, trembling. The thing that had been his daughter opened her mouth and screamed darkness.

CHAPTER THIRTY-FOUR

Dr. Fields
Another Time

The scream touched him like a burning wind and his hope died. Dr. Fields felt Jacqueline grab his shoulder as darkness poured from his daughter's mouth. Her body shook, muscles vibrating, hands convulsing, as the air around her filled with coils of night. The thing that had been his daughter took a shuddering step forward, her shadow spilling around her, spreading in an animate cloud. Snake-like tendrils of darkness coiled above her head in a twitching mane of blackness. Her hand reached for him and his ears filled with the noise of a hungry scream. He could not move—the empty sockets of his daughter's face held his eyes. His limbs felt leaden. She stepped toward him, arms reaching to pull him into an embrace.

Something yanked him backward.

"Come on, you fool!" shouted Jacqueline.

He stumbled as she tugged him out of his daughter's grasp. He looked into Jacqueline's pale face; her green eyes seemed to blaze.

"No," he snarled, pulling against her grip. Around them, the dusty red light was continuing to vanish behind a spreading pall of smoke-like shadows. He could hear Lemaitre's followers gurgling their last on the stone plinths, and the glass-edged shriek of the shadow creatures that had fed on them.

Amelia is not dead, he thought. Whatever had possessed her body, she was alive somewhere inside its grasp. He would not fail, he could not fail. There was still hope, there must be hope.

"We must get to Lemaitre!" shouted Jacqueline. "We have to get past!" The thing that was once Dr. Fields's daughter stood on the steps now, the door of the temple barely visible in the darkness that surrounded her. As he looked at her, he heard a voice. It was a small voice, the voice of a child caught in a nightmare.

Father, it said. Amelia's head lolled to one side, the sightless pits of her eyes seeming to stare at him from her silently screaming face. She seemed to pause, her body tensing, preparing to pounce. Dr. Fields kept his eyes on his daughter.

I can reach her, he thought. *She will not harm me. There is still hope.*

"Go," he shouted to Jacqueline. "Go and get to Lemaitre."

"But—"

"Go!" he screamed, pushing Jacqueline toward the temple steps as his daughter leapt at them. Behind him, the other shadow predators shrieked.

Amelia flew toward him like a bird diving onto prey. He had a second to look up into the deathly pale face haloed by writhing darkness; a ghost of doubt flicked across his mind, and then her feet hit him in the chest. He fell back, the impact knocking the breath out of him. He felt his ribs crack and screamed. She was on his chest and he could not breathe. Cold hands gripped his head, holding him still.

Darkness ate the world around him, and there was just a pale face above him, inches away. He tried to push it away, but his limbs felt numb and he could not breathe. His lungs felt as if they were filling with ice. The darkness poured from her mouth, flowed into him, seeping through his skin, chilling, deadening.

A burning sensation cut through the cold numbness. Blazing heat radiated across the right side of his body.

The amulet, he thought. The green stone amulet that was still in his pocket wrapped in velvet with the silver dagger...

His right hand moved almost without him thinking, scrabbling for his pocket. The amulet was so hot that it was burning through its fabric wrapping. But even as he reached to grasp it, the raw heat began to dim. The icy numbness began to overwhelm the life that had briefly poured back into his body. But he could feel the haft of the silver dagger in his hand.

Father, he heard the mind whisper again. The creature tilted its head above him, looking at him with empty eyes. He could just allow himself to die. His will began to fade like a dying flame. Just let the shadows eat his being and leave him as nothing, a husk on a mountain of dead gods. *Father, help me*, said the fading voice in his mind.

"Amelia," he croaked, the name pushing its way out of his mouth. He sucked another thin breath and shouted into the face of the creature on his chest. "Amelia!" *She must be alive*, he thought. Inside this creature, she must still be there. He shoved upward, but his arms felt feeble and it batted them away.

Father... The voice was distant, fading.

"Please," he moaned. "Can you hear me?"

The creature wearing his daughter's body clawed at him, its hand fastening around his throat. It brought its face down so that he was inches from it, eye to empty socket. Dr. Fields felt the hand tighten around his throat. He looked into the pits of night that had been his daughter's eyes.

Fath..., came the voice, and vanished. There was nothing in his mind but a sound like the wind blowing through dead trees. The thing looked at him with midnight eyes and he knew his daughter was gone. There was nothing, no fragment of light or hope danced there, just endless uncaring oblivion.

Thoughts of the mistakes that had brought him to this place flooded his mind. He saw his wife's grave open under a clouded sky, his daughter holding a crying bundle and smiling weakly at the husband that would be dead in a few years. He felt hope slide away from him, vanishing into the night that waited in the empty eyes. There was no going back. The choices he had made, all the intentions he had thought good, were worthless. He had done this, he had made this moment. His daughter had been right. Standing in a stinking room in the ruins of her life, she had asked what good he had done. He saw now that the answer was nothing. He had hoped that he could undo the mistakes that he had made. Now he saw the truth of that hope.

He could not feel his body. The world faded, contracting to the pale face of a daughter that he had failed and who was no more.

"I am sorry," he said. From the fading reaches of his memory, the accented voice of Lemaitre rose: *there are ways to change anything.* The words echoed through his mind. It had not been a lie. He had seen things done that defied explanation. The laws of science were false, and the bounds of human knowledge were the bars of a prison. He had seen both shattered at the command of a man. The laws of the uncaring universe could be wielded like a blade to cut through the limits of space, of time. Lemaitre had come here to find the key to wield greater power than he could comprehend, to turn back time. There was hope for those who could seize it, for those who could pay the price. The power to make things anew existed if you could grasp it, if you could pay the price.

He felt the weight of the silver dagger in his hand, the dagger he had not used. With the last dregs of his will and strength, he gripped its handle. He looked into the face of his daughter vanishing into darkness. To solve the past, he had to have a future.

"There is hope," he said, and stabbed up into the body of his daughter.

CHAPTER THIRTY-FIVE

Raker

French Hill, Arkham

Blood had blinded Raker. He brought his hand up and wiped the warm, sticky fluid from his eyes. He stood in the wreck of a study, a shattered mirror at his back, the ruin of fine furniture tangling the floor amongst the lifeless forms of people. The heavy corpse of Hugo Bradbury lay on the floor at his feet, blood pooling around the ruin of his skull. In the gloom, the blood looked black. Helena Bradbury stood a few paces away, a revolver clutched in both hands still pointing at where Hugo had been, at where Raker stood now.

"He...," she began, her eyes wide and glittering in the flickering light.

"Thank you," said Raker, keeping still, his eyes on the shaking muzzle of the gun.

"I just wanted her back," said Helena. Raker noticed the tremble in her voice, the edge of mania. What had she experienced in these last hours? Murder? Certainly, and she had done it willingly, had conspired to kill hundreds of people. But there was an edge of desperation in her words, the plea of someone who had leapt into the void willingly and found terror on the way down. "I just wanted my daughter back. It was supposed to be all put right."

"This cannot be put right," said Raker, shifting his gaze to Helena's eyes.

"They were just supposed to open the gate; that was all." Helena did not lower the gun. Raker flicked a glance around the room at the bloodstains, ruin of furniture, and splattered white walls. There was something beyond those walls, something at the center of the great house like a pulsing wound. He could feel it like something lurking in the corner of his eye.

"What gate, Helena?" he asked, keeping his voice steady.

"A gate to another place, to another time. They were supposed to have come back with it, so that we could put it all right." There were tears rolling down her face, and Raker thought that she looked cracked and broken. She had always been a woman of poise who commanded the respect of those around her. The woman who stood pointing a gun at him looked old and withered, the steel in her broken. He would have pitied her, but the air stank of sorcery and the blood of people she had helped murder.

"What were they supposed to return with?" he asked, keeping his face calm.

Her jaw trembled as she spoke, and he could see pain flash in her eyes, the pain of someone who had destroyed themselves for a lie. "The key, the Obsidian Key, the key to enslave a god."

"That's what this was for?" He could not keep a note of anger from his voice. "These people died for that?"

"It should have been made so that it never happened. Don't you see?" she whined.

"No, all I see is that you have murdered for a lie." He could not help it; the words came out in a rush of anger in spite of the gun still in her hands.

"It was not a lie." She sounded as if she was pleading.

"It was, and you bought it with blood, Helena." He took a

step toward her. The gun barrel wavered. "Lemaitre killed Vivian. He killed her because she found out what he was."

"No, she killed herself."

"He killed her, and then used her death to make you his accomplices." He gestured at the ruin around them. "All this was for a lie." Her finger tightened on the trigger. *The truth hurts her too much. She will kill to believe that she did the right thing.* "Shoot me," he said softly. "You killed Hugo to save me, but kill me if you cannot hear the truth."

"Hugo…" She glanced at the corpse on the floor, its grey robes saturated with blood, the face pale, the back of his head a shattered ruin. "The things that have happened, the things that we saw…" The gun barrel dropped a few inches. Raker forced his rage down, made his voice calm. There was more at stake here than his anger.

"And you, Helena? What about you?"

She looked up at him and shook her head. "I never thought…" She looked at the gun pointed at Raker, and around at the blood pooling around them. "It was supposed to be put right."

"That cannot happen, all this cannot be changed." He took a step forward, feet squelching on the blood-soaked carpet. "It has to stop. Whatever is going on here, there has to be a way of stopping it before it hurts more people." He reached out a hand and slowly pushed the barrel down until it pointed at the ground. Helena did not resist. "That is something that can be done."

For a second, he thought that she would try to bring the gun back up. Then she looked at him and he could see the need for hope in her eyes.

"How?"

"You said that the rest went somewhere through a gate into another world." Helena nodded, pushing ragged grey hair out of her face and blinking the tears from her eyes.

"Everything we did was to open the gate, to open a way to

another place, another world. When the gate opened, that was when this began." She gestured around at the ruined house, at the marks of rot spreading on the walls. "Everything changed; it was as if we had spilled nightmares into this world."

Raker nodded; he had felt and seen the effects. "Can it be closed?"

"I don't know."

"You must," he snarled.

"I don't, or don't you think I would have tried?" She looked at him, anger now flashing in her eyes. Raker held her gaze, his face unmoving. "He did not explain everything." She went suddenly still, her eyes staring into space as if looking at something in a memory. "The devices," she said quietly.

Raker opened his mouth to ask a question but she cut him off. "The things that Lemaitre brought with him. They are sort of machines. There is one on this side and one on the other side, in the world they went to." He could sense the eagerness in her, the return of some of the old, hard energy.

"They were part of what you did to create this 'gate'?" he asked.

"Yes. Lemaitre called them anchors. 'Made by a great race that walked the stars,' that was what he said."

He rolled the words around his mind and reached the possibility she had seen. "Anchors?"

Helena was nodding, something that might have been the ghost of a smile on her face. "As if they were to tether something."

"Where's the anchor on this side?"

"In the Great Hall, with the gate."

Raker tore a strip of cloth from a curtain and wrapped it around a candlestick to make a torch. He lit the fabric with his matches and walked toward the arched door to the Great Hall, the light of the torch casting a shifting shadow at his feet. He had taken two steps when Helena Bradbury called to him.

"You mean to destroy it?"

He looked back at her, a frail woman, stained with blood and guilt. She stood near the same spot that he had confronted her only a day before in what seemed like another life. He did pity her, he realized, but he could not forgive her.

"I mean to try," he said.

"I do not know if it can be destroyed, or what will happen if it is," she said.

He shook his head. "I have to try. If there is any hope, I must try."

Helena Bradbury came to stand beside him, the gun still in her hand but not pointed at him. He looked at her, the hard edge of determination once again in place on her features. He gave a curt nod, and together they began to run down the tangled corridor toward the wound in the world.

CHAPTER THIRTY-SIX

Jacqueline Fine
Another Time

Jacqueline ran up the black steps of the temple without looking back. Behind her, she could hear the cries of the doctor as he struggled with the creature that wore his daughter's skin. The man had made his decision and bought her an opportunity with his life; she would not squander his sacrifice. She shut off the instinct to turn back and focused on reaching the arched door into the temple.

The door waited a dozen yards away behind vast pillars of black glass that rose to support the roof. It was three times her height, an arch of dark stone set in a wall of smoothly cut blocks. Inscriptions covered every inch of every surface, lines and lines of texts in languages that she did not recognize circling the pillars and texturing the floors and walls.

Flanking the doorway were two statues carved from glistening black stone. Both were humanoid figures, their arms by their sides, fingers splayed. Neither had any features or faces; they were like three dimensional silhouettes drawn around a shadow. Slowing her run to a careful walk, Jacqueline passed between them and into the temple. For a moment, she felt as if the statues turned their smooth heads to follow her. She remembered the shadow man, the man cut from night in her dreams. She gripped the haft of the knife she'd taken from one of the dead cultists and hidden in her sleeve, and looked into the gloomy temple interior.

It was quiet, the air still as if the chaos and horror outside could not cross the threshold. Light fell from openings somewhere high in the ceiling above, filling the temple with shafts of light and expanses of shadow. Squinting as her eyes adjusted, Jacqueline peered around. Fine, pale dust rose around her feet as she moved across the white marble floor. Rows of black pillars stretched into the distance in front of her and to either side, their tops vanishing into darkness.

Something moved in the shadows on the edge of one of the distant pools of light. Jacqueline slid close to one of the wide pillars and edged toward where the movement had been. The dust muffled her steps and her grey robe blended with the shadows so that she moved like a ghost. Occasionally she saw the pale shape moving ahead of her, passing deeper into the temple.

It must be Lemaitre, and somewhere in here is the thing that he has come for, the thing that he has spent the lives of hundreds to reach. He would not get what he'd come for, she was determined of that, and she would make him pay for the blood he had spilled to get here.

She saw it before she saw Lemaitre. The rows of pillars curled around an open space. It was at least fifty paces across. A shaft of light shone straight down on the center of the open space, illuminating a narrow plinth of white stone no taller than a child. The plinth was plain, unmarked by the carved script that wound across the floor around it in spiraling patterns. On the smooth top of the plinth sat a cylinder of obsidian, its surface reflecting the light that fell on it. Jacqueline guessed that it was no longer than the span of her hand and two finger widths wide. Coming to the edge of the pillars circling the black cylinder, she saw that its surface was irregular, cut with angular symbols that winked in the light.

From the other side of the circle of pillars, Lemaitre stepped out, seeming to coalesce out of nothing as he entered the light. His hand was rising, the thin fingers open, reaching for the black cylinder, eyes fixed on it and it alone.

"It was a lie, wasn't it?" Jacqueline's voice echoed in the stillness of the temple. Lemaitre's hand stopped inches away from the cylinder, his bright blue eyes fastening on her as she stepped into the light. "There was no way of undoing those people's suffering. They paid your price to get here, and for a lie."

Lemaitre looked at her with surprise, his eyes glittering in the sunken ruin of his face.

"You are right. This is no key to undo the past." He smiled and looked at the black cylinder inches from his fingers. "This is something more, something much more." Jacqueline sensed the intensity of his desire in that look, a raw, desperate hunger. She shifted her grip on the knife beneath the sleeve of her robe. This monster would not leave with his prize, but she would know the reason for what he had done. She needed a reason, hungered for it as if it would heal her past. She would have that answer before she ended this.

"You killed Vivian Bradbury because she knew who you were."

"Yes," he said, licking his lips, his eyes on her as if judging what she would do if he grabbed the cylinder. "I needed the Bradburys. Their house was built on ground where old gods once touched the earth. Such places are rare, and I knew that to reach this place I would need their house and their cooperation. I began to associate with them, but their daughter did not trust me. She found out my secret." He shrugged. "Killing her protected me and brought the Bradburys into the Hand of Solace as willing allies."

"What could be worth the price they paid for you?"

He snorted, his hand drifting away from the cylinder, a distant look in his eyes.

"You think you know of suffering? You think the people I used knew of true suffering?" His lip curled. "What is worse than pain and loss and lies? Many lifetimes ago, I asked a question of something that exists beyond any understanding of man. I was given an answer, an answer that I live and understand in every instant of my life." He snorted. "I am cursed to live without end. I have seen and feasted on everything this world has to offer, over and over again. There is no greater curse that could have been put on me." Jacqueline heard the bitterness in his words.

"The taste of ash is all that is left to me. You think I am a monster, but I take no pleasure in what I have done." He smiled and Jacqueline realized that it was hollow, like the grimace of a puppet's mask. "Once, I would have delighted in slaughter and power; now I just wish to reach an end." He raised his hand toward the black cylinder. "This is a snare to catch and bind a god. The god that granted me the gift of endless life." He gave a humorless laugh. "With it, I can bring him to me at the appointed time and force him to give me release."

Lemaitre looked up at her. "It is what I came for." He smiled his death mask smile again. "And now you have the answer you came for, Elizabeth Bell." Her real name hit her like a physical blow. She realized he had been talking to give him time to invade her mind, to prepare. She had listened to his lies and given him all the time he had needed.

Lemaitre was shouting words that sent pain through her flesh, wracking her where she stood. She saw Lemaitre's hand close on the black cylinder and felt cold rage run though her body.

Lemaitre was backing away from the white pillar, the black cylinder in his hand. She screamed, convulsing where she stood. He had tricked her, spun lies for her. Anger filled her, blotting out the pain.

She lunged toward him, the knife in her hand.

"You lie!" she shouted, and rammed the knife up under his ribs. There was a warm gush of blood, and his eyes went wide. He opened his mouth and blood spilled over his chin and down the white fabric of his suit. Jacqueline held the knife in him and twisted, she was close enough to smell the hint of expensive cologne clinging to his clothes. Red foam bubbled at his lips as he mouthed, struggling to form words.

"I did not lie," he whispered as he died.

Pain filled Jacqueline like molten fire pouring into her soul.

Chapter Thirty-Seven

Dr. Fields
Another Time

The dagger twisted in Dr. Fields's hand as it bit into flesh and bone. The creature that had been his daughter shrieked with a sound like the cry of a thousand crows. He brought his hand back and stabbed again and again, feeling blood spatter down out of the darkness. The cries rose to a single combined note of pain and fury and then began to fade. The animate darkness surrounding him began to break apart, dissolving into smoke-like patches, soaking back into the earth and air.

The dead red light of the sun fell on his face. He rolled to one side, setting the bleeding corpse down on the white marble paving. The dagger still protruded from the last wound he had inflicted, the spreading blood stain almost black against the grey of the robe. He left the dagger where it was, and looked at her face. Amelia looked whole again: her eyes were no longer empty pits and the blond hair that fell across her blood-stained face no longer writhed with snake-like shadows. In death, she looked like his daughter again.

Slowly, he leaned in and kissed her forehead as if she was falling asleep. Her skin was still warm, he thought, not yet faded to the clammy cold of the dead.

"I have to leave you here," he said. A low breeze blew across the mountaintop stirring her hair. "I will put it right, Amelia, this and all that came before it." A cold emptiness settled over him, all thoughts of anger and grief fading. He had something he had to do, a distant light flickering like a flame before a storm. It was all that mattered. He had been weak before, unwilling to see what was possible and what sacrifice was required.

Gently, as if not to wake her, he unfastened the clasped hand amulet from around her neck and pulled the ring from her finger. He looked at it, at the two silver-worked hands gripped together as if for comfort.

"I am sorry, but I will need these," he said to her, and slipped the ring over his finger. It felt tight and cold against his skin. He stood, straightening so that he stood tall, his shadow falling over her face. When he saw her again, there would be no need for sorrow or forgiveness.

"Goodbye." He strode up the steps and into the temple.

As the cool darkness of the temple folded around him, he heard a voice. It was distant, echoing through the long lines of wide pillars. The words were lost, but he heard the strange, accented tone to the sound, the accent of Lemaitre's cultured voice. He began to walk toward the voice, his stride quick and firm, and as he got closer he could feel the decision he had made hardening into something unyielding, something iron hard and blade-edged.

A scream of pain echoed through the still air. He began to run, hearing the strange noises of alien chanting rise in pitch, and an acidic texture fill the air. He ran toward the screaming, not bothering about concealment or noise, the pillars flicking by him, determination overriding age and the pain of injuries.

The pillars parted in front of him, revealing a circle like a clearing in a stone forest. At its center, two figures stood in a shaft of ruddy sunlight on either side of a low stone pillar. One was Jacqueline, her face contorted in agony, her body jerking as if being tugged by strings hooked into her flesh. She was screaming, the sound of her pain an echoing howl. Lemaitre had his left hand raised, his fingers arranged in a crooked shape, guttural words spilling from his mouth. In his other hand he held a short black cylinder. Neither noticed Dr. Fields as he paused at the edge of the circle.

Dr. Fields's eyes fastened on the cylinder, remembering the thing that the Hand of Solace had come here to find: the Obsidian Key, the key to snare a god and turn back time. It was no more than twenty paces away. Lemaitre had cared nothing for those he had used, but he had shown the way, and now the key to all was in his hands. Dr. Fields looked about for a weapon. Jacqueline shouted something, and Dr. Fields looked back to them in time to see the silver length of a blade disappear in Lemaitre's chest.

The black cylinder dropped from Lemaitre's fingers. Dr. Fields was already moving, watching as the black cylinder hit the ground. Jacqueline still held the dying sorcerer's weight on the knife blade. He could hear Lemaitre cough some broken words to her, too quiet for him to hear as he ran forward, hand already reaching for the cylinder. He was a pace away when Jacqueline screamed again. Ethereal light haloed Jacqueline and the slumped body of Lemaitre. Dr. Fields's eyes met hers and he saw terror in them, pleading and desperate. He dropped his eyes, turned away from her scream, and picked up the black cylinder from the temple floor.

It felt cool in his hand, the texture of the symbols carved in its surface rough to the touch. A grim feeling of triumph flooded him as he straightened and looked at the two figures locked together: one dying, one screaming as some spiteful sorcery ate her life. He felt nothing for them, no hate, nor pity. For a second, he thought Jacqueline tried to mouth something at him, but he could not tell what it was. It was as if the possibility of caring had been burned away. He gripped the cylinder and looked into Jacqueline's eyes without blinking. In time, this key would allow him to remove both her death and the man who'd caused it. In the face of such a purpose, even her dying screams seemed hollow. He turned and walked away without looking back.

When he reached the outside of the temple, he looked out at the plain stretching away from the mountain. Down there, by the road that led from the mountain, was the gate back to his world. It was a strange thought, one that would have struck him as insane before. But that was another life, a life close in time but separated by revelation and terrible truths. Power over the forces of nature, and powers like those he had witnessed, would be his first endeavor. He did not know the secret to the Obsidian Key, but he would learn. When he knew it, then the storm would come and wash away the past of suffering. He felt the ring that he had taken from his daughter's body, the metal tight on his finger. He would need others to help, others who would understand what needed to be done and why. It would take time, but he was a patient man.

With a grim smile, he began to walk down the mountain.

Chapter Thirty-Eight

Raker

French Hill, Arkham

They ran through a silent house by the light of a burning torch. Light and shadows flickered around them, and the only sounds were their steps and their sucking breaths as they ran. Torn free from the tethers to reality, the house could show many faces, many slices of time. As they ran, it flickered between instants of dust-covered floor, flaking white walls, and ash-filled rooms spattered with blood dried to brown streaks. Gun in hand, Raker felt acid fear fill his guts every time they turned a corner, and looked over his shoulder with every other stride. Corpses dried by time and shrouded by cobwebs huddled at the edges of walls and in darkened rooms. Raker did not know why, but he felt as if the house was not still but poised, waiting.

"Look," gasped Helena in a half-whisper, and Raker felt her tug on his sleeve. Slowing to a walk, he looked ahead at where Helena had pointed. An arched doorway framed the top of a wide flight of stairs that led down. The carpet had faded and rotted to tatters and the marble was grey with grime, but he recognized the stairs. He had climbed them from the Great Hall to confront Helena in the study. It had only been a few hours ago.

He swallowed. Pale light flickered around the archway, shining up from what waited in the Great Hall. This was the center of the wrongness that had swallowed this house, the focus of the vile things done by Helena and her fellow cultists. And he had no choice but to walk into its presence.

I can only go forward, he thought, *there is no going back.*

"Come on," he said, and strode toward the light, the gun gripped tight in his hand. He heard Helena follow, but did not look around.

Step by step he walked down the stairs, the ethereal light growing in brightness around him. There was a smell of burnt sugar, hot metal, and ozone so thick he almost gagged. For a moment he thought he saw the lurid light coalesce into a luminous tendril at the corner of his eye. He did not look, and tried to shut away the sensation of something caressing his skin. He took the last steps at a run, feeling his terror rise even as he tried to outpace it.

He landed on the stone floor and looked up. The gate gaped above him, a shifting kaleidoscopic tear in space, glowing with unnatural light. He felt a hot, tinny taste in his mouth, felt a buzzing inside his ears. The space flickered like celluloid film cranked too slowly through a projector. One image replaced another with stuttering speed: a brightly lit room glittering with light and gilt, a gutted ruin covered in frost, a bare hillside beneath cold stars. His body felt dull, disconnected, and distant. He could not remember where he was, who he was. He was nothing but a grain of dust caught in the flickering flow of time.

"Raker!" The voice was close to his ear, a shout that yanked him back into the Great Hall. He looked at the face of Helena, so close that he could see the terror glittering in her eyes. "Look," she said, pointing behind him toward the shadowed edge of the Great Hall.

The dead stood there, silent and still. A pale death light wreathed them, pulsing in time with the flickering beat of the gate, a close-pressed throng of dried flesh hung with tatters of fine clothes like a carnival of the damned.

"Can you see the device?" asked Raker quietly, not taking his eyes from the dead.

"Yes," said Helena, her voice almost a croak. "Thirty paces away, under the...the gate."

Raker nodded without looking at her.

"When I say, run for the device." Helena made a low noise of agreement. He held the torch steady above him, its yellow light glinting from dark metal as he raised his pistol. The dead stared back with empty eyes. "Run."

There was a moment of silence and the sound of Helena's running feet. Then the dead came forward with a sound like leaves blown by a winter wind. Raker pulled the trigger, a corpse with a rotted stole jerked off its feet. Another roaring shot, another long-dead body falling back. He turned around, seeing the ring of dead faces closing in toward the torchlight and the pulsing glare of the gate.

"Helena!" he shouted, glancing over his shoulder. She had had to crawl to reach the pyramidal device without passing through the gate that hung above it. Her body was covered with trails of energy; her eyes were running with blood. She reached forward, her fingers stretching for the metallic surface of the device.

Raker looked around; the dead were paces away. He shot again and again. Corpses dropped, but the gaps filled with more. He glanced behind him again, saw Helena's hand close on the side of the pyramidal device. There was a sound like the beating of countless insect wings. Arcs of electricity flowed over Helena. She began to spasm, her hand locked onto the device, her mouth open in a scream that was lost in the screech that came from the gate. It screamed like a living thing, growing and shrinking in wild pulses, its sickly hue moving through color and darkness. Raker felt his senses blur, bile rising to his mouth, eyes prickling with bloody tears. Around him, the dead came on, their bodies shifting between the stages of death with every pulse of the gate: dried cadavers, bloated bodies streaming corruption, fresh and bloody with sightless eyes. He tried to raise his gun but they were on him, dead fingers raking him, corpse slime smearing his face.

I have failed. The thought stabbed into him as he felt dead hands close over his mouth, filling his last breath with a grave stench.

There was a sound like a thousand panes of glass shattering. The touch of the dead vanished. The floor came up to hit Raker as he fell, unsupported by the press of attackers. A scream filled the Great Hall, ululating higher and higher. Raker felt as if he was on the deck of a pitching boat tossed on the sea. He raised his head.

The gate was unmoving, frozen in the air like an explosion caught in a still frame of film. Beneath it, caught still in the moment of bringing the pyramidal device down on the stone floor, was Helena, her mouth wide in a never-ending scream. The gate imploded, folding through impossible dimensions. Helena Bradbury came apart like a shredded picture. Around where the gate had been, things broke apart, dissolving into dust that sucked back into the gate.

Raker pulled himself to his feet and ran. He ran under the archway into the hall lined with its shattered mirrors as the molecules of the house unknitted in his wake. He felt sick, thoughts and images flicking through his mind from a million possible futures and pasts that would never happen. He ran toward the front door he had come through on a summer's afternoon a lifetime ago, his limbs becoming weak and insubstantial. He had the vaguest sense of someone running just behind him. He reached the door, wrenching it open.

The night sky above burned with red, alien stars. Raker took two steps and fell into a vortex of numb oblivion.

CHAPTER THIRTY-NINE

Jacqueline Fine

Another Time

Jacqueline looked into the dying face and felt her soul burn. Lemaitre's mouth was open, flapping like a fish drowning in air, his eyes wide and staring at her, his blood gushing over her hands as he shuddered on the blade of her knife. She could not move. It was as if they were locked together. Pain filled her, burning to the ends of her nerves and through her blood. She wanted to scream but found that she could not draw breath. The fire flooded into her mind, burning away thoughts in a spreading tide.

I did not lie, said a voice in her mind. *I cannot die.* She felt its burning, alien touch beside her own thoughts. She recognized the voice: it was the voice from her dreams, the voice that had seemed to beckon into the future. It was the voice of Lemaitre, not beautiful and cultured, but guttural and sharp. His soul tasted of ashes and smoke, edged with calcified lumps of dead emotion. It flowed over her consciousness, enveloping and killing her thoughts and memories where it touched.

I will live, girl. My death is not in your gift. In her mind, Jacqueline screamed.

The temple faded from her vision, crumbling under intense white light that seemed to come from inside her. She felt her body fall to the floor of the temple, but it was far away.

No! she shouted in her mind. Somewhere far off in a dusty temple, she thought she heard herself cry out. She pushed against the burning tide, refusing to let it advance, holding it back with her rage.

It withdrew, rippling back from the iron of her mind and soul. Then, the voice came in a low chuckle, echoing through her.

There is no solace, it said. *Your life is mine.* For an instant, her consciousness held, resisted, holding onto its existence. Then Lemaitre's soul was all around her and she broke, her mind crumbling like a castle of sand in the path of the tide. She could feel herself dissolve piece by piece, her consciousness retreating through layers of memory and identity. Memories flicked past: *Walter lying on the red sand, a man's laugh, the door of the Curiositie Shoppe creaking open, a touch of breeze across her skin.* Then they were gone, vanished into the flames that crackled with Lemaitre's voice. *She was on the stage, trying to ignore the man leering in the front row. She was alone on a dark street, her last coin cold in her hand. She was bending over her father as he spluttered yellow puss from his lungs, the stink of liquor heavy on his breath. She was on the edge of a stage, hidden in the curtains, watching her father flick cards between his hands to waves of applause. She was...*

No! she shouted with the last of her will, grasping the last fragment of her soul. She would not go, she would hold this back, she would...

The girl with green eyes and dark hair opened her eyes. She stood unsteadily. Her limbs were shaking and her movements clumsy. Blood had splattered her face and soaked into the rough fabric of the robe she wore. She looked at her hands, eyes struggling for a moment to focus. Blood covered them, still wet. She let her hands drop and looked at the corpse at her feet. It was the body of a man: blond hair, pale skin, lined and veined as if aged prematurely. He was curled up, his long-fingered hands touching the handle of the knife that was embedded in his chest. His eyes and mouth were still open, staring at nothing. The girl shook herself, flexing her hands as if testing them. She looked down at the corpse and gave a grim smile that did not reach her cold eyes.

"I did not lie," said Lemaitre, and walked away.

The woman sat on the bench and wept. Swathed in funeral black, she tried to make as little sound as possible, pressing a handkerchief to her nose as the tears rolled down her face. People passed her, hurrying to and from trains, their eyes looking at anything but the woman who sat alone crying to herself. She was well-dressed in a coat and hat that spoke of money, if not happiness, and the creases around her hazel eyes said that she was only just edging into middle age.

There had been a train that she was supposed to have gotten onto an hour before or maybe more. She had tried to get on it, had even opened the door of a first-class carriage. But then the tears had started and she had let go of the door handle, leaving the waiting baggage boy confused, her case in his hand. She had found the bench and let the tears come. The train had left, but she had not moved. She did not want to be on it. Leaving Arkham would somehow make it real, would mean that it was true. Her mother was gone. She knew it as a fact, had seen her mother's face in the open coffin, but she could not bring herself to accept it as real. She kept on thinking that if she went back to her mother's house, she would be there with her books and gossip about the local families.

"Excuse me." She looked up, startled by the voice and the thought that she had been watched without realizing it. The speaker wore a black coat over a tailored suit of charcoal, so dark that she wondered if he had not come from a funeral himself. He had a thin face, framed by a silver-grey beard and set with bright blue eyes. His hand rested on a black cane with a silver top worked in the shape of two hands clasped together.

"May I help?" The voice was kindly, the sort of voice that could tell you that something was nothing to worry about and would be fine in a day.

"No, no," she stammered, smearing away tears and blinking. "Thank you, though."

The man smiled and sat down at the other end of the bench, hands resting on the top of his cane. There was something about him, something powerful and reassuring.

"I know I may be intruding, but you seem distressed. Are you sure that I cannot help you?"

She dabbed at her face, trying to hold back the tears so that she did not cry in the face of this stranger. "I don't think so." She looked again at his somber garb. "Are you a priest?"

He smiled again. "No, I am a doctor," he said, and handed her his own handkerchief. "And I may be able to offer you better solace than a priest."

* * *

The police sergeant opened the door, spilling light across the man who sat on the iron-framed cot. The cell was small and stank of the countless drunks that had spent nights in it over many years. The man looked up as the door opened. The sergeant paused, looking at the paperwork in his hands. There was something about this one that sent his policeman's instincts into overdrive. The man was calm, just like he had been when they had questioned him, just like when he had walked in off the street and asked to talk to Sheriff Engle.

"What did the sheriff and the officers say?" asked the man, his voice steady and polite. The sergeant chewed his lip and glanced at the paperwork again. The man was all wrong and it set his teeth on edge. Crazy men should howl and scream, not sit there politely and say crazy things as calm as a lawyer laying out a case.

"The sheriff's still in hospital." He looked at the man. He wore the remains of a cheap suit, and looked like he had been in a serious fight, or maybe several. Blood and dirt stained the fabric and it was ripped in several places.

"But you talked to him?" asked the man.

"Yeah, I talked to him."

"So, he told you about what happened up at the Stonegroves place?"

The sergeant sighed; it was late and all he could think about was getting home to some sleep. "Look, son, he has no more idea of who you are than I do, and has less idea about what this crazy party or ceremony thing is that you keep talking about." The man rubbed his hands across his face.

"But, he is in the hospital? With a gunshot wound?" The sergeant nodded. "So he must remember how he got shot? And what about all the officers? They don't remember? They don't remember how a lot of their friends died last night?"

The sergeant had had enough. He thought of himself as a patient man, but it had been a bad last couple of days for the sheriff's department in Arkham. He walked over slowly and crouched down so that he was eye to eye with the man.

"The sheriff caught a bullet from a raid on a gang of bootleggers out on the Dunwich Road. A lot of the boys did not come back from that raid. If you know anything about it beyond your weird stories about rituals and monsters, I would say so now, or shut up before you have an accident."

The man's eyes darted around the cell in confusion. "They don't remember me? None of the officers?"

"No, they have no more idea who you are than I do," said the sergeant, standing back up. "If I were you, son, I would leave Arkham, leave the county." The sergeant stood to one side and thumbed at the open cell door.

"What?" asked the man, frowning. "But what about all the people who were at the Stonegroves mansion? All the people who died?"

The sergeant reached down and pulled the man to his feet and gently pushed him out of the cell.

"No one has any idea what you are talking about, son. No one is missing, there was no party, and no one has heard of anyone called Helena or Hugo Bradbury in these parts."

The man turned to look at the sergeant, the light of the corridor outside the cell streaming past him so that he was a dark silhouette against the light. The sergeant cut off any further questions with a shake of his head.

"There is no mansion called Stonegroves around here. There never has been. Where you say it was, there are just fields." The sergeant thought he saw a tremor pass through the man. "No one knows what you are talking about, Mr. Raker."

The man was still for a second, as if working through what the sergeant had said. Then he nodded and walked away toward the police station door and the waiting Arkham night.

* * *

What you desire will not come at small cost, said the mouthless figure in a whisper that passed from mind to mind without sound. It sat on a jade chair in the shade of the mountain which was its home. Around it, the gigantic forms of its attendants stood still while their master bargained, the yellow cloth of their robes stirring in the dry wind.

This will help, the figure said, extending the tip of its twisted staff to almost tap the pyramidal object of shimmering metal. *Its twin is a loss, but its creators knew much and their artistry in such matters is a boon.* It inclined its head at the bargainer who had come down from the shrine at the top of the mountain.

A thin face, young for one of the short-lived human type, green eyes and a mind like a pit of fire. The flesh looked like the human thing it had seen before ascending the mountain with another of her kind. The other had fled the mountain and back to where they had come from before their gate had collapsed. This one, though, was not the same as the other. Surviving pilgrims to the temple of the Hungering God were rare, but it could sense the power in this one.

But it will not be easy, it said, *and so the payment must be great, whether it comes now or later, when you have returned to the world you came from.* Withdrawing its staff, it turned its mouthless face and blue eyes to the bargainer. *Do you still wish to leave this place, and are you willing to pay the price?*

The human woman nodded, her green eyes flashing in the dead light of the sun at the end of time.

"Yes," she said. "Any price."

End of Book Two

About the Author

John French is a writer and freelance game designer from Nottingham, England. His work can be seen in the *Dark Heresy*, *Rogue Trader*, and *Deathwatch* roleplaying games, and scattered through a number of other books, including the New York Times bestselling anthology *Age of Darkness*.

When he is not thinking of ways that dark and corrupting beings could destroy realty and space, John enjoys talking about why it would be a good idea… that and drinking good wine.